The Victorian Vampire

by

Nick James

Contents

Also by Author

Acknowledgements

I wish to thank my partner in crime and life, my darling wife Sarah. And of course, my beta readers Dawn Walker, Layla Bennett and Amanda Spreadbury. Thank you for all your help.

Finally, I hope that my grandparents are looking down at me proudly, as their bodies have been lost to time, their memories and souls are still with us, although Grandpa Woolcott will be watching The Arsenal instead.

To Frank & Margaret Woolcott and Arthur & Margaret Plumridge, I miss you every day, the world seems duller without you somehow.

Alone. Yes, that's the key word, the most awful word in the English tongue. Murder doesn't hold a candle to it and hell is only a poor synonym.

Stephen King

Chapter 1

A lot of people do not believe in souls. But when you no longer have one, you certainly know about it. You have a void in your body, which gnaws away at you. Drink, food and loose women, I've tried them all, but nothing will ever fill that hole. Although, feeling the love of a good woman almost makes me feel human.

Then when you add a lack of heartbeat and pulse, your body feels like a shell, a half-filled suitcase that you drag your organs and brain around in. Then you add the need to feed, which consumes you, your friends, family, and even your true love. You will tear them asunder, sometimes destroying several generations.

Sometimes I think the reason we do not have a soul is because God knows what the demon inside will drive you to do. So, he took his gift away. But then again very few choose this existence, because you couldn't call it a life.

My name is Albert Nathanial Morris. I am a vampire and, like many others, I did not choose to be a vampire. I grew up in London around the Whitechapel area in a little house on Middlesex Street. I was born 24 August 1868. My father, Nathanial, was a well-respected painter and decorator, and deeply religious. His wife of many years and my mother was called Anne. At only five feet tall and petite, it meant she had a difficult pregnancy, to which she told me on a regular basis, so I was their one and only child. That upset them both.

The early years were not too bad: school and chores, and the odd beating here and there, especially if I took the good Lord's name in vain. Well, what would you say if you were twelve and stubbed your toe on your bed and you hadn't learnt any swear words yet?

At the weekends I helped my father with his business, decorating the rich families' houses around the boroughs of London. My main duty was to push the barrow containing my father's tools and paints as we didn't have the money for a horse and cart. Even if we did, in our part of London the horse would be stolen within the hour, and every household and pub within walking distance would be eating stew for the next few days.

When I did manage to break free from my family's bonds, my best friend and I would run riot through the streets trying not to be caught by the police, or the other names they were called: copper, slops, scufty, bulky, rozzers, old bill, and crushers. Our favourite was 'bastards', not witty or catchy, but shouting 'the bastards are coming' sounded just right for us.

My best friend, Adrian Michaels, was the one who always got caught and given the back hand of justice. When we reached sixteen, I topped out at five feet eleven inches, which was a couple of inches above my father, but Adrian carried on until he reached six feet two. Between this, his flame-red hair and being the width of a beanpole, the Peelers could see him in any street, day or night.

In the summer of 1885, I had been working with my father for two years, but no money had come my way as I was in training and had to pay for room and board. Some parts of the job were fun, being inside all the nice houses and seeing all the exceptionally clean housemaids, who would sometimes give me a kiss and a cuddle, especially if I had seen them about when I was growing up. But apart from that, the day-to-day work was dull and boring. I wanted a new life – one of fun and adventure.

I was sat in our local pub, The Slaughtered Lamb, having a pint with Adrian, who was working at a local abattoir and was covered in blood and pissed off.

'We gotta get out of 'ere, mate, this place is boring me to death,' he said, taking a large draught of dark brown ale.

I shrugged and looked at the barmaid behind the bar. She was in her fifties, but what could be seen spilling out of her top was worth a look.

'What do you want to do? I'm sick of it, too, but what else is there, apart from robbing?' I asked, catching the eye of the barmaid. The look she returned was not pleasant to say the least.

We were being jostled in every corner. It was one of those times of the day when there were shift changes from the surrounding factories, so tired men wanted a pint to drown their sorrows before heading home to the family or drinking their fill and getting some paid company before going home.

I will not act all pious like my father and say I have never paid for sex. Living in Whitechapel, you won't find a single girl from a good respectful family, especially in the pubs Adrian and I frequented. The company was nice albeit brief (my fault). I left with less money, but without my virginity.

'What about the army? My cousin Bill went to India and loved it there, all the women and curry you could eat,' Adrian said with a gap-toothed smile, which he acquired after pinching a woman's bum one night in the pub. Let's say her husband didn't appreciate his hands-on approach.

I frowned. 'Didn't he die over there?' I asked.

He gave me a thoughtful look, which looked like a donkey eating a salty carrot. He wasn't a pretty boy, despite what he thought.

'Well, yeah, but that wasn't the army's fault. The postcard we got said he was drunk and decided to climb up a building to some woman's room,' Adrian said.

'Did he fall? I can't remember,' I admitted, taking another sip from my pint, hoping my mum would forgo the 'you're such a disappointment' speech when I made it home, although the reason I drank was to get through such conversations without losing my temper.

Adrian chuckled. 'Yeah, he managed to get to the window, and the husband was standing there inside the bedroom window and punched him right off the ledge,' he said, straining his memory back to when they received the postcard from his cousin's friend who had served alongside him in the army.

I rubbed my face and looked around, same old people, same old smell. You had more chance of getting a knife in the gut around here than finding a girl to marry. Unless I do what Mum says: go to church and find a nice Catholic girl. *Sorry, Mum, look around you. If there is a God, he's not doing a good job.*

'Do you think the army would take us?' I asked.

'Well, my cousin was as flat-footed as an elephant, so if he can get in, I don't see why not.' He grabbed my now empty pint pot and headed off to the bar.

As I waited, I thought about my future. I could work with my father until he dies and follow his slow and methodical working practices while he belittles me at every turn, or I could save money from my on-the-side work and build my own customer base, starting with places my father wouldn't touch, like pubs and knocking shops.

Adrian finally returned. He had been trying to chat up the barmaid to see if she had a back room they could play in, but he was given a forceful no. 'So, what do you think, Bert, want to fight for Queen and country?' he asked before starting to assault his new pint.

'My father would kill me, or worse,' I said, pulling a scared face.

'What could be worse than that?'

I rolled my eyes. 'Mum would cry, then pray for me, then they would talk to me for the rest of my life about what a disappointment of a son I am.' I took a draught of my pint, which was so unpleasant I felt like I could chew on it.

An old toothless man with a bloody apron came stumbling into us. 'You two boys wouldn't…wouldn't…' he stuttered while looking like he was going to be sick over our drinks. '…Wouldn't make it in the army. Ugly 'ere told me his plans.'

The old man started to laugh, and then started to poke my friend in the chest while laughing.

Now, I grew up with Adrian and we classed each other as family, but even I wouldn't get away with doing that to him.

First thing to notice was the vein in his neck, which was pulsing so much it looked as though it was outside his skin. The next thing was him handing me his half-empty glass. And the final hint I had that something was about to go bent was the old man's nose being splattered across his face. Plus point was that Adrian knocked him down. Not so good point was his three friends who came to his aid.

Adrian launched himself at the three, headfirst into a fellow ginger's face. I used the two pint glasses to blind the other two – having chewable ale thrown in your eyes is not nice, especially followed by cheap glass pint pots. I managed to take one down with a quick kick to his bollocks, but his colleague caught me with a punch, which felt like granite knocking me flat on my arse.

Once again Lady Luck was on my side – or, in layman's terms, it was the barmaid. My assaulter crumpled, which left her standing over me with a truncheon she had taken from an ex-lover. I never did dare ask if he was a policeman or not. As the man who hit me was in the realms of unconsciousness, a voice barked a slang word which I hadn't heard in years, not since my schooldays, 'Peg it, mutton shunters!' (Run, police!)

Using the knocked-out man as somewhere clean to put my hands, I managed to get up just as I heard a whistle blast coming from the charging police. What I didn't know at the time was that the fight had already spilled into the road.

Catching sight of the bloodied but weirdly smiling Adrian, who seemed to be fighting all comers, we locked eyes. 'Peelers!' I shouted, and we bolted to the door and into the street which was awash with brawlers and police. I watched my friend dodge the truncheon from a newly arrived copper, but that didn't stop us running.

We stopped two streets over panting. 'Well, that's me out of a job.' The redhead chuckled, then cleared his nose of snot and blood which splattered onto the cobbles scaring a nearby rat.

'I'd better get home; they are going to be angry anyway,' I said, knowing that a night-long lecture was coming my way. 'But as you're jobless, go and find what you need to join up. I think my future as a painter is coming to an end.'

Adrian agreed, and we parted laughing as always.

Chapter 2

'WHERE HAVE YOU BEEN, BOY!' boomed my father as soon as the city noise had been shut away by the front door. He was standing at the end of the hall, still all prim and proper as was Mother standing behind him.

'Well, Albert, where have you been?' she asked.

Clearly, they weren't going to be understanding. 'I had a drink with Adrian, but something happened,' I admitted, and then waited for the floodgates of tears to come from Mum. 'But it wasn't our fault.' Yes, lying is a sin, but according to my parents everything is.

'Taking the demon drink. You remember what that did to your uncle,' Father spat angrily. Uncle John had walked in front of a carriage after a skinful. 'You bring this family name into the dirt; you're an embarrassment to us, boy. If I didn't need you tomorrow so badly, I would cast you out so you can join the dregs of society that you love to associate with,' and with that statement he stormed back into the front room, just leaving my mother standing there with tears running down her cheeks. But, for once, she didn't say a word and just walked away to join Father.

I headed upstairs to my small room. As ever, the house was in pristine shape, even the stair carpet was as clean as a nun's dream. My room had also been tidied, so I filled my wash basin with fresh water and washed the bloody remnants from the fight before undressing and getting into bed, hoping that Father would be in a better mood on the morrow.

The next morning, I quickly learned I was wrong. I pushed our barrow for over an hour in stony silence with the London early morning mist clawing at my face. Father just walked in front of me, not even casting an eye at me. Breakfast had been bad enough, Father said nothing, and Mother told me it was time

I started to act my age. Clearly, they didn't understand the irony that giving me the silent treatment was hardly acting *their* ages.

With a sheen of sweat now covering my skin, we finally arrived at the three-storey town house belonging to Mr and Mrs Alistair McAdams. I parked up the barrow by the kerb as my father walked around to the servants' entrance situated at the rear of the property. I waited for him to return. Thankfully the weather was mild today, which meant I didn't have to empty the whole contents into the house, but then again Father might just make me do that as punishment.

I could see the odd curtain being twitched from the surrounding houses. If you weren't a tradesman, our type of person wasn't wanted in this area; and workmen from the houses would arrive to turn you off the patch, sometimes with menaces.

I was pulled out of my musings by my father. 'Albert, start bringing the stuff in, and hurry up about it,' he shouted from the side of the house. He obviously wasn't going to help today.

I grabbed the folded-up dust sheet, headed towards the back of the house and walked into the kitchen. The well-rounded and red-faced cook just flicked her head towards another door.

'Thanks, ma'am,' I uttered and walked past. I found my father talking to a tall, balding man, clearly the butler to the property. 'Where do you want these, Father?'

They stopped and stared at me. 'In there, boy, we are painting the cellar, it's all cleared out ready,' he said and pointed to a side door with stairs that descended into darkness.

As the creaking steps dropped away, there were oil lamps burning on cupboards allowing me to see the vastness of our job ahead – a good few days' work.

It took me several trips to empty the whole barrow and, as I thought, Father was using it as punishment. The benefit of this toing and froing was that I bumped into one of the housemaids, a blonde giggly girl called Emily Barker, but she scuttled away quite quickly when the cook shouted for her. Things were looking up.

Father walked off the job to see a new customer to give him a quote, leaving me to start preparing the room for painting, mainly making sure it was free from dust, so washing down the walls here we come.

This part of the job was always hard, especially as you're trying to rid the place of all the dust while you had heavy-footed sods banging around above and flexing the floorboards letting even more dust float to the ground. 'Bloody hell!' I swore, throwing my washing rag back into the bucket of water.

'Now, now, Berty, that mouth of yours will get you into trouble,' said a soft voice coming from the stairs.

I looked over and saw the typical black and white uniform of a housemaid, not the curvy girl from earlier, this one was tallish and thin.

'Don't you recognise me, Albert?' The girl walked slowly down the stairs holding a sandwich and a glass of milk.

I squinted in the oil lamp-bathed room, then the flickering light illuminated her face. I smiled. 'Annabel, Annabel Abbot. Well, this is a nice surprise,' I said. We had gone to school together for a few years, but then one day she never turned up.

She smiled putting down the plate and glass, and then she placed her hands on her hips. 'How are you, Berty? You look well,' Annabel said, but she kept her tones low so the upstairs staff wouldn't hear us talking.

'Yes, I'm good thank you. You are looking well, too. Why did you leave school?' I asked, and then looked at the food and drink.

Her uniform rustled as she shrugged. 'The cook sent those down for you,' she added and walked a bit closer, flicking her dark eyes upwards. 'My father owed a lot of money, so he pulled me out of school and managed to get me a position here,' she explained. There were tears in her eyes, but she had always been a strong girl. Many boys had limped away from her at school after trying to pursue her.

'How are they treating you here, are you enjoying it?' I asked, hoping it was all okay, but I watched her still and shoot a quick look towards the stairs.

'It's okay, I have a place to eat and sleep,' she said and gave me a weak but beautiful smile. 'I have it better than most.' She placed her thin-fingered hand on my bare but wet arm. 'Enough about me. I see you are working for your father. I thought you wanted to do something different?'

I sighed. 'Yes, we all thought we could do better, but there's not much else to do,' I admitted, putting my other hand on hers and giving it a squeeze. 'Living with my parents is getting too much. We have to live by the Good Book,' I explained and saw her roll her eyes.

'Berty, you need to lead your own life. Get out if you can,' she said softly.

'WILL YOU GET YOUR BAG OF BONES BACK UP HERE, GIRL! YOU BOTH HAVE WORK TO DO!' someone shouted down, must've been the cook.

It made Annabel jump. But before running off, she leaned in and gave me a kiss on the cheek, and then she was gone. I could hear her being chided by the fat cook.

I sat on a packing box and ate the sandwich. The bread was a bit dry, but along with the leftover beef it did the job.

Father came back and helped with the cleaning, but clearly the cook had got to him. He didn't say anything while we were working. But when I was pushing the empty barrow back home, as we had left all our stuff in the basement, he told me off all the way.

I'd had enough. 'So, all I did wrong was talk to a girl who brought me lunch?' I argued back, making my father bristle, but I didn't let that stop me. 'You and Mother say I should find a nice girl, but when I speak to one, who I know from school, you shout at me about it!'

Father balled his fists. 'I have had enough of your disrespect, Albert. If you are not careful, you will have to find somewhere else to live!' he said angrily. 'I wanted you to take over when I got too old, but you just don't seem to care.'

My body sagged. 'I'm sorry, Father, but I want to find my own path in this world. I want more than putting paint on walls for a living.' It was then I saw that this little comment broke the small connection my father and I ever had. He just turned and walked away. I didn't know at the time, but those words I shared with my father that day would be the last.

I was dreading going back home, but it was something that had to be done. I parked up the barrow and headed indoors. There stood my mother expressing the normal cold look with a hint of disappointment; at her feet was a bag with what I guessed contained my belongings.

'Mother, please,' I begged as tears filled my eyes. I started to tremble. 'I didn't—' I was cut off by Mother raising her hand.

'Albert, I gave birth to you, fed and clothed you, yet all you have done is disappointed your father and me. All you had to do was be a good son and follow our words, as well as the word of the Lord our God,' she said in such cold tones that I felt ice particles in the air between us. 'But now you have broken our hearts for the final time. You want a new life, there's the door.' She pointed to the door that I wished I hadn't entered. 'There is some money and sandwiches in the bag. Goodbye, Albert.' With a sniff she walked away into the front room, leaving me alone with my thoughts.

Although I saw them on occasions, they never once acknowledged me. After walking out of the house I was born in, I headed to Adrian's to see if they had any space for me. Thankfully they did, so I slept on a threadbare chair as my red-headed friend snored a tooth-rattling snore. But as sleep claimed me, all I could think about was the warmth of Annabel's lips on my cheek and the regret I felt as I wouldn't be going back there now.

The very next day myself and the red-headed beanpole walked up and joined the army. Surprisingly enough the London regiment numbers were down, so now we had a future, a roof over our head and a nice warm bed, although we spent hardly any time in it. The basic training was brutal, and the training officers were something that I don't think could ever have been born of a woman. They were created in hell and banished to Bunhill Row drill hall in Finsbury to continue their evil works.

Adrian and I stood in our uniforms as we were inducted into the 8th London Regiment (Post Office Rifles). We were proud of what we had accomplished. I hadn't received a single letter from my parents, even though I sent them some money every month. We were never sent anywhere hot, to the point our battalion didn't even move that far from bloody England.

What can I say? I thought I would see the world with my friend. If you're the kind of positive person most of us mortals hate, especially first thing in the morning bouncing around the barracks excited for the day ahead, that kind of person I am not. Adrian and I spent two soggy, wet-footed years in Ireland, trying not to upset the locals, especially as our government was doing a bang-up job of achieving that without our help.

Going on long patrols through depressing-looking towns and soggy countryside, some hailed us and treated us fairly, the next treated us like murderers. There were a few skirmishes, and we lost one or two boys on our patrols, and we even had a deserter. Tony Watkins just stood up one night while we were kipping in a barn in the countryside and said, 'Fuck this shit,' and then walked out. We found him stripped and gutted the next night. We were never sure which side did it.

Normally, life was boring. There were some nice local girls who would take care of a soldier's needs for a fair fee. But during the early months of 1888, Adrian stopped, saying he had found love. He would never tell us who she was. But during that time he was winding up the regiment's sergeant major, which meant he took his fair share of licks from the man and his friends, which were numerous. He was an evil man who had repeatedly been knocked down in the ranks for going too far with punishments against the troops.

After the Watkins affair, the regiment was being replaced in Ireland and we were being sent back home to smoggy old London. I was hoping we could stay in London forever when we got back there. I would have been happy with that; travel was highly overrated if you ask me.

We were all excited about going back to home barracks. Adrian's mum had written when she heard, overjoyed about her son coming back and again agreed to let me kip on the floor. The letter was full of news and gossip of recent events in our area of London. There had been a murder of a local working girl, Martha Tabram. There had been a spate of other murders, too, but hers was laid at the feet of a man they were calling Saucy Jack, or the more publicised Jack the Ripper.

What can I say except that my army career ended the same weekend that my best friend Adrian died. On 30 August 1888, the stupid red-headed idiot had spent the day enjoying some more one-on-one manoeuvres with a busty blonde – his words, not mine. Unfortunately, it turned out she was the wife of the regiment's sergeant major, a big brute of a man from the East End of London, and he was well known to be a good knifeman in a close-quarters battle. Unfortunately, he came home early and showed the rutting pair both his temper and how good he was with a knife. At least my friend died doing what he loved. It turned out it had been going on for months, but Adrian couldn't help teasing the woman's husband, which turned out to be his death sentence.

That day I took as much money as I could find, walked out of the barracks, headed back to the streets of my birth, started to drink, and midway through took some company into the alley before resuming drinking again.

I somehow managed to find my way out of the pub in the very early hours, and that's how I stumbled into Buck's Row in Whitechapel. It was then I saw in my drunken haze a man on top of a woman with her skirts pulled up to her waist. Personally, I didn't care. I had been doing the very same thing earlier over an old beer barrel – less chance of getting a rat in your breeches.

As I got closer, the man seemed to be out of place. This wasn't a man of my ilk; he looked like a toff the way he was dressed. But what stopped me was the flash of a knife in the gaslight that barely lit the street.

'OI, OI, WHAT YOU DOIN'?' I shouted, making the man still as I approached, my army hobnailed boots echoing on the cobbles.

'This doesn't concern you, human, move along and live,' he said and kept on doing what he had been doing to the poor woman.

What did he mean 'human'? I dismissed that thought as my army training kicked in and I ran towards him. Although, clearly, the drink told me I was going faster than I was. I balled him over, both of us crushing down on the poor girl's body, but I didn't know she was already dead at that time.

His knife skittered into the darkness as we collided and punches were thrown. My vision blurred even more than it was as he connected with my jaw. 'You shit,' I muttered before thumping him in the face. It was like hitting a brick wall not a head, and I felt a bone snap in my hand making me scream out, which seemed to panic him slightly.

'You will pay for this, human,' he growled, and then sank his teeth into my neck. The pain shot through me like nobody's business. What are we, kids again? Who bites in a fight? Once again my training kicked in, and I pushed my thumb into his eye making him cry out a piercing scream as it popped under the pressure I applied. As he raised his head, I decided to play him at his own game and drove my mouth towards his neck and bit down savagely. I gagged as the warm blood filled my senses with a metallic smell and taste.

His scream echoed through the streets, bringing shouts from the surrounding houses. He repeatedly hit me until the pain and punishment were too much. I dropped to the ground panting, my face awash with his lifeblood. That's when I saw the angry man's face with dark eyes and a trimmed moustache almost looking like a posh gentleman. I watched him collect his knife and disappear into the night.

I tried to follow, but my stomach was on fire and my feet slipped away from me as the world turned upside down and I hit the deck. The pain spread throughout my body rapidly; it felt like my skin was burning. I tried to crawl away. Even in my bad state I knew that I shouldn't be caught with the body of that poor woman. What disturbed me was the sweet smell all around which made me want to linger.

The world had started to move slowly and my vision had improved, but the pain in my stomach was still there. But not only that, I felt anger; a fury was building up inside from where I knew not.

Finally, I managed to get back on my feet and weave through the tide of people coming from all quarters. Now there was something else hurting me: a cacophony of rhythmic sounds, not just from one place, it was everywhere. What was it?

So many things were happening to me all at once: anger, tiredness and pain. I saw a rundown shop down an alley which hadn't seen much foot traffic over the years. I leaned against the door as my vision started to swim. Using my weight, the brittle and rotten wood cracked. I fell through the door, hitting the floorboards hard, scattering rodents and sleeping pigeons alike, before the pain overtook me. I managed to roll further into the ruined shop, and that was it. The darkness suffocated me into unconsciousness and more.

Chapter 3

Rage. Pure unfiltered rage was flowing through my body as I shot up and looked around. My vision was tinged with a red hue and the clarity was perfect even in this pitch-dark room. There was still the burning in my stomach, a hunger that matched the rage I felt, but hunger for what? I didn't know how long I had spent in this damned place. My head snapped to the left and my mouth filled with saliva. There it was, voices just outside.

I silently moved to the still broken door and heard two different sounds of the same rhythmical-type noises that overcame me earlier. It was heartbeats, all of them together but never once synchronised, just a mass of noise that threatened to shut down my brain.

But now there were only two, and the human voices filtered towards me, which then turned into grunts and groans. My mind screamed, *food, kill and feed.* I was struggling to remain in control. One part of me told me to burst out and rip them both to pieces. The other, a calm and calculating part of me, said to take the man and let the woman go. I didn't know how, but I had a sense of who was out there and their genders. An instinct inside told me so.

My stomach burned while one word continued to repeat forcefully inside my brain: feed, feed, feed. I craned my head through the doorway and saw the back of a man as a woman laboured on her knees to fulfil the details of the verbal contract they had agreed to. The smell of the man's lust disgusted me. Yet her feeling of hate and desperation had no effect on me at all, although I didn't know why.

My movement was like lightning. The dust barely moved as I darted from the doorway in a fraction of a second to the man. I felt a pain in my fingers and then I saw that my nails had grown into something alike claws as my hand went to his neck. The man's scream was cut off quickly as my left hand crushed his larynx. Then my right hand dug into his shoulder, pulling him back into the darkness from where I had come. The prostitute, a youngish girl with long blonde hair, didn't even scream. All she did was stare into the darkness with what seemed to be a piece of her client hanging from her mouth. Cleary, I wasn't quick enough and she had clamped her mouth down in shock.

As the girl ran off, leaving her gift on the floor, I forced the struggling man's head to the side and clamped my mouth onto his neck. I could hear the pop as my incisors pushed through his skin and into his pulsing jugular, letting his lifeblood fill my mouth. I drank and drank until his racing heartbeat decreased, getting slower with every tired beat. At the same time the burning in my gut and the rage I had was now dissipating, along with the man's life.

I fell onto my backside and scuttled backwards on all fours away from the corpse. The dead man's sightless eyes judged me in the darkness. My mind, which had started to work again, seemed sharper. I closed my eyes, trying to calm myself and enhance my senses. All I could smell was blood and where the man had voided his bowels as his soul was returned to his maker. I needed to leave just in case the girl called for help.

Knowing that my funds were limited I took what money the man had and ran into the night without a destination in mind. Again, I didn't know why but not only could I see perfectly in the dark but somehow I could also feel the moon upon me, and I knew how long I could be in the fresh air before the sun returned and the pain would come.

Luckily, in the depths of the West End there are many abandoned houses and businesses. I just needed to be alone and think with somewhere to shelter. Then, there it was, like a beacon in the night, a shop that had been foreclosed by the bank. At least that's what the poster pasted over the window was telling me.

I waited in the shadows caused by the flickering gas-fuelled streetlamps until the stream of people walking through the street had cleared enough so I could force open the property door. My new strength impressed me, but the rest just flat out scared me.

As the door closed me off from the world, I looked around and took in the room before me just containing bare tables and chairs, so it looked like it had been a place to eat. I moved a table in front of the door to stop any nosey bugger from coming in.

I moved through the property and found an old bed with an even older mattress. I couldn't sense any heartbeats, so that meant I wouldn't be laying my head onto a rat's nest. With the screams of rusty springs, I lay down, stretched out and closed my eyes, even though I was nowhere near tired. The moon still had a few hours left gracing us with her presence, but I needed to think.

Adrian was dead, and I had left the barracks to drown my sorrows, which I had done proudly. Then I'd chanced across that monster killing the woman. No, not killing. Torturing. But why the hell did he bite me? *I did get the bugger back*, I thought to myself, making me chuckle. *But the question is, what was he?*

So, let's think about this. I'm stronger than I have ever been before. I can see in the dark and move quicker than any person should able to. I have extreme anger and a burning need to feed. Where the hell did that come from? That monster must have infected me with something. But what? While in my musings, the sun had started to rise, sending rays through the moth-eaten curtains. I smelt smoke, then I felt pain.

'Bloody hell!' I screamed, jumping up and looking at a small hole burned through my hand by the sunlight. Then, just as I started to examine the wound, it began to change. A scab formed and then quickly fell away to show my perfectly healed hand.

Things were getting crazy. What had happened to me? I walked about and managed to find some other rags to cover the holes where the sunlight was encroaching on my rest. Finally, I could once again settle down to think and plan.

I thought back to my schooldays and a book that my friend Annabel had lent to me, it was by John Polidori called *The Vampyre: A Tale*. Surely, they were just the ramblings of a drunk or a man with a gift for telling tall tales.

As I thought back to the story, I shook my head in disbelief. There were too many similarities to the book, but it just couldn't be. I refused to accept that I was now a demon of a man. Somehow, I managed to calm myself and allow sleep to claim me, but the dreams that came were not pleasant.

When I did wake, the sun had finally started to hide itself beyond the city limit. I walked to the window and watched the scuttling forms of Londoners going about their business. When the darkness claimed the world again as its own, the rage which had started to build was accompanied by the burning in my stomach. I gripped the windowsill as a wave of anger flooded me, causing the rotten wood to fragment beneath my hand, the splintering pieces scattering into my face.

How I hated that man who had done this to me. How I hated my family, that bastard who killed Adrian and all those who flaunted their normality at me while I watched them through the red hue. 'I must feed, kill, destroy.'

It was time I needed to go. I ran down the stairs but slowed my descent as I could feel that the monster within me wanted to burst through the door and rip the world asunder. I had to rein this demon in. I could sense that the street was empty, so I moved the table aside, slipped out and closed the old door before starting to hunt.

It was busy as normal. All that blood. The food that was on offer: Man, woman and child. Black, white and even an old Chinese woman shuffling along with a bundle in her arms. The burning was increasing, but I needed to stay in control, yet I was struggling and panting like an overheated dog.

I slumped against a wall as the demon inside started to take over. It was then that a red-haired girl ghosted past me, her scent was like honey to a bee. It was divine, and once again the predator I was came to the fore. I stalked her as seagulls do fishing boats. I registered a flash of light as she entered a door on a small side street. I stood opposite and unknowingly reached out with my senses. There were four people in the house: plenty of food.

It wasn't too late, but the burning felt like it was devouring me from the inside out. I had to do it. I walked towards damnation and knocked on the door. I heard a few curse words, and then the door was opened by a man in his forties.

'What the bloody hell do you want?' he barked.

The darkness within me descended. My true self was only an observer as the beast punched the man. The crack of his neck could be heard as his head was thrown backwards, killing him instantly. Evil had entered the house. It didn't matter how much the good in me screamed, the monster went to work.

A woman came running out of a door brandishing a knife, which I caught easily. With a twist shattering her wrist into mush before pulling her towards me, I sank my fangs into her throat and drank. But the demon needed to move quickly, so the middle-aged woman was quietened with a quick snap of her neck, separating her spinal cord and body from her soul.

I then moved swiftly up the stairs where the last two heartbeats could be found. As I crested the stairs, a red-haired young girl covered in freckles walked into me. Before she could even draw breath, my claws had torn out her beautiful throat. From my right came a piercing scream. I spun around and there she was, the red-haired angel who had led me to this house. She tried to flee and hide behind her bedroom door. It didn't work. The monster wanted his prize, and he won out that night. Unlike her family, her death wasn't quick or easy. The demon wanted to play, and play he did.

I slept throughout the day at that house and woke late afternoon. I didn't want to see what I had done, but the cold, naked woman told me all I needed to know. The monster had had its fun with the poor girl.

I got up and walked over to the water jug and bowl sat on a table in her room and washed my naked body. I threw sheets over her as a funeral shroud. My clothes were ruined by claws and blood, so I went in search of clothes and hopefully some money – they wouldn't need it. The father had some old work clothes that fitted me as well as a few pounds around the place.

The house was now devoid of life; nothing good resided there anymore. Adults were lying just where they had been felled last night. The youngest had fallen down the stairs, spraying arterial blood down the walls as she went. As the light started to fade outside, I spread paraffin oil from the lamps throughout the house before placing candles under the curtains at the rear of the property. No one on the street should notice the fire too soon, allowing the newly moved bodies to be burned.

Just as I walked out through the door, I scrutinised the flame-bathed house and vowed in honour of that family's life that I would kill the man who made me into this abomination. Then I walked away from the house of death and into the night.

As I walked, I noticed the need to feed was no longer there. So, clearly, I had fed enough, even though I had killed innocents. It was then that I decided I would never take the life of an innocent person again. I would track down this so-called Jack the Ripper and as I did, I would feed upon the wrongdoers of London town that plagued this city.

That night I decided to right a wrong and avenge the death of my friend, Adrian. I walked back to the army barracks and skulked around in the shadows before breaking into my commanding officer's office and riffling through his mountain of files. I found my personnel file, slid it in between flesh and shirt, and then continued my hunt through his office.

What I found in his desk drawer well and truly brought back the rage. I lifted out the paperwork and read it. It was the report of my friend's death. Damn them, they had painted him as a murderer, and the bastard sergeant major and the old boy brigade agreed to let it happen. The rage might have flared, but this time I was in control as I walked calmly through the night and headed silently to my destination. Luckily, as I had spent most of my service life here, I knew the guards' routines and where I could find just the thing I needed for my night's work.

The front door of the house was unlocked, although that wouldn't have stopped me. It just proved that he was a foolish, arrogant man. I could hear his walrus-like snoring filtering from upstairs in the small house. I stepped slowly thinking that he would be ready for anything with all his years of service. In reality and life, he was ready for nothing. He was at least six foot five, with a big bushy beard and a nose that was pointing in a direction that Mother Nature had never intended.

By the looks of the empty whisky bottle on his bedside table, he had been drinking hard. I am guessing that's what you do when you get away with murdering your wife and her lover, my best friend. I stood over the bear of a man and struck him in the face, just hard enough to wake him. He woke fast. But my second hit was faster, sending him back into a forced sleep.

I was prepared. I had brought rope and handcuffs. When the man woke up, he was tied spread-eagled on the bed and unable to move. A match flared to life as I struck it, bathing me in the light it had created. I put the match to the oil lamp on the bedside cabinet, and that's when I saw his eyes go wide, not with fear but surprise and then anger. And don't I know something about the latter one.

'Hello, Sergeant Major,' I said softly as I put a bayonet to his throat. 'I see murder agrees with you,' I sneered.

The man outdid my sneer. 'Morris, come crawling back, did ya?' he said in a mocking tone. 'You're lucky I didn't kill you as well.' He laughed.

I sat on the side of the bed and looked at him. 'Maybe so, Gibson,' I snapped, knowing that anyone using his name without his rank would send him into a fury, causing him to rant and spray spittle around the place. That was certainly the reaction I received, so I shoved an old sock into his mouth. 'Well, if I'm lucky, that makes you unlucky because, my dear Gibson, you will not survive this night,' I stated calmly.

That did the job as his eyes widened and he started to panic. He thrashed around until a slap with the bayonet quietened him down, splitting his scalp, sending blood into his eyes – and the burning within me to return, damn it. I pulled out the file that had earlier filled me with so much rage.

'So, it appears the colonel has defended your story that Adrian raped and killed your wife, which sent you mad, making you kill my friend,' I recapped, staring at him. 'Truth is, they had been seeing each other for months and they were in love. But that doesn't matter as they are together now, and neither you, Gibson, nor I will ever join them.' I bared my fangs, making him struggle even more.

I bit into his wrist just to sate the need to feed but not yet wanting him killed that way. We locked eyes as I pulled away, and I smiled allowing my blood-soaked fangs to drop his blood onto his bed. Unfortunately, that's when the smell of urine overran the potent smell of his whisky-imbued blood.

It was a bit weird, but I stripped naked. I think in the end that scared him more than the bayonet ever did, but I couldn't keep changing clothes, and I knew this one was going to be particularly messy.

'Now, Gibson, you killed my best friend and your wife,' I said and stuck the bayonet into his thigh, drawing a scream from him and allowing me to drink. 'You should've been a better husband to your wife, and maybe I should've been a better friend to Adrian.' I stuck the bayonet into his other vast thigh; the sock continued to keep his screaming muffled nicely.

As the time went on he was struggling to remain conscious, so I decided to grab his attention by slapping him roughly until he could focus.

'Gibson, you were always a shit, and you will die like one too.' We locked eyes as I slowly pushed the bayonet into his chest cavity, and there it penetrated his black heart, removing another monster from this cold world.

I left the bayonet in him, cleaned myself up and decided to check for any money, of which there was a good few pounds. Clearly, he must have had some kind of racket going on. Another plus point was the Enfield MKII along with twenty .476 rounds. *Try outrunning a bullet*, I thought, my mind returning to finding the monster who had done this to me. I smiled as I put the pistol into my belt and walked away from the barracks for the last time.

What I found out later was that the police had visited my parents to see if they knew my whereabouts, which obviously they didn't. But they had showed off their new adopted boy, and what a good boy he was too. Well, that's what Adrian's parents told me when I visited and handed them some money. I told them that the man who killed my friend, their son, was now in hell. They knew what I had done, but it wouldn't be voiced or talked about. We embraced, and then I went out into the night and back to the shop where I had made my home, if you could call it that, while I hunted for the monster.

Chapter 4

The newspaper was still full of the Jack the Ripper killings. I pieced together the knowledge that it was the murder of Mary Ann Nichols who I had drunkenly stumbled across at the Buck's Row stable. Not that I could save her, or myself as it played out. No longer did I have to name the man who bit me then, he was now called Jack the Ripper, public enemy number one, and I knew that I would kill him.

As the nights went by, I spent my time walking the dark streets, feeding on the street toughs and wrongdoers near the Thames, that way I could let the body float away, keeping any police searches far from my home.

As the days turned into weeks, victims were still coming. Thanks to my nightly activities I managed to keep the rage and hunger at bay. The regular feedings kept the criminals scared and money in my pocket, to the point that I could afford to rent the shop I had been living in, and at a cheap rate as this area of London was classed as a piece of shit.

At the end of September while hunting, I caught a hint of the Ripper's scent. Many people pulled away from me as I moved from shadow to shadow, and it was then that I heard the piercing whistles of panicked coppers. I moved quickly through the crowd, ending up in Dutfields Yard. I could hear chatter that it was another body. But his scent tailed off somewhere else. My pace built as it became stronger, and then another scream could be heard far off in the fog. A knife gleamed in the fog-filtered lamplight. I ran into the Ripper, knocking him from his most recent victim. The knife he held clattered onto the street as we both went sprawling. He pulled another knife from his coat. As I grasped for my pistol, I found it gone.

'You,' Jack growled angrily. 'Why do you hound me, boy?'

'You turned me into a monster. I've killed innocents all because of you!' I cried furiously as we circled each other around the corpse, which was creating steam from the torn open belly.

His teeth glistened as they were bared. 'You should be on your knees, boy, thanking me. I have made you immortal. A god amongst these cattle,' answered the Ripper in superior tones as we continued to circle each other.

But once again there was a scream echoing from my left, then another before the whistles started. My eyes had left him for a split second, but when I turned back he was gone, with knife and bag. I found my gun in the gutter amongst the blood and filth. I gave it a shake before disappearing into the night.

My hunt for the man and monster they called Jack the Ripper would continue. I knew our paths would cross again, but for now I had to live and start the future I had always hoped for. Although, it would be by moonlight and not in my father's shadow. It was time to start my own business.

Thankfully, with my previous skills as a painter/decorator, I had the place looking good as the month of November started. Morris Pawnbrokers was now open for business. It seemed ideal as I had plenty of cash thanks to the criminals, especially when I hunted the gangs down by the river and docks. When the wrong sort turned up in the dark hours to sell something they had stolen, they would be a handy meal too. Through all this though I had two constant thoughts in my head: kill the Ripper and contact Annabel. She had become a permanent fixture in my dreams which calmed the sleeping beast that resided inside me.

I was on my usual night-time wanderings in the very early hours of November 9th, walking down Dorset Street in Spitalfields, when I heard a scream. None of the other night owls reacted, so I knew it was my superior hearing. Could it be him again? Or just the normal domestic? I walked quickly into Millers Court. My blood was boiling and the rage embraced me. My vision turned red as I followed the scent of blood.

When I reached number 13, I could see that the door was open a crack. I could hear movement behind the door, but it all went silent as I moved closer. My rage was eager to escape. As I moved in, the monster came out with a bloodied bag and knife which glinted in the lamplight spilling in from the street. Jack was startled as he realised who was in front of him, again.

'YOU!' he growled. 'Leave now, boy, or die!' he cursed, and with such dexterity he spun the weapon around on his finger.

'You monster, tell me what have you done to me?' I demanded, feeling my incisors and claws lengthen ready for the fight. 'You've ruined my life.'

The man just laughed a guttural laugh. He was nearly my body double but sported large sideburns, his fangs were out and his eyes were now totally black.

'Ruined it, boy, I made your life better. We are the shepherds, boy. These mortals are our flock, to kill at our pleasure,' he hissed, mixing his metaphors. I'm sure he used a different one last time.

'But why are you cutting them up? You're sick!' I shook my head in confusion and tried to stare him down, but he was clearly a madman. He not only had blood dripping from his jaw, but he was also salivating. He just laughed at my amazement, and then in a blink of an eye he ran at me. He was moving too quickly for me to dodge out of the way. His blade slid into my shoulder with ease, making me fall back, but thanks to my army training I allowed him to follow through and rolled him over the top of me, sending him out into the street.

As I spun around to get up, he was already on his feet. He gave me a feral grin as I pulled out his knife with a slight hiss of pain. Then he ran, and the rage took over as I got up and made chase. Pain be damned. He was quick; both shops and people were left in our wake as we ran.

Neither of us tired, but the rage lessened just enough for me to think. I felt for the pistol in my coat that I had always carried since that night at the barracks. I ran with it in my right hand, cocked ready to fire. I just had to wait for the right moment, which came a few minutes later as he headed down a narrow alleyway, barely enough room for two to walk side by side.

As I turned into the alleyway, I saw him bouncing off a drainpipe, which was knocked to the floor with a clatter. I stopped quickly, raised the gun and fired three shots one after the other.

With a scream, he fell clutching his legs. I started to run to him. Then he leapt up again and tried to flee, but this time I was much closer. I shot him twice in the back, knocking him down. I finally managed to reach him and kicked him over with my foot, seeing him cough up blood whilst still smiling at me.

'That won't kill me, boy. You know nothing.' He gave me a bloody chuckle.

I watched as the bullet seemed to be pushed from his chest. I placed my final bullet into his forehead. Everything stilled. The air was the typical smoggy but crisp type, and then I saw his chest wounds starting to heal themselves, which meant the bastard was still alive. So, the book was true: only the sun and a stake to the heart would kill.

I scanned the area as his body started to stir once again. Then there it was, my salvation, a broken chair leg amongst the usual trash found on London's backstreets. I grabbed the nearest piece. Just as his eyes opened and locked with mine, the timber broke through his chest cavity, rupturing his heart. Before he could react, the alley was illuminated as his body was engulfed in white flames that burned him and everything around him: body, medical bag and any evidence that he even existed.

I stood over the ashes of the monster that had ruined my life. I had hoped that the rage inside me would've lessened by despatching him, but it still lingered, albeit in the shadows, and just as powerful. I had my soul taken from me. That was my penalty. I hoped Annabel was okay.

The air was now full of police whistles and shouts. So after putting the now empty revolver away, I fled into the darkness and far from the scene of my revenge. The burning in my stomach had returned again, but not the rage this time, it must have been the smell of my blood from the rapidly healing wound in my shoulder. Although the killer was now gone, I was certain that the stain of his actions would linger for years to come.

Even though that monster was no longer alive, bodies continued to be found. These were all attributed to the man named Jack. Concerned that somehow Jack was not in fact dead, I scanned each murder scene, but not once did I catch a whiff of his foul scent. However, the remnants of the murderer's scent lingered and led me to them. Take a life, pay with your life.

In the New Year I employed a local woman call Suzanne Atkinson to work in my pawnshop. She was a mother of six in her thirties, so I knew she was a strong woman. Suzie, which was the preferred moniker she chose to be called, worked the eight-to-five shift, then I would take over. I set up the shop to cater for my specific needs with the counter nearer the back, as there was never any direct sunlight there.

Taking this job worked for Suzie as she lived close by. I allowed her to bring in her children if they were ill; she could keep them in the back as I rested upstairs in my room. The downside to this was finding strands of Suzie's hair all over the place. Long black and grey tendrils attaching themselves to you, when you least expected it. Although it was nice to have some female company, it had always been ghostly quiet when I started up the business, now her voice was echoing around the place when I rested in my pitch-dark room, whether she had customers or not. The money rolled in with both of us running the shop. And in the evenings, so did the food.

When I did start embracing the criminal fraternity into my shop, I had an issue with waste management, but then I had a eureka moment. The shop had a small garden and yard out the back, so I bought a pair of breeding pigs, which did the trick.

I found that my condition settled down as time went on. To keep the demon at rest I had to feed every couple of days, but this was dependent on the energy I had used. Luckily, thanks to the nice dark cellar and rope, where Toby the Ice Pick Thompson or others of his ilk tended to hang, such specimens could last over a few nights. And I found that not draining them dry allowed me to keep them alive and juicy. When their hearts failed, they then became piggy food.

After the first litter of piglets arrived, I moved the sow and her babies into another run so the piglets would feed on the mother's milk and normal scraps. Then I left the boar, who I nicknamed Killer, to carry on with my waste removal needs. Suzie would sell the piglets at a later date, mainly to her friends and family, and I gave her family the biggest as a thank you. It was either that or she would've stolen it anyway.

One evening we sat in the back room together, it was now March 1889 and the business was thriving, so I bought us a nice bottle of wine to share. Although Suzie admitted to being a beer-loving girl, it didn't stop her trying it. I had learnt that I could eat and drink in the usual way of humans, but it just didn't give me the energy I needed.

'Albert, when you gonna do some courting, love?' she asked in her no-nonsense way. 'What about that girl…? What's her name?' She tapped her lone front tooth. 'Anna?'

I had to smile. 'Annabel, she's a maid in a house on the Strand,' I replied and took a sip of wine.

'Ah, I see. So why don't ya walk out with her, then? You talk about ya schooldays all the time.' She then gave her vast cleavage a scratch with a broken nail, where she had punched the pig named Killer because he nuzzled her where she didn't want him to.

'I wish I could, but you know my condition with the sun. You can't go knocking on doors in that part of town at night,' I explained, to which she gave a forced laugh. I frowned. 'What's so funny?'

'There's something going on with you, Albert. I have seen you out and about but never once in the bloody daylight. You sleep most of the day, then you wander the streets in the early mornings,' she said, narrowing her eyes at me.

I heard something metallic being slid out of something leather. I knew she had a knife, so I guess she was worried. I ran my hand through my hair and sighed. 'What can I say? I do have a condition that stops me going out in the daylight. That isn't a lie,' I explained sincerely, looking at her. 'And I do some of the best business in the early hours. What do you think I am, a killer or something?'

She shrugged her large, well-rounded shoulders. 'I've been around, Albert. I have seen some shit and stood toe to toe with some real bad men, and you, son, are not a bad man,' Suzie replied and took another draught. 'But something is off here. And if you want to continue our partnership, I want the truth.'

A dark laugh escaped my lips, which made Suzie slam her knife onto the counter and growl like a feral dog.

'Somehow I think the truth is somewhat scarier than any lie you or I can think up, Suzie.'

'I doubt that. Just remember this, Albert, I will keep your secrets, but if you lie to me again I will bury you!' she snapped before draining her drink. 'Oh, and Killer doesn't eat everything you throw in there, so think on that before you lie to me.'

I nodded. 'Okay, you got me, watch my mouth,' I instructed. As she looked, I lengthened my incisor.

She grabbed at her knife and threw it at me as she scrabbled back, sending stock to the floor. 'What the fuck are you?' she shouted, wide-eyed.

'Well, Suzie, take a seat and I will tell you,' I said calmly and watched her lift up her chair and sit down, but noticeably further away. 'Did you want your knife back?' I asked, pointing to the handle protruding from my shoulder.

Her eyes got even wider. 'Shit. Doesn't that hurt, Albert?'

'Emotionally and physically, yes, I guess it does, but not that much if I'm honest.' I smiled, and with a squelch I pulled the knife from my shoulder and placed it onto the counter. 'Well, not so long ago I was bitten in a fight and infected, which turned me into what you see before you.'

I saw her nod as she slowly picked up the knife and held it securely in her meaty hand.

I continued to explain, 'Have you heard the term "vampire"?'

'Wot, like in the stories? Sucking blood from virgins and such like?' she asked with fear in her voice and sweat on her brow.

'Yes. Although, to be honest, you'd be hard pushed to find many virgins around here, Suzie,' I said and laughed, which did bring a faint smile to her face. 'I feed on those who break the law, and mainly the ones who hurt people. They deserve it.'

The room went quiet for a long moment.

'So, what happened to the bloke who bit you? Is he still out and about hurting people?' she asked, her mouth open aghast at what she was hearing.

I shook my head. 'No, he's dead. I killed him myself,' I said and sighed. 'I am sorry, Suzie, I wish I had told you earlier, but, as you can imagine, it's a difficult topic to bring up.'

Suzie visibly relaxed at this point, realising that she was certainly not in any danger from me. 'Don't worry about it. There's plenty of monsters in this world – as long as you eat them and not me or mine. I guess we won't be having a walk in the sun, then. If the stories are right, that is.' She smiled.

I was surprised that she was so receptive to this shocking reality, but she always was a quick-minded woman. 'Your family are safe from me, that I promise you; and yes, you're right, the sun is hazardous to me,' I stated.

She just smiled and drank another whole glass of wine. I feared for her husband, as Suzie had previously declared that alcohol made her loins tingle. That was one weird conversation.

'Anyway, when are you going to see Annabel? It's time for you to share your life with someone,' she slightly slurred before lifting up the bottle to see if there was any left – the answer was no. Her husband really was in for a hell of a night.

I watched Suzie sticking her tongue into the neck of the bottle. There was nothing classy about this woman at all, but that's why I liked her. Suzie tried three times to get up. On the fourth she managed it and then rebounded off the wall, showering the floor with plaster dust. She walked through the shop before turning back to face me.

'Go and see your girl, Albert. Start a new life,' she instructed, and then fell through the shop door and started to shout at people in the street, making me laugh. But I knew she was right.

Later that evening I closed the shop and went for a walk. The foggy air of London town made me bark a few coughs making the locals laugh, but they soon scuttled away when I gave them a stern, cold look, which I have been told is scary in gaslight. I made my way to the McAdams' house where I had worked with my father that last time. I stared up and searched the windows wondering if I could see Annabel. I knew the servants' quarters were on the top floor. The hour was late, but not so late that the servants would be sleeping.

I knew I was alone on the streets, so I slowly took step after step, my heels making clicking sounds on the cobbles. The curtains were drawn at the front of the house, but I could see shadows in the back garden, which meant the kitchen and back rooms were occupied as lamps were on at this time.

The shadows were my friend as I moved into the back garden. I could see through the kitchen window and there was the gobby chef. She was giggling as the butler had reached around her and given her chest a grope. He then turned quickly and barked some orders to whoever was behind him. I had known men like that in the army – pure bullies. My father had told me that just because a man fights for his country, it doesn't mean he's a good man.

The back door then opened, bathing the garden in a glaring bright light. And there she was. The rage in me peaked as I saw Annabel had a black eye. She was bringing something out to be scattered onto the vegetable garden. No one else was with her, so I tried to catch my old school friend's attention. '*Psst*, Anna,' I whispered.

She turned like a snake; I noticed a knife in her hand. 'Who's there?' she hissed while scanning the deep shadows.

I could tell she wasn't scared; it was anger. That made me smile, which tamed the demon, for now. 'It's me Albert, Albert Morris,' I whispered back and moved into the light.

Her eyes softened, but the knife never moved at all. 'What are you doing here, Berty?' she asked, using the name that only she had ever called me. Her eyes darted back towards the house; there was fear in them.

'I came to see you. I didn't want to annoy your employers,' I explained, moving closer. We were now within two or three feet of each other. 'I missed you.'

A blush ran riot across her beautiful face. 'I miss you, too, Berty. I was worried when you never came back, and your father was so angry when I asked where you were,' she said before sliding her knife back into her pocket. She then stepped forward and hugged me, but what surprised me more was how frail she felt.

'Anna, you're so thin. Don't they feed you?' I whispered into her ear.

She leaned back and looked into my eyes. 'They do, but I share mine with Emma and Stan,' she whispered back and placed her head onto my chest. 'Berty, why can't I hear your heart?' she asked, even though her hold didn't lessen.

I sighed. 'It's there, just very faint. It has always been a problem,' I said, trying to brush off her concerns. 'Do you have any days off?' I placed a gentle kiss on the top of her head, which made her arms tighten around me.

'No, we don't have much free time,' she said, and then looked back towards the house again. 'If you can wait till later, I will sneak down.' She then pressed her warm lips against mine. 'Blimey, even your lips are cold. You should get home into the warm, Albert Morris.'

Laughing, I reassured her, 'I'll be okay, Anna, I'm a big boy now.' I cupped her cheek, nodded, then silently moved away and watched Anna continue with her tasks in the garden. Like an angel she drifted back into the light of the house with a small smile on her warm lips. So, now to wait.

It must have been a good couple of hours before the back door opened silently. She stepped out wearing her ankle-length nightgown with a woollen shawl wrapped around her and black shoes on her otherwise bare feet. This time there were no nerves. She just slammed into my chest, squashing her body into mine. Her heart was racing.

'Miss me?' I chuckled.

'Forever,' she whispered from my chest and then pulled me towards the garden shed.

I followed her into the spider-ridden place where she bent down to light a candle. She had clearly been here before.

'A regular meeting place?' I laughed. I could see her smile in the darkness.

'Not like that, Berty. We just use it when Big Mack the butler gets drunk while the master and mistress go away.' She lit the candle.

I sat on a large bag of God knows what, which allowed Anna to sit on my lap and give me another kiss.

'Firstly, I'm sorry to hear about Adrian. He was crazy but fun.'

We hugged. 'Thanks,' and once again she captured my lips. It was warm and loving, nothing like I had felt before in this lifetime so far. We parted and locked eyes.

She pointed a finger into my chest. 'You Mr, owe me a story – from the day you left here to now,' Annabel said happily.

'Indeed, I do, but then you tell me how you got that shiner,' I replied, pointing to her black eye.

Her hand instantly moved to her eye and her fingers stroked the discoloured skin, which looked even worse in candlelight. 'That's easy. Big Mack grabbed something he shouldn't, so I slapped him and I got one back,' she said in a nonplussed way.

Mental note: kill the butler. So, I told her my story. After which, in her defence, she never shivered or pulled away. She smiled when I told her about the Ripper's fate, then frowned about the rage I battled with every day. But I reassured her that I now had a routine: feeding on wrongdoers. Finally, I finished by telling her about Suzie and the shop. 'And that's my story,' I concluded.

She just sat there looking me up and down. I could feel the turmoil inside her, whether to flee or not. 'Well, Berty, your story is better than mine,' she said in light tones, which gave me hope. 'But I need to sleep and think about what you have said. It's a lot to take in.' She gave me a quick peck on the lips, stood up, then bent down to put out the candle, which offered her backside in all its cotton-covered glory. I don't know even to this day if she did it to tease or test whether I was a gentleman or not. Every time I asked in the future, she just smiled that little smile she had. It was so innocent that I swear she could've started the Great Fire of London with that match and with one smile the police would have let her walk free.

I stood up quickly. 'Okay, when shall we meet again?' I asked, worried that she would leave and I wouldn't know if she wanted to ever see me again.

'This time and place in a week. By then I would've thought it all through,' she said carefully. We both headed out of the shed holding hands, then she turned and kissed me again. 'In a week, Berty,' and with that she ghosted away into the house.

I headed home but was waylaid by a pair of muggers who darted out of a side alleyway. Any other night I would've sensed them, but my mind was full of Anna and my nose full of her rose water scent. I grunted in pain as a knife slid into my side.

'Give us ya money!' the man with the knife spat with his whisky-fuelled breath.

I fell to my knees. Despite any new abilities as a vampire, wounds still hurt. That's when I heard a second heartbeat approach, the first man's accomplice. Now I knew it was going to be messy, and I liked this shirt. Suzie was going to be upset because she offered to do my washing and cleaning around the place for a bit more money. My thoughts were interrupted by the knife slammed into my back.

'ARGGHHHHHH! Please stop!' I cried.

The second man gave me a kick to the ribs. 'Hand over your cash now and we'll leave you to die in peace,' he growled in a gravely tone.

I coughed up some blood, but I could feel my wound knitting together. It's a weird feeling, a bit like a human zip. 'Firstly, I have no money!' I said sternly. I coughed up a bloody lump and spat it onto the man's dirty work boot. As I looked up, I realised that my whole suit was ruined. That let my rage flash. 'You are so dead!'

Both men had knives pulled which glinted in the moonlight.

'And who's gonna do it? You?' the second man mocked and gave me another kick.

This time it was my teeth not a knife that glinted in the darkness, making them freeze. Before they could utter another word, I was up on my feet. My right hand, claws adorned, swiped across the stabber's throat, sending arterial spray into the night. The man instantly dropped to the floor clutching his ruined throat, making bubbling sounds. The rib kicker tried to run, but my left hand grabbed his left shoulder and pulled him back while digging my claws into his flesh, making him scream. I then finished him off by plunging my fangs into his neck and drinking. With a quick twist of his neck, he was dead.

I stood there looking at the mess around me. 'Bugger,' I said to myself and quickly took any money they had before using my clawed hand to tear out the noticeable fang puncture marks. Hopefully Mr Rat and his friends would come a calling. I soon headed into the night, leaving the muggers to their self-made fate.

The next day was bad twofold. Firstly, my suit was ruined, and it was my favourite. Secondly, a tired and hung-over Suzanne found out about the said suit. She was very loud and vocal about it. In my time I have killed many people and vampires, but still to this day I am glad I never opened my bedroom door as she pounded her meaty fist on it. All I had to do was wait until she went back downstairs to open the shop.

Time passed slowly for me that week. My mind had only one thought: Annabel. Even Suzie was laughing at me wandering around with my sad, woeful face. I tried to scare her by baring my fangs at her, but the woman just laughed and carried on about her duties.

The shop was carrying on steadily enough. The good thing about crime is that when one of the criminals move away to another astral plane, thanks to me and Killer the pig, there is always another person on the wrong side of the law to step in. So, we get a regular stream of stolen goods. Obviously, I give anything too high profile straight to an old school friend. He had come into the shop one night and we became reacquainted. Mickey Edwards was his name. He was a beast of a man, at least six foot two, and the same again wide. But he was always polite, even to the people he was snapping in half. He was a perfect copper. I always remembered him being a total hit with the ladies. As a result, he married his sweetheart from school, the one and only Tabatha Hawkins, a pretty, petite blonde who barely reached five feet.

Mickey and I had a good working relationship. I gave him the goods and a description of the said robber, but Mickey never looked that hard, not that he knew I had fed on them. To him it was just the fact that people had their goods back, so why bother? But it was nice to see him when he was on a night shift; we could have a cuppa and talk about the old days. Although, he seemed to know more about what my old friend Adrian and I used to get up to than I knew about him.

When I mentioned to Mickey that I had seen Annabel at her job, I saw his face straighten. 'What's up? What do you know?' I asked.

There was clearly a war being fought in his mind. Should he say or not? Mickey rubbed his bald head. 'It was a couple of years ago, me and my colleague "No Knees" were on a late patrol around the Strand when a maid came running over and told us there had been screams coming from the house next door to her employers,' he explained, taking a sip of his tea before looking me in the eye. 'We found Anna on the kitchen floor badly beaten. The butler had lost his temper with her, but that's as far as it went. Anna wouldn't press charges, plus the owner of the house pulled some strings, so that was it.'

I growled internally and the monster inside me wanted to dispense justice on the bastard butler. 'How badly was she hurt, Mikey?' I asked coldly.

His face dropped. 'The rumour was that she was found in bed bleeding by the other maid, so the next-door's cook's sister was called, her being a midwife. It was the best they could hope for,' he said, knowing that most housemaids couldn't afford a doctor. 'The midwife said she had been hit hard in her lower abdominal area. She had been pregnant at the time, which of course she lost, but she was hit very hard to the point where Anna might not be able to get pregnant again. But, of course, they wouldn't call a doctor for a servant,' he said, raising an eyebrow. We both read in between the lines there.

After that night I was fighting the fury not to run over there straight away and tear the man's manhood away from his body while looking into his fear-filled eyes. I told Suzie about what I had learnt, but she just said it was commonplace that either the master of the house or another male would use the young girls for fun. And if they got pregnant, they would try to get rid of the scandal before it became too prominent – either through a back-alley doctor or a simple beating to the stomach.

It disgusted me what had happened behind those closed doors of the so-called social betters, but tonight was the night I would find out the truth and hopefully that my dear Annabel would choose to be with me.

'Right, this is not a date, so you can put on some old clothes, just in case,' Suzie demanded.

'Just in case what?' I frowned at her insinuation.

She put her hand on her well-rounded hip and raised a quizzical eyebrow.

Okay, maybe she did have a point, but what did surprise me was the fact that she hugged me and placed a warm kiss on my cheek.

'Good luck, Albert. Try not to kill anyone,' she said with a hint of love and caring. She then proceeded to push me out of my own shop so she could have a drink, then head home and either fight or have sex with her put-upon husband – or both, who knew.

I headed out into the fog-covered streets of London. People had once again melted into the shadows as my shoes clicked on the filth-encrusted cobbles. It meant that they hadn't done anything bad enough to bring my ire to bear upon them; it was only the truly evil ones that ended up in the pigpen.

My journey was calming, although the fog did seem to claw at me like it was trying to hold me back from doing something, albeit a good cause.

But nothing was going to hold me back. Whatever she wanted this night, I would deliver. It was nice to have purpose again, even though blood may be spilt.

Chapter 5

I stood in front of my destination. The fog had thickened on my journey, but no one had the desire to heed my progress. A couple of Peelers saw me, but they just nodded and saluted with their truncheon brought to their helmet brims. They knew I had helped out my friend by tracking down some criminals who were in The Slaughtered Lamb – and like the handy vampire I was, I tracked them to a desolate warehouse by the docks.

The gas street lighting burned away, but it hardly illuminated a thing through the thick fog, which may be beneficial for my purposes this night. I headed across the street and into the grounds of the McAdams's. The lamps were still lit downstairs, so the housemaids were still working while the cook and butler relaxed and the master and mistress were asleep.

Annabel and Emily could be seen through the kitchen window talking about something. They look tired but content in their work, although their white aprons looked dishevelled. I knew I was early, so I took a seat on a garden bench which was cloaked in darkness. I could see them but not vice versa.

In time, most of the lights in the house were extinguished, so it was a case of waiting until my late-night visitor turned up, to either give me that which my dead heart desired or crush it with her words. I sat down on the sack which I had used as my seat last time and waited. The door creaked open thirty minutes later. With my enhanced vision I could see the nightdress-adorned Annabel.

'Berty, you there?' she asked hesitantly, putting her hand out trying to find me in the pitch darkness.

'Yes, Anna, I'm here,' I said softly, but it still made her jump. She looked so frail as I took her hands and pulled her into a hug. 'How are you?' I asked, and then watched her bend over and scrabble about for the candle and matches. Soon enough, after some only just silent swear words, we were bathed in candlelight, but her nervousness was evident.

'Berty, I've missed you.' She sighed and captured my lips with hers. They were so soft and warm. In that moment, I could almost feel my heart pulse again. We parted and looked into each other's eyes; our arms were still wrapped around each other. 'You're so cold, Berty. How have you been?'

I gave her a smile. 'Working hard; the shop is doing well.' I flicked my head towards the house and asked, 'How are they treating you?'

Anna shivered in my arms. 'It's okay, let's sit.' She pulled up a crate, so I took up my station again. 'Mack and cook are a pain, but that's about it,' she explained, but I could tell there was more to it.

'My friend Mickey said he was called here once when Mack got a bit angry at you and you were hurt?' I asked.

Her face fell. 'He should know to keep his mouth shut! Typical copper!' she spat angrily. She moved closer to me and leaned her head on my shoulder. 'But, yes,' she continued, 'that was a bad time. I was ill for a fair old while, but I'm better now.' She gave me a brittle smile, which looked even worse in this light. Her skin was parchment thin and her eyes dull and sallow.

I kissed the top of her head and pulled her into my side. 'Have you decided, Anna, about you and me?' I asked with worry, my stomach acid trying to melt everything in its way.

'Yes, I want to be with you, Berty, but…'

I felt the bottom drop out of my world as I feared all my plans and hopes would be destroyed in the next few moments.

'I can't leave Stanley and Emily here.'

I lifted her up and placed her onto my lap. Yes, I was strong, but she was also so light. 'What do we do, then?' I asked, looking for a resolution to the problem before us. 'The shop isn't profitable enough to buy a house for all of us yet.' I felt her nuzzle into my neck even more.

'Why is life so hard, Berty? Those old sods upstairs don't go out, they don't have visitors, but they live like kings and queens,' she said while tears dripped onto me.

We sat in silence as shadows danced around us and rogue drafts toyed with the candle flame. 'Anna, I have an idea,' I said softly, and then looked down as she looked up. 'I can get rid of them, all of them. And you, Stan, Emily and I can take the house over, and—' She stopped me by pressing her hand against my mouth. It was then I realised that I had pushed too soon. The air turned thick; our eyes never wavered from each other.

'You're talking about murdering people, Albert,' she gasped, shaking her head quickly. 'I was willing to give us a try, but to offer to kill someone who puts their trust in me every day, are you mad?' It looked like she was shaking with anger. Anna just kept on muttering repeatedly, then she suddenly stood up and looked down at me. 'Don't ever come back. You're not the boy I knew. Leave me alone, you…you…beast!' she spat with tears flowing freely down her face. Anna turned and walked out of the shed and away into the night.

I put my hand onto the flame that flickered, which my sore eyes were drawn to as my heart shattered into a million pieces, even though it hadn't worked since that fateful night.

I had read it so wrong. The demon inside was mocking me for being weak. The fury was building and telling me to feed on the household. But not just them, to tear the whole world asunder.

It was thirty minutes until I reined in the beast enough to walk home. My head was down as I left the shed. I knew she was watching me, and that she was still crying, but I didn't look up or back as I melted into the fog, allowing it to eclipse my body and despair. It was naïve of me to think that I could find happiness in this world. I only had one stop on the way as another ghost drifted out and slid a knife into my back. I knew the mugger was coming as I could sense his presence, but I deserved the pain, so

I allowed him to slide the knife into me repeatedly. I then let myself drop onto the filthy path.

His hands searched my pockets, but unfortunately for him I don't carry money. And what was even worse for the foul-breathed murderer? My beast wanted to play. What was left thereafter not even God could identify as one of his creations.

I awoke the next afternoon. By the noise coming from downstairs, I guessed my employee, Suzie, had found my clothes and was once again as angry as a summer thunderstorm. I was in limbo be a vampire and dominate the woman and bring her to her knees, or just hide up here.

The beast gave me a poke, so I washed and dressed. Then, with fury building up inside me and a job to do, I stormed into the shop like a Viking warrior, who was then cut down by a flying coal scuttle.

'What did you do last night, you beard splitter (penis)!' the banshee who was Suzie shouted. She stood over my prone self, tearing strips off me. Not once did she wait for me to answer, she just continued with her diatribe until she stormed out, leaving the mighty vampire lying on a dusty floor in shock. It hadn't been a good few days.

Suzanne came back the next morning with a missing tooth and a black eye, but she was radiant with a glow about her that only an angel would dare have. After leaving me, she must have gone to the pub, proceeded to get drunk, and then fought and rutted all night with her husband, poor bugger. I saw him once walking with all of his children; he was as thin as a butcher's pencil and had less teeth than his missus.

She slammed two bottles of beer on the counter and opened them both with her teeth and then handed one to me. 'Spill it!' she demanded. 'What happened?'

I sunk into my seat and told her everything. That's when her empty beer bottle wrapped itself around my head, sending me to the ground.

'You really are stupid, Albert. Let the girl plan. She wanted to be with you, and she might have suggested that in the long run!' She then started to drink my beer as I was on the floor covered in the brown glass. 'It's like going from a kiss to taking your kids to school!' she said incredulously while shaking her head and gulping down more of my beer.

'What can I do to fix it?' I begged, still lying on the floor.

For once a softness came to her face; I wished it would happen more often. 'You can't, just leave the girl be,' Suzie instructed and opened a third bottle, spitting the cork into the shadowy corner. 'Let her come back to you – if she wants to, that is. Pursue her, and you will have no chance at all.'

I nodded. 'You're right, but I know her, she's as stubborn as you.' I cracked a smile up at the larger-than-life woman.

'Then it's a good job you're immortal, because the good ones make you wait,' she said dismissively before tossing the bottle over at me, breaking my nose. She chuckled at my screams and left for the day.

As the months went by, I stepped up my work with Mickey and his police friends. As ever, they were outnumbered by wrongdoers. Suzie was running the business like a demon, and surprisingly she hadn't become pregnant again. I put it down to her alcohol to blood ratio, or perhaps her age, but she wouldn't change herself for anyone.

It was early February 1890 when a letter came addressed to me, but Suzie flicked a mirror pointing the sun's rays in my direction, causing me to flee to the back of the shop as she read the letter bathed in sunlight. That woman was an evil genius. The employee gave me a smile that she only gave when I took back her empties and returned with full beer bottles.

She walked towards me with a slight limp. Five months ago she was kicked by a carthorse. Let's just say it cost me a day's takings to pay for that horse to be taken away to the slaughterhouse. I also had to pay the driver. But I blame myself.

I should never have let a bloodied and dirt-covered Suzanne walk out of my shop after picking up a sabre from the 1812 Napoleonic War. There was blood everywhere on the road, and Suzie's family was eating horse for a week; but then again, so was most of the street.

I took the letter from her and sat down to read it with hope.

My dearest Berty

I'm so sorry for calling you a horrible name that night. It only scared me so much because of where my thoughts and dreams had taken me. And hearing it coming from your mouth and hearing it out loud scared me to the core. I convinced myself that it was you who put those thoughts into my head, not me.

Please forgive me, my darling Berty. I need you in my life so we can be a family in this wonderful house. Even if you choose not to do it, we can runaway somewhere together.

Please come and see me soon. I miss the feel of your lips on mine.

I shall visit the shed the same time for the next week. But after what I called you, I wouldn't blame you not to come. I just hope that you do.

Lots of love
Your Anna xxx

I looked up with a smile. 'Where are my work clothes? I will be going out tonight,' I announced.

She shrugged dismissively. 'I dunno, you messed up your last lot. I'm not your housekeeper,' she said before walking out muttering.

'You have no heart, woman!' I shouted as the shop door clicked shut.

I saw her stop dead and slowly turn, her hair flowing in the wind. She gave me a look through the glass window that adorned the top half of the door, like a Valkyrie warrior from Norse mythology who were believed to swoop down upon a battlefield to decide who lived or died. For a moment I thought I was being judged. In those few seconds time didn't flow as normal; a fly was held stationary in mid-air. But then she was gone into the flow of people. I released the breath I didn't know I was holding, not that I could suffocate, but still, it was a scary moment.

She came back in an hour with some used work overalls and boots. Not a word was shared until the end of the day after she took some money from the till and went to head out again.

'Be careful, Albert,' she advised. 'This is your one chance to win her over. Let her take the lead.' She then headed out into the street again. Once more she stopped just outside the door, almost daring me to say something, but this time I kept my mouth shut.

The hours crept on, business was light but flowing, yet my mind was busy playing through the scenarios again. This time I kept all my hopes and dreams in the realms of reality. I pushed through the late-night crowds. It was a drinking night, which meant a busy day tomorrow as the local thieves and pickpockets would come to the shop to sell their wares. The locals knew I would buy, but not if the owners of the goods had been hurt or killed. There was always one who thought the rules didn't apply to him; they never got a second warning.

I stood opposite the house on this frosty night. I could see nothing but stars in the sky. Looking at the pathway with its layer of new frost, it looked as if I was walking on diamonds. My footsteps crunched as I walked across the road and headed to the shed. The house was only spotted with one or two lamps, so the servants were readying themselves for bed.

The shed door creaked open; nothing had really changed in the time I had spent away. But instead of sitting, I stood at the far end amongst the garden tools. My knuckles cracked as I flexed my fists while the time ticked by. Maybe she had changed her mind. She was right about me being a beast, but it was one that could be controlled, at times.

A smile crept across my face as I heard the brittle, frost-ridden grass shatter underneath a kind, gentle-footed soul: my Annabel.

She opened the door and instantly smiled. Although it was dark, the moonlight shone past her shawl-covered shoulders and lit my silhouette.

'Berty,' she whispered and rushed forward encompassing me in a hug. 'I'm so sorry, my love.' Tears then flowed.

'Shush now, Anna, that's in the past,' I soothed and kissed the top of her head as she sobbed into my chest. 'How have you been?'

It obviously hadn't been good as she sobbed even harder.

'Hell, Berty. Mack and the cook are just plain evil, especially when they get the drink in them.' She sobbed, wiping her gaunt face with her sleeve.

'I've missed you, Anna, but what can I do to help you?' I whispered, and then felt her cold tear-covered lips against mine. As our lips parted, I felt the warm air from her mouth hit mine.

'I agree with your plan, if you are willing,' she whispered conspiratorially, her eyes shifting around even though it was pitch black and there was nothing for her to see.

My eyes widened. Was I really hearing this? 'But if I do it, we can't go back, you know that?' I questioned, knowing that killing wasn't an easy thing, especially those who were still blessed with a soul. 'I don't want you to think of me as a monster, or Stanley and Emily.'

Anna shook her head. 'I will not lose a single night's sleep when Mack dies, or that nasty woman Bertha. She hits us if we are too slow, even poor Stan,' she said, pulling me back into a hug. 'Emily is a bit of a girl still, but she'll understand. But Stanley, we'll just tell him the master and madam have gone away, leaving you and me in the house.'

'And they don't have any visitors?' I checked with her.

Anna gave a dark laugh into my chest. 'As I understand it, they are known to be very brusque. In life and business in my years of being here only tradesmen come, and cook and Mack look after them,' she stated. 'They had a few parties, but they died out quickly enough.'

I nodded. 'What about money and the mortgage?'

'I've heard talk in the house. The mortgage is paid off and there is a large safe in the master's office – he never liked or trusted banks,' she explained. 'And bills are paid by us…well, Mack, but that won't make any difference as long as they get their money.'

It seemed almost too perfect. 'Seems like a dream,' I said, rubbing my face. As Anna parted to light the candle I took my seat, and then she settled onto my lap. 'What about the bodies? And what if the other two lose their nerve?' I asked, sounding Anna out with the possibilities of things that could go awry.

'Errrrr, I have drugged Emily and Stan, just enough for them to sleep soundly,' she said, looking into my eyes. 'I prayed you would come tonight.' Anna relaxed when she saw me smile. Although, she was shaking, but I think that was due to the cold, not me. 'The bodies, I'm not sure. Do you have any ideas, Berty?'

I sighed. It was something I had thought about over the time at the shop; the pigs were huge. 'Well, there is something we could try. I read the vampire book again,' I mused out loud. 'If it doesn't work, it's cold enough to keep them in the cellar for a time.' I saw her pull a face. 'But hopefully it won't come to that.'

'What first, Berty?'

I kissed her neck, making her squirm. 'Where are their rooms? Mack first, then the cook,' I asked, pulling her in tighter.

'Both Mack's and Bertha's rooms are just off the kitchen. They decided not to rut tonight as she was in a bit of a dither.' She looked at me with a worried smile.

I pressed my lips against hers and then pulled away again. 'Shall we, my love?' I asked, holding out my hand.

I saw a flicker of confusion in her eyes, then Anna nodded, got up and wetted her finger before extinguishing the candle. We headed out into the night hand in hand, her breath crystallised in the air as we walked to the house. The back door opened with only a slight squeak, but it wasn't loud enough to alert anyone.

In front of us were two doors. I looked down at my frail-looking Anna as she pointed to the left-hand door. I nodded, looked around and saw the look of confusion on her thin face as I picked up a large wooden spoon. I gave her a wink and slowly opened the butler's door. No such care was necessary as he was snoring like a pig; I could've kicked the door open and not disturbed him. Anna made to follow, but I held up my hand and mouthed, 'No.' She looked disappointed but hopefully she understood.

I stood over the man who smelt of whisky and feet. I raised my fist and punched the bear of a man straight in the face. Clearly, it wasn't hard enough because the snores finished instantly and his eyes shot open ready to see the second hit. Then that was it; he was out like a baby.

I moved the slumped body and bit into his neck, filling my mouth and throat with his booze-flooded blood, but not too much. I then bit into my wrist and let some of my vampire blood drop into his mouth to start the change.

The man just lay there, so I walked out straight into the cook's room. I recognised her from the visit with my father – a big red face and snoring just as loudly as the butler. Only one punch stopped the noise. She tasted slightly better than he did. Maybe it was the whisky. I gave her my blood and headed back to the woman-beating Mack.

His chest was still moving, but it was getting slower. I placed my hand above his heart and could feel the beat slow down. Leaving my left hand on his chest, I grabbed the spoon with my right. Then, in an impressive show of dexterity, I spun it in my fingers. As I smiled at my spinning spoon, his heart stopped and once again his eyes flew open.

'Oh shit,' I muttered as he turned to look at me. He opened his mouth just as the spoon handle ruptured his chest cavity, then his dead heart. With my hand clamped to his mouth, he screamed as he was consumed by fire.

My clothes were now covered in bloody ash. But hey, that's why I was wearing the overalls Suzie had bought me, so she can't bitch about it. I lifted the spoon; it was charred but okay. I shook myself out of the revelry and ran off scattering ash everywhere.

Anna jumped and coughed as I headed into the cook's room, who was just getting up from the bed.

'Oh no you don't!' I announced, making her turn as I lunged and slammed her back onto the bed.

'NO, PLEASE DON'T!' she called out as I plunged the wooden spoon into her heart, eventually covering myself in ash…again.

I broke into a coughing fit. Having ash particles in your nose and throat is not the best feeling. I then stumbled out. 'Water,' I gasped to a panicked and warmer-looking Annabel.

She ran to the pitcher and poured me a glass full, which I downed quickly. With a gesture of the glass, I received a second glassful.

'Thanks, Anna, that was a bit messier than I thought,' I explained and sat down on a chair.

Anna pulled up another chair and looked at the smoking spoon. 'What did you do, Berty, stir them to death?' she said before bursting into giggles.

I rolled my still gritty eyes. 'Oh ha-ha,' I said dryly, although smiling at her sense of humour despite the event. I took another sip of water. 'I bit them and started the change from human to vampire, just like the book we read as kids.' I saw her nod and creep out to observe the scenes.

'Oh, Berty, what a mess.' She chuckled and closed the door. 'That's a whole day's work.' She walked back and placed a kiss on my nose. 'Maybe cover them with a sheet before you stab them,' she said with her hands on her hips.

'Yes, dear,' I said obediently before standing up and claiming another wooden stake/spoon. 'How do we get into the safe, do we need a key or combination?' I asked, hoping luck was staying with us.

Despite the circumstances she smiled a big smile. 'Key. He knew his mind was more of a passing acquaintance than a friend.' She chuckled while taking my hand and walking me slowly upstairs to a large ornate door.

I slipped in and saw the house owner and his wife sleeping away merrily. They didn't even wake as I pushed my incisors through their rice paper-like skin. If I'm honest I think they welcomed death, which is what I delivered. But as suggested by Anna, I made sure they were covered with a cotton sheet before plunging the stake into them.

'Shit, ANNA!' I cried out. The door flew open. 'The bloody sheet's on fire!'

Anna ran and got the water jug and threw it over the flames that was once the lady of the house. As she did so, we were covered in ash. When the husband burst into flames, she shot me a harsh look, but that just disappeared and turned into one of amusement. Clearly, she held a lot of grudges against the people I killed that night.

'What now, Anna?' I asked with a smile.

The beautiful ash-covered brunette walked up, wrapped her arms around my neck and kissed me. 'We need to talk to our kids when they wake up,' she said with a playful grin.

'We'll send the boy to school, don't you think?' I asked as we walked back downstairs to the kitchen where we sat for hours making plans.

Things were still new, and I spent my time between the shop and the house. Anna and I went out on some dates, but she admitted she wanted her body to heal a bit more from the punishments handed out by the late cook and butler before sharing a bed together. I didn't mind as I had all the time in the world.

As the days and weeks went by, Anna found a man who could forge the deeds to the house into my name and Stanley was sent to school as promised.

Two months later when Stanley was at school and Emily had gone to lunch with some new friends, Annabel came to my bedroom. She still sported her crooked grin that seemed to be a permanent fixture now. I went to get up as she closed the door behind her.

'What's the matter, Anna, are you okay?' I asked, concerned.

She walked closer, and that's when I noticed she was wearing her favourite silk dressing gown I found in a shop I had robbed one night. Okay, my moral compass had shifted a little since the night of the wooden spoons.

'Everything is more than all right, Albert, and this will make things perfect,' she whispered, letting her robe slip off her shoulder.

I could hear the silk rasp against the fine hair on her body. She was naked, and thanks to a decent diet she had filled out, no longer did her ribs show. She was beautiful.

'Is this wise? You know what I am?' I asked as I watched her lithe form crawl onto the bed. She captured my lips and the kiss grew. We parted panting from the kiss.

'Albert, you have saved our lives, and I love you for that alone, and also many other things,' she said and kissed me again. 'There are monsters in many forms – you, my Albert, are not one of them. You didn't ask for this, and you only kill those who do wrong on this earth. So as long as you keep on doing that, I will love you forever until I take my last breath.' She then placed her hand over my mouth. I was just going to offer to change her, but she said, 'No, I like me, and unlike you I have a choice, which is no. I want to grow old with you. It will be hard on you, but you're my tough and beautiful Albert.'

That day we made love for hours until the other occupants of our home arrived. Anna sat them down later that night when I went out to feed and told them that we were now together, and about my condition. In the end they didn't care; I had saved them and given them a home to call their own and money in their pocket.

The following winter Annabel and I were married by a vicar who was willing to come to our home to perform the service. We lived together for over twenty years. She gave me hope that the curse I carried hadn't taken my soul away – it had just darkened it. Between the two of us and my shop, we also bought three more properties that we could rent out. We made a very good future nest egg.

My wife and love, Annabel Marie Morris, didn't wake up on the morning of 15 November 1913 at the tender age of forty-five years. To this day I blame that household who abused and scarred her. May they burn in hell, then when it's my turn to visit the pit I shall find them again. My heart may not beat, but on that day my heart was truly broken. I had commissioned a family plot, which I had brought my parents to only recently. They couldn't argue being dead, but they joined my wife, my one and only Anna. She was laid to rest with my children around me, although they did look older than me. It was a lovely service on an overcast day. At dusk, money stopped the vicar from complaining.

That house was never the same after my little Anna left, but the memories were there and I couldn't leave them. Annabel made me a loving home, which I would never leave. I loved her to my core; she would never leave me.

Emily had long since married an accountant and moved to Nottingham, but she still wrote every month and called me Dad. She had three children and passed away at the age of sixty-six. She had a happy life, and I held her hand as she passed. I pretended to be a cousin so her extended married family would not be suspicious. It hurt when she whispered, 'Goodbye, Daddy.' Then her eyes closed, her heart slowed and her spirit departed.

Stanley never got on at school. He was expelled for headbutting a male teacher who had hit him with a ruler. But we arranged for a tutor, and after that he found a home in the army and rose to the rank of sergeant major. I always told him how proud I was of him, and like Emily he called me Dad. Unfortunately, he never came back from France. He died in an explosion from a German shell in 1917. But at least he didn't have to take that walk into the light alone; his poor platoon went with him into the heavens.

Chapter 6

The years after Anna's death were difficult for me, but I still had my shop to run. After the Great War, where I had lost my Stanley, I made Suzie my business partner. With the help of her kids we opened another three around London where I would share my time between them. Suzie had lost one of her sons in the war and later her husband due to ill health in 1921.

With all the shops running well, Suzie could finally be a lady of leisure. That meant moving into the flat above our original shop. Her youngest daughter began running the shop with her husband. Suzie spent the rest of her life drinking beer and chatting to me and the pigs.

'Albert, you need to find someone else,' Suzie said from her sickbed. She had contracted TB in the winter of 1929.

I opened another beer and handed it to the pale woman. The illness had taken all of the fight out of her, but it had to fight hard to do it. 'I don't think I can, Suzie.' I sighed and pulled out my own cork and spat it into the far corner to collect dust with her other beer bottle corks.

'Don't be bloody stupid, Bert. You have loved once, you can do it again,' she said so forcefully that she fell into a coughing fit.

I took the bottle from her hand. If she had spilt it, she would have been savage as hell. I handed it back and watched her down half the bottle. What a woman she was.

'I'm not saying go courting or anything like that, but in time somebody will turn up, just don't push them away,' she explained.

I took her hand and squeezed it. 'I'll try, Suzie. But watching you all grow old; it hurts so much.' I pulled her hand to kiss it but found it connecting with the back of my head. 'Shit! Your bloody ring!' I exclaimed, rubbing my head.

Suzanna cackled away happily; you could hear the damage to her lungs. 'Shouldn't have bought it for me, Berty,' she retorted.

This time it was her turn to show affection, which was rare and fleeting. The bruiser of a woman cupped my cheek.

'I can't imagine how you feel, Albert. You may not have chosen your lot in life, but you have done a lot of good, especially for Anna, those kids and my whole family,' she whispered with tears in her eyes, and then she started to cough again into the handkerchief that I pressed to her mouth. I dabbed the spittle and blood from her paling lips. 'My family owe you so much – remember, we may die but we'll always be with you.'

Suzanne Atkinson died in her sleep that very night of 17 February 1930 at the ripe old age of seventy-five. Her family, knowing about my condition, arranged an early evening funeral. Again, it's amazing what money will buy you. As she was buried with her husband, we all joked about him having at least a decade of rest. I placed a crate of her favourite beer onto her casket, much to the disgust of the vicar. The next day I signed over my share of the shops to the family, but I stipulated that I wanted my name to remain on the business signs, to which they all agreed. And so, I started to pull away from public life. Don't get me wrong, I didn't stay held up in my house just looking at pictures of my family – well, not all the time.

My old school friend Mickey Edwards' son was now a police officer, and by the sounds of it, just like his old man, he was a damn fine one. His name was Sergeant Stuart Edwards, and his circle of friends kept me busy. When they couldn't find someone, or there was a particularly nasty murder, they passed the case on to me to look into, in an unofficial capacity. Sometimes they wanted them alive, but they wanted the really nasty ones to just disappear – and that's what happened. So, it worked out well for everyone, except the lawbreakers, of course.

The years passed in a blur. It was November 1940 and the Germans were at it again. We were kicked out of France, but then again everybody saw the writing on the wall, and we hadn't prepared. So, when we did declare war on Germany, we sent those poor boys over there, undermanned and outgunned, but they did their best. And now the Luftwaffe were bombing us nearly every night. So far, I had lost one of my houses to the bastard Hun, but thankfully the family who were renting from me survived. I moved them to another property that had been empty for a while.

I was sat in front of a roaring fire with a bottle of red wine. I could almost hear Suzie calling me a tart already. There was a banging on the front door. I closed my eyes and reached out with my senses; my control of them was getting better and better as the years had gone by. There was a man of my age, who seemed to have lung problems on account of the late nights chasing down criminals, another one who I didn't recognise in his early fifties and a third man in his forties. I put my glass down, walked to the front door and opened it.

'Mickey, Stuart,' I said with a smile to the father and son team. I then locked eyes with my now very old-looking school friend. 'What are you doing out on a cold night like this?' I asked, shooting his son a look that made him step back.

'Oh, leave him be, mate. Now, where is that rum of yours?' Mickey chuckled, shaking my hand as he walked past straight into the lounge and to the drink's cabinet.

He had lost his wife, Tabatha, three years previously, and unfortunately his own health was slipping. But he still came around every week to swap stories and drink me dry.

'Sorry, Uncle Albert, he insisted on coming, you know what Dad is like,' Stuart explained, shaking my hand as I looked the third man up and down.

He was tall and thin with a pencil-thin moustache and hard grey eyes. He was wearing a dark pinstripe suit with a bowler hat, but his demeanour screamed army.

'This is Major Matterson, from the Foreign Office,' Stuart introduced us.

We shook hands as Stuart walked past, hopefully to save my rum from his dad, but from the tinkling sound I heard I was mistaken. Like father, like son.

'Good evening, Major, please come in.' I smelt a whiff of gun oil on him, strong enough to show that he was armed.

He removed his hat, showing off his perfectly cut hair which shone the purest silver. 'Thank you, Mr Morris, you have a lovely house,' he said stiffly, in the typical way of not meaning it and just keeping up appearances.

I closed the door behind us and walked past to show him into the lounge where the Edwards family were sat on their usual sofa with two glasses and a bottle of rum. This was the same rum that the navy uses. It's good to be old sometimes.

'Please, take a seat,' I said and pointed to the chair that I had left only moments ago. 'Would you care for a drink, before they drink it all?' I smiled while thumbing at the copper and ex-copper.

The man nodded stiffly. 'The rum does look quit inviting and warming,' the major replied, and then he looked at the drinking pair who smiled and clinked their glasses together.

I poured him a glass and settled down in Annabel's chair. I could still smell her as my weight pushed the air from the seat cushion and into my nasal passage, igniting my memories, flashes from the past filling my mind. I was so happy once.

I looked around the room and raised the glass. 'The King,' I toasted, which they all replied and took a sip of their rum. 'So, what can I do for you, Major?'

The man looked down into the thick dark rum in his glass as he swilled it around, allowing the firelight to dance on the glass. 'May I call you Albert?' he asked respectfully.

I nodded in agreement and enjoyed the drink warming my throat as it trickled down.

'Good,' he replied. 'Please call me Samuel. I work for the Foreign Office, as the drunks over there said, and as you know this Hitler fellow has become quite a pain.' He smiled ironically and looked up into my eyes.

'Bit of an understatement, but I concur,' I stated with a wry grin. 'Please, continue.'

'Well, I am part of a department called the SOE, Special Operations Executive. We have been tasked to set Europe ablaze by Churchill himself and make ourselves a thorn in the Germans' side,' Samuel explained. He placed his glass down on the chairside table and leaned back in his chair, crossing his legs. 'I'm sure you are wondering why I am telling you this. It's simple, I want you to work for me.'

The room was silent apart from the crackling fire. I raised a quizzical eyebrow. 'And the Edwards boys think it's a good idea?' I asked, looking over and seeing my old school friend asleep, but his son smiled and nodded.

'I think it's a perfect fit, Uncle. You need something to keep your mind and body active,' Stuart said happily but with a slight slur.

I rolled my eyes. 'Take your dad upstairs to his usual room and get yourself home, kiddo,' I instructed and watched him manhandle the brute of a man whom he called Father. 'And try not to drop him this time – he doesn't bounce as well as he used to.' Samuel and I just listened to the grunts and curses. Then I walked Stuart out to the front door and we embraced. 'What shit have you got me into this time?'

He gave me a cheesy, drunken grin. 'I won't force you to do anything, Uncle. Well, I can't, you'll snap my spine.' Stuart chuckled before falling into the bush in my front garden, and that's where I left him. I did hear him move about twenty minutes later.

I walked back into the living room and straight to a countryside painting created lovingly by Thomas Girtin of

Kirkstall Abbey in Yorkshire. It resided above the fireplace. I did think about getting a portrait of Anna commissioned. But even though she had passed, I could feel the slap around the back of my head and her chiding me for wasting money on such a pretentious item. The picture was mounted on well-oiled hinges; it swung open noiselessly to reveal a wall-mounted safe.

I spun the dial to the relevant numbers and opened it with a heavy metal clunk. I reached in and took a bottle from the back; it was a pure black bottle without a label. After closing the safe and covering it with the picture, I pulled out two fresh tumblers and poured a good measure of the syrup-like liquid. Still in silence, we drank.

'That is beautiful,' the major commented with his eyes closed.

'Somebody bought this amongst other naval items. It came from HMS *Victory*, supposedly from the Battle of Trafalgar,' I explained whilst enjoying the burn from the drink. 'There were several metal tankards with the ship marks on them too.' I pointed to the dulled metal items on a shelf.

Silence reigned as we enjoyed the drink and the major looked at the tankard. Once he settled down again, he started, 'Before joining the Foreign Office I was in the police force, under Mickey, then in charge of Stuart,' he stated and looked at me. 'I saw you many times, of course, but you never aged a day, unlike the rest of us.' Then we both heard the warthog-like cadence coming from Mickey's room as he slept off my booze.

'I admit I have aged well, but what of it?' I asked in colder tones than I had intended.

The man smoothed down his moustache, clearly not realising the danger he could be in if the meeting went awry, but I would hear him out.

'Unfortunately, coppers talk, but not as much as a drunk one, and Mickey is one of the worst. He told me about the run-in with the Ripper. Although something horrid happened to you that night, I thank you for despatching such a monster,' Samuel said sincerely and gulped.

My eyes blackened. 'Some say I am a monster, too, Major, although my wife found it within herself to love me, which took a piece of darkness from me,' I admitted and took another draught of the rum. 'But you wish to unleash me upon the world?' It was then that I could hear Stuart crawling from my garden.

'No, Albert, not the world, just the enemy, home and abroad,' he clarified and placed his now empty glass on the side table. He steepled his fingers. 'You have a talent for finding people and not being seen while doing it.' He shot me a quick look before continuing, 'I want you to hunt down spies here at home. We will give you a list, and we ask that you check our information on these people is accurate. If it is, then despatch them.'

I couldn't help but agree with his plan, and it would keep me busy and fed. 'What about abroad?'

He nodded. 'The idea I had was just some trips to France, intelligence gathering and the odd assassination,' Samuel stated and smiled.

I copied him and steepled my fingers and placed them on my top lip as I thought. 'Okay, but I will not kill women or children. If a woman is a spy, I will bring her to you.'

'I agree,' he said and clapped his hands together. 'Well, as I understand it you are ex-army, so no need for training or a medical.' He then stood up, giving a slight wobble as he found his feet, the rum was a potent one, and handed me a card. 'Can you come over tomorrow? We can get all your kit together and your uniform.'

I stood in front of him and we shook hands. 'My true nature will be kept secret. Do we understand each other?' I stipulated and stepped closer to him, allowing my incisors to protrude.

'Not to worry, Albert. I will be your only point of contact and you will work for me,' he said, steely-eyed. We shook hands; the deal was agreed.

The next day I walked into a nondescript town house in Tottenham and then walked out as Captain Albert Morris. I took my journey home via my old shop to show off my uniform to Suzie's granddaughter, who was the spitting image of her grandmother, to the point where her parents had given her the same name.

Although I didn't run the shops anymore, I always kept in contact with Suzie's family. Most of them liked me, but the rest thought of the monster who slept in me. It was on one of these visits that I saved young Suzie from a robber. Since that day I had shared her bed from time to time; her personality was too forthright for the men around here. She was born in the wrong century.

As I walked in through the shop door, I heard Suzie giggle.

'Well, don't you scrub up nice, Berty.' She chuckled and ran around the counter to hug me.

'Thanks, Suzie. I bought you a gift,' I said, handing her my hip flask. 'It's the good stuff,' I added with a grin.

She followed her namesake in most of her pursuits, although the twenty-something girl hadn't killed a horse yet. That said, the original horse's head was adorning the wall in the shop alongside the sword and newspaper article.

She took a draught. 'Bloody hell, that's gonna turn my future kids boss-eyed!' Suzie exclaimed before taking my hand and dragging me into the back room. She pushed me onto a chair, sat on my lap and wrapped her arm around my neck. 'What's this all about, Berty? I thought you were happy?'

I gave her buxom form a hug. 'I was, but the Edwards boys gossiped about my condition, and you know what the government is like, they will use anyone to get ahead.'

She pulled up my chin and locked eyes with me. 'Did they threaten you, Berty?' Suzie growled, but I shook my head.

I have always liked her; the girl reminded me so much of my friend. It warmed me.

The young lass stood up and straddled me, pulling me into a long, slow kiss. 'I missed you, Berty.' She placed her hand onto my lips to stop me answering. 'I know why, and I know it wouldn't work between us,' she said before pulling my face into her soft cleavage. 'But it works at the moment. I don't have time for a relationship or a family, so come and warm my bed.' She did not take no for an answer.

I laboured over the girl for most of the night, until she changed the rules and took control, and then sleep claimed her. I placed a kiss on the smiling girl's face and like the other times, I left her a note saying how much she meant to me.

I put on my uniform, collected all the buttons which Suzie had torn off my tunic and headed home as the bombs were dropped on the docks, and the nail marks healed on my bum and back.

It took a whole week until I was contacted by the major; he sent over a file of a target. It was on a middle-aged man who called himself Ian Baxter who had managed to get himself a job at the Woolwich Arsenal as a floor manager. The file said he was half German, although that wasn't mentioned in his employment file.

I headed out early evening just as the accursed and much-missed sun said goodbye and the lands were bathed in the winter cold and dark nights. I donned a heavy work jacket, overalls and heavy boots.

I waited for the man to leave work. Being a manager, he left his place of work alone and made his way back to his flat nearby. It happened like that night after night. During the day and every other night I stayed with Suzie, but her irritation of being smothered soon pushed me back home with a smile. Clearly, she would never settle down.

It was a fortnight later when instead of heading home, my target changed direction down an old cobbled street. The man was very conscientious in his journey, sometimes doubling back, but finally after forty-five minutes he knocked on a door. Mr Baxter was bathed in light when the door opened. As he stepped inside, the light was taken away by the door closing just as quickly.

I moved closer to the property using the shadows and reached out with my senses. There were four men and one woman; they were speaking English, not German.

'So, they have upped the output on the anti-aircraft shells,' a man said.

'Yes, I have the numbers here. Also, they have upped tank shell production for Africa.' That was Baxter speaking.

They were obviously all guilty. All five people were at the table talking about matters which had no place in conversation during this time of war. I walked around the house and saw the power cables attached on the front right corner of the building. I knew I had to be quick. I made a last check to make sure they were all still in the same room, which they were.

With my vampiric abilities I jumped up and slashed at the cables with my claws, slicing them clean through. Screams of shock came from the woman in the house as they were bathed in darkness. She was then slapped and told to be quiet.

I forced the back door open with a loud crack.

'WHO'S THERE?' a man shouted.

They didn't stand a chance; I was in the room. The woman was still prone after being slapped. There was only one man with a pistol, so I put him down hard and punched him out, sending him against the wall. A noise like an egg breaking followed, his skull being crushed.

Unfortunately, my beast wanted to play. I had to fight the spies and him, so that didn't help, but a kick in Baxter's bollocks put him down, giving me focus. One tried to run, but he was caught. I twisted him around quickly before holding his head in place, and with a snap he was done. The last one managed to strike me, who knew how in the darkness, but a headbutt to the nose sent him off to a peaceful slumber.

I stood over the crying woman. The beast told me to take her, then feast on her.

'Wwwwhat do you want?' she sobbed.

I crouched over her staring through my monochrome night sight. 'To feeeeeeeeeed,' I growled.

The beast was panting and my lust was engorged, but once again I managed to reign the monster back in. But I wondered for how much longer. It clearly wanted to stretch its claws. So, a hard slap quietened the woman. I walked around and bound all of them, even the man who hit the wall, despite his head being way too flat at the back, and his eyes were open and bulging.

There was paperwork all over the table from munitions to troop movements, this alone would've sealed their fates. I headed out to the hallway and found a spindly-legged table with letters stacked haphazardly upon it.

'Gotcha,' I muttered as I saw the house address on the letters. Now I could call in the cavalry to clean this lot up.

I headed out of the front door, taking the letters with me to the nearest telephone box and dialled the major.

'Hello, do you know what time it is?' the posh man growled on the other end, which made me chuckle.

'Well, you wanted me to work for you, Sam, and I work nights,' I joked.

He grumbled, 'Is that you, Albert? What's wrong?'

I gave a bored yawn. 'Yes, it's me. Baxter is guilty as hell. I found him with four others, all tied up and waiting for collection,' I explained and then gave him the address.

'All right. I thought you would kill them?'

I wish he could have seen me roll my eyes because it would've hammered home the point. 'You can ask more questions to the living than the dead, Sam,' I stated.

He replied that he'd be there in an hour, and then slammed down the phone angrily – he was clearly not a night owl.

I headed back into the house to see who would wake first and complain, or who was dead, at least they would keep quiet.

It was just under an hour when an army truck turned up with a car in front and a very tired Samuel in it. I gave him my best salute and received a salute and a glare in return.

'What do we have, Captain?' he growled officially.

'One dead, four alive. They were discussing the munitions output from Baxter's work,' I explained as we walked into the torch-lit house.

The live ones were gagged and frogmarched with bags over their heads towards the lorry and an unknown future, which was most probably a long drop from a short rope. It turned out that Sam was very happy with the arrests, and with the myriad of other arrests after that night which tore down Hitler's information gathering in the London area for months to come.

I popped in to see Suzie on the way home with a case of beer, which we polished off in bed, and she caringly allowed me to stay as the sun was out. She was too kind.

Chapter 7

Hitler was now bashing the hell out of London, but that was better than bombing the airfields. The rumour was that one of Hermann Goering's bombers accidentally bombed London first, so we retaliated against Berlin. My work was keeping me busy, mainly just ones or twos now. Some guilty, some not. I had to 'ash' a few as they were way too feisty, real Nazi do-or-death types, and they tasted like crap.

It was late March, and I had to go into the office for a meet and greet by Hugh Dalton. The SOE was his brainchild, so I had to don my officer's uniform and clean myself up. He clearly knew who and what I was because he flinched when we shook hands. I quite enjoyed myself. But instead of hanging around eating finger food and rubbish wine, I said my farewells and handed a small tumbler full of my Trafalgar rum from my hip flask to Sam before heading out into the chilly night.

An hour later the sky was alight as London was burning, bringing misery and death. With my quickness I made it to the nearest shelter, which so happened to be a crowded tube station. I made my way through looking for a space to call my own. Some old soldiers from the Great War moved to let me sit down, but I just waved them back down with a smile and a slap on the back – and, as usual, an offer of a nip from my flask. Soldiers love booze.

I saw a space between an old woman, who was falling asleep against a wooden fire cupboard which held axes and similar equipment, and a young blonde woman, who was very pretty with vivid ice-blue eyes.

'Excuse me, are you saving that place?' I asked politely.

The old woman snorted like a pig and continued sleeping, but the blonde giggled and patted the space. 'Nope, it's all yours,' she said, as the whole place shook with German bombs dropping onto the city.

I smiled and took a seat. 'Albert Morris, nice to meet you,' I said, offering my hand.

She gave me a brittle smile as more ordnance hit the ground above making her duck slightly. 'Veronica, Veronica Jenkins.' She shook my hand gently. We sat in silence for a time until the next load of death bringers. 'So, do you come here often?' she asked, making me snort with laughter.

'Only to meet girls,' I said as the woman next to us belched. 'Yep, she's one of mine,' I responded and winked at Veronica.

She jammed her hand over her mouth to stop laughing. 'You only go for high-class women, then?' she commented with a huge smile.

I clutched my heart. 'What the heart wants, the heart wants. I'm a slave to my emotions, I'm afraid.' That's when I lost sight of her as she fell off the wooden bench laughing so hard.

Once she regained her composure, and as the bombs seemed to have moved on, she asked, 'So, what do you do, General Morris?'

I straightened my back. 'How dare you, I am a captain…in the Salvation Army, the watery tea section, I'll have you know.' I then saw a snot bubble fly out of the girl's nose as once again she lost control and had to hold onto my arm for support.

I offered her my handkerchief, which she frowned at. I pointed at her nose, and she took the handkerchief in a hurry. After wiping, she was mortified.

'I'm so embarrassed,' Veronica mumbled with cheeks as red as a stop light. 'I'm not normally like this.' She handed back the handkerchief, which I grimaced at and held with pinched fingers.

'Maybe I should burn this; not even the Germans drop anything this deadly,' I commented, and then shielded myself as a hail of slaps came my way. I was smitten. 'So, what do you do for a living? Children's entertainer?' *Slap!*

Veronica crossed her arms and took a minute or two to answer. 'I'm a secretary at the *Daily Express*, Mr Captain, sir,' she said, still displaying a cute pout on her face as she mock saluted me. Her look softened when I smiled.

'Do you like it?'

The woman shrugged. 'It's okay, it pays my rent. Well, if my flat is still there, mind you.' She gave a dark chuckle.

'Ah, you'll be okay. You're a lucky girl – you met me, after all,' I said, giving her my best smile. I was doing my absolute best not to listen to her heartbeat, and of course not go on a killing spree – all these bodies with heightened emotions.

She laughed again. 'So, what do you really do, or can't you say?'

I sighed. 'I know it's what everyone says, but I can't tell you.' I saw her sag. 'But what I can say is that I look for naughty foreign people.' Veronica's eyes sparkled with mischief.

'Well, you caught me, Mr Captain, sir.' She chuckled with her hands held up in surrender. We then heard the old woman grumble about kids and the lack of respect. 'So, what are you going to do with me?' she asked with a wink.

It was then that the all-clear signal echoed throughout the streets above, and now the heart-breaking search for loved ones and clean-up would start. I could see some people heading out, but those with families seemed happy to continue to hunker down for the night.

'Would you like to go to the cinema one night?' I asked.

Veronica flicked her blonde hair over her shoulder. 'How about you take me to a dance? There's one near work just off Fleet Street,' she suggested, almost bouncing with excitement.

'Sure, I'll get my dancing shoes on,' I responded, and for the first time in years I felt excited. 'Would you like me to escort you home? A young lady shouldn't go anywhere alone at this time of the night.' Even in the bad lighting I could see her blush.

'That would be nice, thank you, Captain,' she said, and we both heard the old woman continue to grumble.

I stood up and held out my hand; her dainty fingers wrapped around mine as I pulled her to her feet. I led her out of the tube station hand in hand like a mother elephant leads her young. She followed me closely, and finally we were out into the not so fresh night-time air, and that's when I finally saw Veronica in her monochrome best.

The lady that caused me to feel hope again stood at a mighty five foot six with a classic hourglass figure. She looped her arm through mine and we walked off into the night. We chatted about her family. Unfortunately, her mother had passed away during childbirth and her father died from a heart attack in 1935. That's why she came to London from Buckinghamshire. Veronica had no family and neither did I. When it was time to tell my story, I started to spin my web of lies and half-truths, but I had a feeling she wasn't convinced.

'Well, Mr Captain, this is me,' she said, pointing to a red door with number 37 on it. I felt her squeeze my hand. 'Pick me up here, say seven on Friday?'

I nodded. 'I'll be here.' Giving her hand a squeeze back, she then surprised me by going on tiptoes and placing a kiss on my cheek.

'Goodnight, Mr Captain,' she said with a smile before heading in through her front door.

I held my breath as the door clicked to and she ascended up to her flat. I could feel that her pulse was racing – and if I had one, mine would be, too.

The smile on my face didn't leave for days, even as I tore the head off Edward Perkins, or Stefan Krueger as was his real name. He did seem somewhat confused as I tried to question him with that permanent smile taunting him. It only left when he said that all the English women would be used to fill all the brothels in the Reich. The monster who slumbers inside me painted his flat with blood and internal organs.

Friday night arrived. I put on my freshly cleaned uniform and walked out into the failing daylight. I just hoped for a bomb-free night. My travel through London was uneventful, getting respectful nods from coppers and air raid wardens alike. I made it to my goal, number 37, in one piece and with zero spots of blood on my face or clothing.

I gave the door a knock. I could feel her excitement and heard her rushing around her flat. But I also heard another couple arguing, and somebody having a very loud bowel movement, so I pulled back my senses. It really does have plus and minus points.

'Albert, you made it,' Veronica said after throwing open the door. She looked stunning wearing an over-the-knee red dress with low black heels.

'You doubt an officer of His Majesty's armed forces? How dare you, young lady,' I stated in mock disbelief, and then received a slap with her hand which sported freshly painted nails.

She then pulled me into a hug and gave me another kiss.

'Are you trying to corrupt me, Miss Jenkins?' I asked, raising a quizzical eyebrow.

A slight blush crept over her cheeks. 'Well, maybe a little, Mr Captain, sir.' The tones she used for just those few words were like liquid silk that infused themselves to my bones.

She looped her hand through my arm and we walked off towards our destination, one of the many dance halls nearby.

We chatted softly as we stood in the queue shoulder to shoulder. Other servicemen gave me respectful nods knowing what my insignia meant.

'You will have to tell me what you do one day, Albert?' she asked while cuddling into my side.

'But if I did, I would have to kill you…my dear.' I gave her an evil grin, which earned me another slap. All the women in my life have been hitters. Makes you think a bit, but not for too long.

Her blonde hair ruffled as a breeze blew down the street. 'You're way too good at that look, Albert, so I won't press you tonight,' she said with a little laugh as the crowd started to move inwards.

'Would you like a drink, Veronica?' I asked as we entered the huge hall.

She didn't answer but instead took my hand and pulled me amongst the crowd filling the dance floor as the band started to play. As the rhythm of the songs changed, we did not. Our bodies fitted perfectly together, our eyes were locked and we retreated into our own world. We didn't hear the grumbles as we danced to our own music at that moment in war-torn Britain. There were only two people on the planet, and that was us.

We were sharing a coffee when the call of nature caused Veronica to shuffle off, so I went to place another order at the hall's café. I saw her red dress and blonde hair first, then her smile, which instantly wavered as a couple of suited men barred her way through the crowd, and from what I could hear they were not taking no for an answer. I looked over at a sailor and his date at the next table.

'Excuse me, but would you mind looking after my drinks while I retrieve my girl?' I asked politely.

The burly ensign looked over. 'Do you need help, mate,' he boomed. Clearly, his time on the ships was noisy and he knew what I was looking at.

'No, thank you, just look after your lovely lady and our table?' I asked.

His date, a pretty little redhead who had a smattering of freckles all over her face, blushed. The big man nodded and grasped his date's hand.

My chair scraped back loudly, turning a few heads, although not the two idiots who were hindering my date. But when she saw that I was on my way over, the look of panic on Veronica's face turned to mischief. I could hear them demanding a dance and then a drink outside, but at every request she pushed back slapping away their hands and telling them that she had a boyfriend.

'Hello there,' I said coldly, making the men turn. 'Are you okay, Veronica?' I held out my hand to her. She was about to take it when the cheap-suited twenty-year-olds pushed it away.

The bigger one, whose nose seemed to point due west, took a step forward. 'Piss off, mate, the lady is with us now.' His grin showed off very crooked teeth.

I held up my hand to placate them. 'Listen, boys, I don't want any trouble, especially with the bloody Nazis bombing us nightly,' I said honestly, seeing other serviceman getting up. 'Let me just take my girlfriend so we can have a coffee.'

The two men exchanged glances and a smirk. 'Nah, I don't think so, mate. You're on our turf,' the bigger man said, stepping towards me.

That's where it stopped. A quick punch to the throat sent him down choking and gasping for breath. Then his skinnier and less lethal friend swung a surprisingly large fist towards my face, which I promptly caught. With a quick twist his wrist was broken.

'You bastard, you broke my wrist!' the crying, skinny man shouted.

I leaned down. 'I know, and you still have many other bones I could break if you don't go away,' I hissed into his dirty ear. 'And take your mate with you. He doesn't look well.' I then straightened up and took Veronica's hand. Instead of looking scared, she just looked amused, especially when she stepped over the man clasping his throat and allowed her heel to hit him on the back of his head.

'Thank you, Albert, I was worried that our coffee was getting cold,' she said loudly, making some of the other patrons laugh as we headed back to our table.

I pulled the chair out for my date and shook the ensign's hand, palming him a few crowns. 'Thanks for that, chap, buy your date some food on me,' I said with a smile. He went to argue, but I slightly increased the pressure on the strong sailor's hand. That simple act impressed him enough to accept and whisk off his redhead for fish and chips. On a plate, not from a bag – it's the little touches nowadays.

After our coffees we were dancing again, twirling ourselves around the dancefloor, our eyes never once leaving each other. We were in our own world again. I hadn't felt like this since sharing my life with my dearest Annabel, and I hoped that she was happy for me.

As the night came to an end, we filtered out with the rest of the couples onto the chilly London streets. I pushed out my senses to find the troublemakers, and those who had ill feeling towards me and my date, but there were none. The crowds started to thin out the closer we got to her lodgings.

'You okay, Mr Captain? A shilling for your thoughts.' Veronica tightened her grip on my arm.

I looked at Veronica's face, which seemed to glow in the moonlight, although it had a ghostly pale to it, but her eyes did glisten. 'No, I'm okay, just making sure our friends are not following us,' I answered, smiling at her.

We chatted about this and that. Several times I checked our surroundings, but we were safe. Then finally we made it to her red front door. I sensed her nerves were afire.

'Well, this is me, Mr Captain,' she said softly. Turning to face me and slightly tilting her head upwards, she gently captured my lips.

I was lost. Her kiss was soft and warm like the rest of her. Then the beauty pulled back.

'Wow,' I mumbled and smirked at her. 'Tonight was wonderful.'

Veronica kissed me again but for longer. 'It was the best night ever, Albert. When can we go out again?' she asked, her heart beating rapidly. 'How about a walk in the park on Sunday and maybe lunch somewhere?'

And here came the lies. 'I would love to, but I work during the days, and as you know it's a busy time.' I hated myself as I saw her face drop with disappointment. 'But would you like to come for dinner? My home is still a bit dated from my relatives, but it's nice enough.' I felt instantly that I had struck gold. Her heart fluttered and she blessed me with another kiss. We made plans before she headed through her front door. I could hear her giggling like a schoolgirl all the way up the stairs to her flat.

I hid in the shadows for a few hours just to make sure the idiots didn't follow us at a distance, but we were in the clear, all except a mugger who tried to rob me. I really don't know why they do it but snapping his wrist and feeding on him while allowing him to change turned the unlucky bugger into ash. Fully sated, I headed home to say hello to the photo of my wife.

There she was in her stoic glory, as was the style of the time thanks to the camera of the era. I looked at the photo of our wedding day. She was so gorgeous in all her black and white beauty. I stared into those eyes that I missed so much and smiled. 'Anna, I miss you so much it hurts. You were my guiding star; you gave me a purpose not to become the monster that dwells inside me,' I whispered as tears started to swamp my eyes. 'I met someone, she's really nice, and I've invited her for a meal in our home. I hope you don't mind.'

I didn't know what I was hoping for, an ethereal voice telling me, the house shaking to its roots, but nothing, which was good as I needed to move on, and I don't mean by gracing Suzie's bed more often. I needed to be part of something again, and hopefully Veronica and I could become as strong as Anna and I were.

I checked all the photos of my family in the house. They would pass any detailed examination by Veronica, apart from our joint one with Emily and Stanley. It was the only time we could get the little bugger Stan clean and standing still long enough. The picture was moved into the chest of drawers wrapped in a homemade scarf that Emily had made me, but it was over four metres long – she just didn't stop knitting. That memory did make me laugh.

Looking at the photos took me back to a moment before Anna passed. We were alone in the house with her favourite Gustav Holst record on the phonograph. I pulled her up from her seat and started to sway to the music.

'I love this, Berty. The music and us dancing together. It warms me, my love,' Anna had whispered into my chest as I held her close.

I placed a kiss on her head. 'I love it, too. It wouldn't be the same if I wasn't dancing with you, Anna.' We had relaxed into the music which surrounded us. I missed my Anna so much, but it was time.

On the Saturday evening I headed to see my boss, Major Matterson. Now, I think that I look clean and tidy, but I swear this man slept under an iron. The tall man stood up behind his desk and offered his hand.

'Good evening, Albert, how are you?' After shaking his hand, he offered me a seat.

'I am well, thank you, sir,' I replied as I settled and put my cap on his desk. 'And you, sir?'

The stress poured out of the man in waves. 'I'm good. Just busy, you know how it is – too many things to do, not enough people,' he said and reached into his desk drawer to bring out the half a bottle of whisky, which led me to bring out my hip flask of his now favourite navy rum. He stilled and a rare smile appeared on his face as the bottle slipped back into the safety of his desk. 'Well, it'll be rude not to,' he said, holding out a tumbler. The major licked his lips as the syrup-like alcohol slowly filled his glass, then mine after.

We both took a small sip in silence as we appreciated the drink. 'So, Sam, what can I do for you? Normally I just receive instructions via courier?' I asked and swilled the thick liquid.

'Firstly, have you got any more of this rum that I could give to the Prime Minster? If Winston likes it, I might get an increase in staff,' said Samuel.

I fixed him a glare but it ended up with a smile. 'Of course, I do have a few bottles of the stuff, but give him a taster first and see if you can trade it for something we both like instead,' I suggested and opened my gasmask bag before lifting out a sealed bottle of the Battle of Trafalgar rum.

Samuel's eyes went wide. 'Amazing, but you want me to haggle with the Prime Minister over a bottle of rum?'

I shook my head. 'No, I want you to haggle with him over a *one of a kind bottle of rum.*' I gave him a winning smile, pushing out my incisors to slam the topic home.

'Fine, but put those bloody things away,' he said, pointing at my mouth.

I laughed as I watched the man cradle the bottle like his firstborn. Somehow, I doubted if it would ever leave this small office ever again.

'Right, the reason I have you here is that the U-boat situation is getting critical, as you know,' he announced officially, looking up to see me nod in agreement. 'The wolf packs have been decimating our poor boys in the Atlantic, and the Admiralty has asked for a favour.'

I squinted at him. 'It must be a big favour given the look on your face, and your heart is racing like an engine,' I commented and chuckled as I took the folder.

'Don't do that either; it scares the shit out of me that you can hear my heartbeat,' he grumbled while still stroking the bottle.

'Sam, should I leave you two alone?' I asked, pointing at him and the bottle.

For the first and only time in our working relationship I saw the man blush and hurry to put the bottle away to join the whisky in the confines of his drawer. I turned my attention back to the file. There were five photos of German servicemen.

'They want me to kill all of these men. They are U-boat captains. How the hell am I meant to do that, pull the plug on the Atlantic?' I said incredulously, slamming the file on the desk before downing my rum quickly and then refilling both glasses from my flask.

He took a big sip of the dark and potent drink. 'The Admiralty seems to think the Hun are going for a big push, and these five captains are amongst their best. At the moment their submarines are docked for repairs and being refitted with new torpedo tubes for this new push. They want the best for their best,' Samuel explained and flicked open his own copy of the file. 'For safety they are staying at five different boarding houses surrounding their harbour with a strong army presence. But every night they have meals together at Casino le Lorient in a private dining room along with their second in commands to plan the coming patrols.'

'So, they want me to take them all out. That's a big order, especially in occupied territory itself,' I admitted.

'I know, Albert, but we plan to parachute you in on Tuesday evening. Hopefully you can deal with them on the Wednesday night. This is particularly important as we plan to bomb the area at midnight on the Thursday night. We just need definite kills of these particular men, you understand?'

I groaned. This was my first mission abroad and clearly time sensitive if I didn't want to get inadvertently blown up by my own country. We discussed further details into the early morning, pawing over maps, and then we decided to meet up again on Monday night for a recap, a final walk through and weapon checking. Afterwards, I headed back to my home to rest and think about the days to come and Veronica.

My date with Veronica came quickly. Thanks to my contacts through the dodgy side of London – well, mine and Suzie's, of course – I procured two joints of meat. My employee would've been put out if I hadn't bought her one, too. It was always best to keep Suzie happy. She was pleased that I had found someone new, although upset that I had left her bed empty. But she did still love me and would do anything for me. It made me miss my family when I heard that.

It was seven o'clock on the dot when there was a knock on the door. Even though I knew it was going to happen, I still jumped. I smoothed down my suit jacket and opened the door. There stood the beautiful Veronica wearing a grey dress that fitted her perfectly. She stepped inside.

'Well, hello, Mr Captain. My, what a lovely house you have,' she said with a smile and pressed her red lips to my cheek.

I could feel the residue of lipstick on my cheek, it was like she was leaving her mark. 'I'm glad you could make it. I'm sorry about the picnic,' I said with a chuckle as I closed the door behind her. I took her gasmask and hung it on a hook on the hat stand, which was followed by her stylish hat. 'I don't get much time in the sun.'

Veronica slapped me gently on the arm as she pulled off her leather gloves. She smelt wonderful. 'Don't be silly, soldier boy, this way I can see where you live,' she said, giving me a wink and then taking a big sniff. 'Is that…beef?'

I gave her a knowing smile. 'Now that, my dear, would be telling. Let me show you around my home.' I proceeded to take her from room to room.

She did blush a little at the master bedroom. But then again if I could've, I would've. By the way her heart was racing, her thoughts were aligned with mine. She saw a photo of me in my uniform when I first joined the London regiment in 1886. She gave me a look.

'Uncanny, isn't it, but that's my father,' I lie with a smile.

And then she took in the rest. I did take out my and Anna's wedding photo after a restless night's sleep as I decided that I didn't like to hide things. If the lies fell apart, so be it. One day I would have to come clean anyway.

'That was Mum, Annabel, and my Aunty Emily and Uncle Stanley, he died in the last war,' I said sadly, but the army was his life.

I could see her drink in the images, remembering every detail, but I think that's just the way women work. Anna was just the same. If I moved even a single ornament on a shelf, she knew by just walking past the room.

My tour of the house brought us both back to the living room. 'Now, Veronica, would you like a drop of wine?'

She tapped her lip with a dainty finger. 'Ermm… Yes, that would be lovely.' She smiled a winning smile.

I walked away into my study and poured two glasses of red wine. Stanley had sent a few cases of French wine to me when he could. He was a good lad.

Veronica was still looking at all the photos and pictures on the wall. I stilled when I saw her staring at the picture of myself in front of the pawnbrokers when it first opened. She smiled at the proffered glass, her throat was tantalisingly close and tender looking as she took a sip of the wine. Our eyes met; her cheeks flushed and her pulse raced.

'So, you own a shop, Albert?' she asked.

'We used to, but Father sold it back in the day,' I answered.

She nodded happily and moved on with her investigation into my past. The questions kept on coming. She loved all the old things that I had kept, like a Trafalgar goblet with an empty bottle of port next to it.

'Right, time for dinner, milady,' I stated before holding out my arm, which she happily took, wrapping her slender arm around mine.

'Lead on, Mr Captain,' she said, giggling.

I noticed her glass was empty. The wine was good, but it had a certain potency that never bothered me; however, my guests were always swept away. I led her to the dining room and seated her at the upper end of the table. I sat opposite her instead of at the head of the table. We were there to eat together, not to entertain royalty.

Veronica gasped when I brought out a plate full of sliced roast beef. I thought it prudent not to show her the joint of beef I was given, just in case she turned out to have morals about the populous being on ration cards. But the way the woman was hurriedly placing slices of the beef onto her plate, I needn't have worried about it at all. She barely had room for the roast potatoes and veg.

Now, I have lived with soldiers in barracks and seen the biggest of men put some food away, but the sight of Veronica eating that mound of food will stick with me until the day I turn into a pile of ash. I don't eat much food now, only for show, but I did always like a traditional roast dinner – and a bloody piece of beef was the best. So, I joined the eating machine which was my date for the night and started to eat.

'I have more beef if you want it?' I offered.

Her cheeks flushed, but then she nodded slightly with mischief in her eyes like a child stealing a sweet.

What truly amazed me was the trifle for pudding; she had a second helping. Her ration book was taking a beating if she always tried to eat like that. I watched as she wiped her bowl clean with her delicate finger and sucked the cream off it, which made my libido jump up like a meerkat searching for predator. If she attacked me like that dinner, I don't think I would survive.

'How was it, Veronica?' I asked with a smile.

Once again her face shone. 'That was amazing. I won't have to eat for a week now,' she said, sporting a big smile and wiping her hands clean with the napkin. 'May I just go and clean up, Albert?'

I nodded and showed her to the bathroom I had fitted when the new models came out. The décor of the rest of the house stayed as Annabel had liked it, to keep her close to me.

The plates were cleared as I waited for her to come back. No doubt she was looking at the other photos I had on the stairs. They were mainly of Emily and her family, and of Stanley and his army mates. The door creaked open and she walked back into the room smiling.

'I am full to burst, Albert,' she said with a slight cackle to her laugh.

I offered her my arm. 'Well, let's go and sit in the lounge. Fancy a cuppa?' I asked as I showed her to the sofa.

'Yes, please, Mr Captain, sir.' She once again gave me a brief salute, so I pushed her onto the sofa, making her giggle like a schoolgirl. She must have been drunk on wine and meat.

When I came back with the tea, I placed the tray on a small table in front of the sofa and poured out the cups.

Veronica took a sip from her cup and then added sugar to taste. 'So, where's this shop of yours?'

I chuckled. 'We owned it years ago and I sold it to family friends who expanded it to other shops around the city.' I took a sip, hoping that would appease the nosey woman, but clearly there was blood in the water. Can't remember where that saying came from, but she wasn't going to give up.

Her eyebrow raised slightly and a small smirk appeared on her perfect lips. 'That's nice. Where is the original shop, then?' That question hung in the air like a barrage balloon, and I was the bomber. She knew I was going to hit, and she was waiting.

'Just off Whitechapel Road, Buck's Row.' I then saw in her eyes that she was storing away the information for future use.

'How is your work?' I asked, determined to sit and hear her beautiful voice for a time.

Veronica relaxed back into the sofa and crossed her legs. Unlike most of the women of this time she preferred bare legs, and they looked smooth as silk. I couldn't pick up the sound of a single rasp of hair on the material. 'Not too bad. Busy as ever, of course. Dare I ask about yours?' she said. 'Or will you have to kill me after?' That was said with a playfulness, her eyes sparkling.

With a shrug, I replied, 'Like yours, really, but I will be travelling soon.' I then locked eyes with her.

'Abroad?'

I nodded.

'Are we talking snails, pasta or sauerkraut for dinner?' she probed.

'The first one, from Tuesday and back… Well, you know,' I said and saw water gathering in her eyes. 'But I will be fine. I'm good at what I do.'

Veronica stood up, took my cup of tea from me and placed it down onto the table, and then slid onto my lap. We kissed deeply. It felt like it went on forever. I knew she could feel my passion underneath her, but we both knew tonight wasn't the night. Particularly not with full bellies and emotions running high. She placed the palms of her soft hands on either side of my head, stared into where my soul had once been and said calmly, 'You come back to me, Captain. Don't get hurt or killed. You come back to me, and we will start making new memories for your walls. You understand?'

'Yes, as soon as I am back, I will come to you. I promise.'

We spent the rest of the evening kissing and talking about the future. Veronica agreed that having children with me or anyone else should wait until the war was over. That saved an awkward conversation for another time.

Chapter 8

Well, I was right: the lying bastard had no intention of taking that bottle of rum to Churchill. I smelt it in Major Matterson's desk. In response to my question, all he did was shrug and send me to an airfield by the coast so that I could carry out a final weapons check and last-minute intelligence briefing.

They had planned a small bombing raid on the submarine pens at Lorient, Brittany. The Mosquitoes would fly in low and fast and drop incendiaries so the high-flying Halifaxes could follow and add their payloads. As the Mosquitoes headed for home, I would be dropped from one after being in the co-pilot seat. What could go wrong…? Everything.

I stood on the edge of the landing field. All the pilots had just come back from their briefing and started to filter away to their own aircraft. Yes, I had concerns about what was to come, but I had a job to do and I would do it the best way I could. I reminded myself that I was merely an asset, as when I was back in Ireland. People like Samuel treated you like a friend, but they weren't. They used your willingness to fight for your country to achieve their goals, and those of their master. But I was really here for Veronica, Suzie and her family, and the Edwards boys and their families.

It was my first time up in a plane and it was fun. It was Flight Sergeant Peter Butler that scared me; he just wouldn't shut up. All he talked about while going over the Channel was the problems with the plane and what had happened to his last co-pilot whom he nicknamed 'No Nose Johnson' after losing his face. The monster in me wanted to feed on him just to shut him up. He thought it hilarious that the plan was for them to drop their bombs and then I was to crawl back and throw myself out of the open bomb bay.

'Well, we've never used these crates for bombing raids. Supposedly, you're a special case,' Butler said with a chuckle, his eyes showing the insanity that lived in his brain.

I decided that silence was a better response, especially as I was trying to centre myself and not rip his head off. My thoughts drifted to Veronica. I could hear her voice in the background as I remembered our night of talking and kissing on the sofa, and the promises of more to come.

I was shaken from my musings when the night's sky was illuminated. I looked at the pilot who was turning his controls. 'What's happening?' I shouted over the noise.

'We just flew over Brittany, starting our bombing run, and they aren't happy,' he announced over the radio, still with a hint of laughter.

There was ground fire exploding all around us, which was painful to my hypersensitive eyes and ears. I felt the plane drop and the whirring of machinery and then a huge explosion.

'Fuck, looks like Barry and Timmy have bought it...shit,' he added, and then there were more explosions from the ground. 'Okay, getting ready to drop our load. Once they go, you better start to move back,' the sergeant ordered.

I felt the plane move up in the air as the bombs dealt out their destruction. Then we were physically thrown into the air within the plane, sparks spitting from the instrument panel, a small fire at our feet.

'Shit, we're hit! Bert, get that fire out!' Peter screamed and pointed to the fire extinguisher between us.

I moved quickly and sprayed the powder, but it was a stubborn one. I managed to look out of the windows and saw that one engine was ablaze and part of the wing had gone. It was then that I knew we were going down.

Butler was fighting the aircraft; his insanity had gone and fear was riding alongside professionalism. I knew that Veronica would be angry yet sad when I didn't make it back, but hopefully I would get to see my Annabel again.

'We're going down, Bert, not far off the area you need, but we will be swamped by the Krauts, that's if we survive!' he shouted through the noise before ripping off his mask as all the systems shut down one by one.

The second engine stopped with a bang and smoke disappeared into the darkness.

'Dumping the fuel, tighten your harness and hold on, mate.' He then went quiet.

All I could hear was the whistling of the wind as we sped towards the ground and the never-ending darkness of death. I closed my eyes and held on. I heard what sounded like branches snapping, then nothing.

First thing I registered was the smell of smoke and then the heat of fire. Was I in hell where I deserved to be? It was certainly hot enough. Then there was the pain shooting through my stomach. My vision came back and I was in Dante's version in hell. The plane was burning; I could feel my skin crisping as the flames licked through the broken fuselage.

I tried to move but I was stuck fast, and then I found out why and the reason there was pain in my gut. It appeared that a part of the plane was in me, and that wasn't good. Either I was going to bleed out or burn to death – if death could still take me this way, of course.

With a crack that came from my neck, I moved my head. My body had clearly gone through the ringer, but not as bad as my pilot. Peter's face was covered in blood, which was intoxicating to my senses. He was still alive, but only just. His legs were in shapes that nothing born of a woman should ever be in. The poor man was not going to make it, and I wouldn't allow the brave airman to burn to death.

I took hold of the piece of aluminium studded with rivets in my hands and yanked it out of my body with a deep breath, squirting blood and what looked like a piece of my liver. 'SHIIIIIIT!' I cursed loudly, placing a hand over the wound. I didn't have much time as the flames were building with intensity. The harness came away easily enough along with my parachute, which clearly was never going to be used, especially by me.

The lack of blood was causing me a problem. Even with my heightened abilities I still felt as weak as a kitten, especially because of the amount of strength it took to remove my skewer.

I eased over towards Peter, searched around his neck and found his identity chain, which I pulled away with little resistance and not a sound, apart from the laboured breathing from its owner. The chain was placed in my pocket alongside his wallet. If I made it back, at least his family would know what happened, kind of.

He was clearly on the homeward stretch of his life, but I had a mission to complete. So, with shouts and torchlights in the distance, I used the last of my strength to position myself across the brave man and sank my fangs into his tough skin. I heard the familiar pop as my fangs penetrated his skin, the artery allowing the life-giving fluid to vanquish my thirst and aid my healing.

The pain in my stomach lessened; as it did, Peter Butler's heart slowed. He must have already lost a significant amount of blood because he passed quickly. I pulled away from the peaceful-looking man and stared into the night at the torchlights coming my way. I looked towards the back of the plane and saw that the bomb bay was empty and the doors had been torn away, but there was still a gap to the outside world.

My last act in the cockpit was to take a hand grenade from my pack that had been stored behind my chair. Dangerous, I know, but not as much as having all those bombs on the plane too. I pulled the pin and let it fall to the floor while still holding a Mills bomb (hand grenade) and the priming lever. I pushed it under Peter's leg. Either the flames would ignite it or a helpful

Kraut would try to get the poor dead bugger out of his pilot seat. Either way, I couldn't have any evidence of my feeding.

I squeezed his hand and felt bad for leaving him even though I had only just met him, but I remembered that many more people would die in this accursed war. The gap to the outside was tight, but I made it. The soldiers were getting closer but only from one direction, which allowed me to move away into a copse of trees and to my escape. I was about half strength as I moved away from the crash site. Keeping low, I made my way out of the area following my compass all the way, hoping that I would soon hit some signs of life. It was then that I heard the thump of the grenade going off, followed by screams and what I imagined were German curse words – that'll teach them.

Two hours later and feeling exhausted, I realised that I needed to cross a bridge which would allow me to remain on the outskirts of the populated area. Hopefully I could find a place to wait out the daylight hours before making a push towards the casino and my target. There was one guard walking along the bridge; I could feel his nervousness from here. I edged closer but there was barely any light for him to see with, just a handheld torch and a small lamp by his guard box.

I crouched and moved through the shadows. The wound in my gut still hurt, but luckily it didn't hinder me too much. As I crept, I slipped out my double-edged commando knife, no teeth this time. I hid by a bridge support and leaned against the iron. It was freezing, indicating that it was going to be a hard frost in the morning. But what else did I expect? Good job it doesn't affect me as much – but, still, I missed my fire.

I spied the soldier getting closer. He was barely a man, but this was war and I needed more food. He was humming as he passed my hiding place with his rifle slung over his shoulder. I moved quickly and came up behind him. With my left hand I reached over, covered his mouth and wrenched his head to the side as my blade slid into his neck on the other side, making him slump. As he sank to the ground, the knife was pulled out with a slurping noise, which was replaced with my mouth as I drank my fill. I had relaxed my left hand and just before the soldier died, I heard him say, 'Mutter… Mutter.' It was only later that I found out he was asking for his mother, but that's war for you.

I drained the poor boy dry. I used his jacket to clean my knife. I took his rifle and ammo along with his pistol before throwing him into the freezing river below. Hopefully he would be found later.

Keeping low, I moved across the bridge and into the darkness. It was quiet as I was now far away from the sub pens and downed aircraft. Any patrols I did see were avoided thanks to my stealth and night vision. The sun was just starting to make an entrance when I found a broken-down old shed on the edge of a field, maybe an old shepherd's lodge. It obviously hadn't been used for years according to all the smells in the air, but at least I had a place to wait out the sun.

Plus point about being a night-time predator? We tended to scare the shit out of any animal, at least the ones who spent their short lives being preyed upon. So, my day of rest in the rubbish-strewn domicile was rodent free – and happily German free also. I did see some patrols in the distance, but it seemed as though they had travelled that route many times as the laughter and the way the soldiers carried their guns showed they weren't worried at all.

As the hours ticked by, both happy and sad memories came a calling. But what was at the forefront of my thoughts was how I was going to get the job done and get back to Blighty. Major Matterson had been a bit vague on the details about how I was getting back, but I would be contacted via messages hidden by the French Resistance in the church of Sainte-Barbe in Le Faouët under the headstone of an unknown French soldier. To get there I had to mainly use my experience. If I kept calm it would all go well, I was told. It was okay for him to say that; I had to get into a well-defended casino, kill some high-ranking officers and get out before the RAF bombed the shit out of the area.

My journey home was just going to be based on luck. If only I could turn into a bat like all the films and books said I could. I took the map and compass out of my pack and studied it. I was about eight miles away from the casino, so I needed to move quickly. It being winter, the days were short, and that meant the soldiers would be wrapped up like that poor bugger last night, so their vision and movement would be reduced.

Finally, the sun disappeared behind the trees. I put the map away and placed the pack onto my shoulders. The rifle was loaded and put on safe. I peered through the murky and cracked windows, my eyes saw through the failing light, there was nothing. With a nervous grin, I stepped out hearing the grass crackle as the temperature was starting to dip. I headed off at a slow jog trying to keep out of sight as much as I could before the light disappeared for good.

I was making good time, only having to divert occasionally for small patrols and a rutting couple against the wall of a bar. It looked like he was going to have a chapped ass in the morning. It did make me laugh so much that I missed a German officer stepping out from someone's outhouse. We both stopped dead. I could see him properly, but he was unsure.

'Halt, Ausweispapiere!' he ordered. But before he could draw his pistol, I slammed the rifle butt into his mouth, sending him down and his teeth out into the night. The man grunted as he hit the frost-covered grass, but before he could say anything more, the rifle was dropped and my knife was driven into his neck, allowing me to feed briefly before picking up the rifle and moving on, leaving him to finish bleeding out. I felt sorry for the local populace who would be punished for my actions tonight.

It took me three hours of zigzagging to finally make it to the casino. It was now nine in the evening, and I had to get moving. The beast that slumbered was awakening and with the taste of the German blood already, it wanted more. It was panting and eager for the murder to come.

In peacetime, the casino would be illuminating the French skyline, but now it lacked its once famous visage. As I moved around the outskirts of its grounds, I remembered the background information I had read in the file. It was once a manor house to a French aristocrat who was beheaded during the last revolution. The property was reclaimed by the people and became a casino and home to high-end women of negotiable affections. Hopefully I could get them out before their workplace got sent to hell.

My luck was with me as the building was guarded by just the normal German Wehrmacht, not Waffen-SS. They did guard every door and there were wandering squads of soldiers around the grounds, men with searchlights were scouring the gardens and surrounding woods. It was on my third time around when I spied my way in. A first-floor window was left open and there were no lights coming from inside, but I wouldn't know if it was empty until I was in there.

Time was getting on as I took my stolen rifle and ammo and hid them under a fallen tree. I feared the rustling of fallen leaves would give me away, like everything else in this damned place. The gun was covered nicely, although I hoped to have time to retrieve it after my mission – unless I was being chased by the damned guards. I waited until the grumbling, heavy-footed guards passed the bushes where I was hiding. I tightened the straps on my pack and focused. My eyes blackened and my teeth and claws lengthened as the glow of the spotlight passed me by. As my feet gripped into the earth, I bounded off focused on only one thing: my leap.

My speed increased and my muscles bunched as I leapt and hit the wall about five feet shy of the window. Chips of brick fell to the ground as my claws gave me purchase; I wasn't caught by lights or any incoming fire. With a final try, I launched myself into the room. After a quick roll over the carpeted floor I jumped up in an empty office.

With a quick look around I checked the room for anything I could use, but there was nothing. The one gift I was given before boarding that fateful flight was a map of the building. It was from 1913, so I was hoping the building hadn't changed too much. My night vision helped as I read the map. The private dining room was next to the large gambling floor; somehow, I had to get there unseen.

According to the map there were two banks of elevators down on the right-hand side and a main stairwell next to them, with fire stairwells at both far ends of the corridor. There were three floors of bedrooms above; the kitchens, restaurant and gambling floors were below.

I should have brought a change of clothes, but things were limited when you had to fit everything in a small backpack. I pulled out my knife and headed to the door, which was unlocked. I could feel that the hallway was clear, although some of the offices and staffrooms on this floor were occupied.

The hallway was lit like bloody Blackpool illuminations before the war. If anyone saw me in my bloody and dirty flight suit, I would have had trouble. I darted straight across to another room, which was empty all apart from a bed and a chair. The next room clearly had a man and woman enjoying themselves; the springs of the bed were taking a hammering.

I slipped out of the room and found their room to be locked, but the lock shattered with a quick twist of the handle and my added strength. I moved into the dark room. The rutting couple were bathed in light which had escaped from the hallway. A large, naked, bald man was in between the skinny legs of his blonde partner. But before he could unmount her, darkness encompassed him due to my fist to the side of his head.

Before his gap-toothed partner could scream, my blade was pressed to her neck. 'Do you speak English?'

Tears filled the woman's eyes as she hugged her lover's (or customer's) large frame like a shield. 'A little,' she whispered.

'Who is this?' I asked and prodded her ample lover.

The woman just shrugged and pointed to a bundle of francs on the bedside table.

I looked around and saw his large pinstriped suit on the chair in the corner. I pointed at the man. 'French or German?'

A sneer appeared on the working girl's face. 'Le Boche, pah!' She then spat angrily. 'I only lie with my fellow countrymen,' she said, and then eyed me up slowly. 'Or maybe 'er ally,' she added, winking at me.

The suit was big enough for me to wear over my flight suit. The woman watched me as I put it on. Yes, I looked stupid, especially with army boots, but how often do people look at the feet of others.

'I need you to escort me to the private dining room, or at least near it,' I demanded.

She gave me a pointed look and rubbed her thumb and forefinger together, which is the international gesture for cash.

I pulled out my mission wallet which had been given to me and handed over one hundred francs, and then with a quick nod I levered the still unconscious man off the petite woman – it wasn't a sight I would hold onto. Naked as the day she was born, the working girl got dressed into a shapeless, faded red dress with a matching pair of heels. Cleary, she was here for the staff not the customers or soldiers.

Wrapping a white belt around her thin waist, she stood in front of me with a smile. But in a flash, she grabbed the money from the table, reached inside my jacket taking the man's wallet and emptied it into her clutch purse. 'For the risk. Non?'

I nodded and patted my chest. 'Albert,' I said and offered her my hand.

She barked out a laugh and gave me a shaky curtsy. 'Gabrielle Decourt.' She then shook my proffered hand. 'You 'ere to kill le Boche?'

'Oui, and when I do you leave and never come back, understand?' I stated and looked upwards. Thankfully she was a fast one and nodded. I placed a small automatic pistol that was in my pack and a grenade in either pocket; my knife in its sheath was pushed in between the boot and my leg.

Arm in arm we headed towards the elevators. As we stood opposite, the one coming down was full. If I had a working heart it would've failed at that moment as I was faced with five SS officers and their women. The lift operator held out his hand and closed the door instantly. Some words came from my escort, but I guessed it was nothing a normal lady would say.

The next lift was empty but for the lift operator. We stepped in and Gabrielle said something. I prayed she wasn't dobbing me in, but by the rhythm of the man's heartbeat she hadn't uttered anything that would cause me harm.

The door parted with a metallic grind to reveal a very busy gambling floor; the clock on the far wall said half past ten. I needed to get going. Gabrielle led me past all manner of card games and slot machines. As we passed the roulette table, I noticed a pair of white double doors that shone between the red painted walls.

She pulled me aside. 'There it is, Albert,' Gabrielle whispered. She turned to face me, hugged me and kissed my neck, which knowing what that mouth had been on only moments earlier wasn't a nice feeling. 'I will 'elp you. They have murdered so many – my father, mother and my 'usband,' she hissed, looking around. 'Wait for my sign, and good luck, mon cher.' She placed her over-painted lips onto mine, and with a sorrowful look she walked away.

I grabbed her hand and pulled her into me and whispered into her ear, 'You don't have to do this. Run, live.' I then stepped back and stared into her war-weary face. 'I can manage this on my own.'

Tears formed in her eyes. 'Non, I will 'elp you. This is my life, and I will go out on my own terms. I will 'old my 'ead up 'igh when I see my darling Sebastian again,' Gabrielle replied and pulled away.

As the blonde walked off, she was propositioned by several customers who must have either been blind or just didn't want to spend too much money. She just waved them away and carried on with her journey.

I was now standing only twelve feet from the white doors when the clock struck eleven. Then something surprised me as well as everyone else: the lights had gone out. I dropped and took out my knife. Running towards the two burly guards, I ran past them and let the sharp blade run against their throats, sending them to the ground.

The door was unlocked and there was shouting and cursing. I pulled the pins on the two grenades and rolled in the first one and threw the other further into the room. I slammed the door shut and stepped away against the walls at the side. *Thump, thump* came the explosions, and then came the screams. I threw open the door and ran in with my pistol in my right hand and the knife in my left. The atmosphere in the room was smoky with an acidic taste from the explosives.

Bodies were everywhere. The doors on the other side of the room had been blown open and were hanging on one hinge each. The last grenade killed the two guards who had been guarding said doors. There were several dead, dying on the floor and slumped on the table. A man with a captain's hat was on his hands and knees being sick; he died quickly with a blade to the base of his skull.

A man ran in with a flashlight but fell instantly with a bullet to the throat. It was a slaughter. Anyone with a heartbeat was despatched with the knife. I threw off the suit and then the shirt and tie. Donned in my flight suit, I quickly went from man to man and retrieved their identity cards. I ran for the door that was hit by the grenade, where another man was taken down by a bullet to the chest.

Alarms and shouts were echoing around the place. As I ran, the odd person came out of a doorway; and it depended on what they were wearing as to whether they lived or died. It was carnage. Then finally I burst through a door and into the night, surprising two panic-stricken guards. One was shot in the eye. As I passed the other, my blade ran across his neck, leaving him holding his throat gargling blood.

Just as I made it to the treeline something hit me, sending me headfirst into the bushes, the pain was excruciating. I could feel blood trickling down my back and in my chest. I staggered further into the trees as branches were destroyed around me. I guess the guards on the roof had spotted me. I left the rifle where it was and carried on with my escape. The bullet was out of my body, so the healing had started. Having to exert myself meant my energy was keeping me running, albeit slower than normal, but I was leaving a bloody trail for the Boche.

But luck was with me that night. I stumbled upon a couple of drunken farmers sat in a barn near Le Faouët. I drank from both after slicing them with the knife. The last thing I needed was the rumour of vampires running around France, although there must have been more of us somewhere. The men died happily drunk, before I set fire to the barn and left to find a place to rest up and heal. I just hoped Gabrielle had managed to get away.

Chapter 9

Veronica Jenkins was worried as she made her way through the city streets; she hadn't heard from Albert in two weeks. The blonde had been around to his house several times but it was still quiet and dark. She had never fallen so quickly for any man. He was strong and funny and full of mystery. She just drank it up and when those thugs hassled her at the dance, it sent her heart into overdrive when he fought for her.

But there was something off about him. His breathing was always shallow and sometimes it seemed like he wasn't breathing at all, and the quickness of how he took down those men was a blur. The thing that worried her the most, apart from not seeing him again, was the love in his eyes when he talked about his family, his parents and his uncles and aunties. There was something strange when he talked about his mum, Annabel; it didn't seem like familiar love, but something more. Nothing perverse like you hear about sometimes, but something she couldn't quite put her finger on.

Being Saturday, the city was busy. The bombings were located towards other cities and the docks at the moment. From their lovely talk at his house she knew he had grown up in London, so when she went to the birth and records department at her work, and flirted slightly with Harold the man in charge of the department, Veronica had obtained a list of all the Albert Morris's in the city of London.

That's how she found herself looking at a family plot showing the one and only Annabel Morris, wife of Albert Morris, who was the son of Nathanial and Anne Morris who had passed in the early 1900s… The maths just wasn't adding up. And the photos she had found of his parents – a photo album about businesses in the Whitechapel area was a rare find indeed. There was a family resemblance, but not like he had told her.

She didn't detect any maliciousness in Albert and the things he had been telling her, despite the glaring holes in his story.

She decided to go to the one place apart from his home that seemed to hold a special importance in his heart. She stood in front of a pawnshop called Morris Pawnbrokers. Taking a deep breath, she walked into the shop. It was nicely set out: glass cabinets with everything you could want from rings, watches, guitars and hats.

'Good afternoon are you buying or selling darlin'?' came a voice from the counter where stood a stocky black-haired girl about Veronica's age.

Veronica smiled at her. 'Hello, I'm just looking around,' she explained whilst examining all the photos and pictures on the wall. 'A friend told me about this shop, so I thought I would have a closer look.'

The girl cackled like an old-world witch. 'What kind of friend would promote a pawnbroker, what kinda friend is that?' she said.

'Albert Morris, we went on a date and he told me that his father started this shop,' Veronica said happily, seeing a hint of recognition on the girl's face. Then she saw a photo. 'Oh goodness, is that you holding a sword?' she asked, looking at the shop girl.

Once again, the girl laughed. She walked over and looked up at the photo with her. 'Nah, that's my gran'ma. We looked so much alike that they called me Suzie after her,' she said smiling while looking Veronica up and down. 'So, you're Albert's new girl, are you?'

The blonde laughed. 'Well, I plan to be, but he went on a mission a couple of weeks ago and I haven't heard anything since.' She placed her hands on the cabinet and stared at the photo and then at a stuffed horse's head on the wall. 'Is that the bloody horse from the photo?'

'Oh yes, Gran'ma was kicked by it, so she ran in here and picked up the sword,' Suzie explained and pointed to the sword mounted underneath the head. 'And then she ran off and killed the bloody thing.' Suzie wiped her eyes. 'Albert had to pay the owner loads of money to save Gran.'

Veronica looked at her sharply. 'Albert, don't you mean his father…Nathaniel?' she probed and saw the girl freeze, but she recovered very quickly.

'Oh yeah, but I was told everyone called him Albert, that was his middle name,' the brunette said quickly, although her face looked a bit panicky and she couldn't hold the other woman's eye for a second.

'I think we need to talk, Suzie. I have a lot of questions,' Veronica said firmly with a stern face. She saw hesitation on shop girl's face. 'Do you have a bottle?'

Suzanne sighed. 'Yeah, we are drinkers, it's the family legacy,' she replied as she walked past Veronica and locked the door, slamming the locking bolts top and bottom before putting up the closed sign. 'C'mon then, I have a bottle of Albert's rum – comes from Nelson's ship, it does.' She opened up the shop counter and waved Veronica through to the sitting room behind a curtain. They were both sat on the sofa at opposite ends as they sipped the potent brew.

'Blimey, did this kill Nelson?' The blonde laughed.

The brunette didn't respond at first, she just drank the booze.

'So, what's going on with the captain?' Veronica asked.

Suzie downed her drink. 'Firstly, I talked to his friends who got him the army gig,' she said and refilled her glass. 'They checked with their sources and…Albert's plane was shot down,' she said with tears starting to stream down her face.

Veronica gasped and put her hand to her face. 'Is he dead?'

'They aren't sure. They won't go into any kind of details with me, though.' Suzie sobbed and blew her nose into a hanky. 'But he will be okay, he's a stayer, and he likes you,' she added, although deep down her heart missed his touch.

'I like him a lot, too, but there are things that don't add up. The pictures in his house of his mum and dad. He said that he looks like his dad, but I found a picture of Nathanial Morris; and yes they do a bit, but not that much,' Veronica explained with ideas swirling around her mind. 'If I'm right, the man we know is over seventy but looks our age!'

Suzie paled, realising this girl was way too quick. 'Well, it's not really my story to tell, but since he might not be coming back, perhaps I should explain. Although, if you repeat this to anyone else, they would lock you up and throw away the key.' She guffawed loudly and threw back another glass of rum. 'Well, it all started with that bastard Jack the Ripper...' She slumped further down the sofa all warm and drunkenly.

Veronica walked back home with a million feelings and thoughts running through her mind. The rum didn't help either, especially as she wasn't much of a drinker. As much as the night was fun talking to Suzie, Veronica could guess that there was more than just friendship between Albert and this Suzanne. But not for a while, maybe.

Somehow, the tipsy blonde made her way home safely, amongst the echoes of bombs landing in other parts of the city and the sky flashing as war was waged thousands of feet above the ground where man and machine duelled to their bloody deaths. She entered her doorway and headed up the stairs towards her flat where she soon found herself slumped in an armchair. The world was spinning slightly.

She tried to sort through her feelings for Albert. It had been such a long time since she had felt drawn to a man, and she found herself falling for him, big time. She kicked off her heels and hung her alcohol-scented dress so she could have a quick wash before bed. Just then, there was a knock on her door.

'Who's that?' she mumbled, hurriedly tying a silk robe around herself that a woman at work had sold her. She moved to the front door. 'Who is it?' she asked and put her hand on the door to either open it or force it shut; a single woman could not be too careful these days.

'Veronica, it's me,' a male voice replied. A male voice that her alcohol-addled mind slightly recognised.

She disengaged the lock and opened it, not caring a jot now who was behind it. Her eyes tried to focus on the man. Her eyes then widened; her pulse raced. 'Albert?'

He sported a small smile. 'That's me. Sorry it took me a while to get back,' Albert started to apologise, but he was quickly silenced by Veronica's lips and tongue as they kissed.

Their passion grew, the door was slammed behind them, and then her back was pressed against the door and her legs wrapped around his waist.

Feeling each other's passion, her hands freed him from the confines of his trousers, she felt her underwear torn away, and then they were one. He carried her towards her bed to continue their act of desire and lust. Her breasts spilled out allowing him to kiss her softness, making her moan with pleasure, and then they locked eyes.

'I missed you, Mr Captain,' she whispered, and they continued their act of love again, until sleep claimed them both. All thoughts of the conversation with Suzanne lost...for now.

As the sun breached through the threadbare curtains that adorned her bedroom window, she stood above her now lover. What happened last night? In all her years she had never acted with such abandonment. She combed out her hair with her eyes locked on his sleeping form. At her dressing table she wrote a short note and laid it on the pillow next to his lightly snoring head. With a faint smile Veronica left to go on a slow but thoughtful walk to see what conclusions her brain would draw from the night.

Chapter 10

I woke with a start. It was the first decent sleep since I had left that accursed mission; getting back was just a series of life and death events. After the debrief I did as I was told and came straight over to see Veronica – and see her I did, what a bloody night. A smile crept over my face and I scanned the room, then I closed my eyes and let my senses reach out. She was not here. That's when I jumped up and saw a piece of paper float gently to the ground. With my quickness, I snagged it even before it settled on the worn carpet. 'Oh shit,' I said as I read the note.

My dearest Albert

I have missed you so much that it hurt, especially as I didn't know how to find out how you were. Since our fantastic date together several things didn't add up for me, and as you weren't here I went all Miss Sherlock Holmes on you.

Your parents are Nathanial and Anne Morris, who adopted another boy and told people he was their son. I'm sure there is a story there somewhere. But after finding pictures of your father, I know now that you have secrets, Mr Captain, although we are all allowed some.

But, my Albert, your age is not what it should be. You look the same age as me even though you were born in 1868. How can that be?

I visited a friend of yours, Suzie, and we chatted and drank as we were both worried about you going missing while on operations. As we talked, I told her

*of my thoughts and feelings about you, and she
grudgingly told me about your history, and your gift
from the Ripper.*

*After the night of my life I had to leave you. No, it
wasn't a mistake, but I let my heart and wants
overtake me, which is normally the male issue, not
the female. Please make yourself at home till
darkness comes, then you can leave safely.*

*I know this has happened to you before, but please
be patient with me and wait for me to come to you,
my darling. I promise it won't be long.*

*Lots of love
Veronica xxx*

I smiled at the letter, folded it and placed it in my wallet. My smile broadened as I saw a small photo of her that she had placed inside with a lipstick imprint on it. I dressed and sat in the armchair reading the paper she had left for me.

The sun had finally gone down. The Nazis had bombed London again, and would most probably do so again tonight. I opened the door to the flat. With a look back, I headed out into the night with only one address in mind.

'Hey, Suzie!' I shouted out as I opened the door and found myself slammed back into the door by the force of the brunette's hug. 'Miss me much?'

She pushed me away. 'Where the fuck have you been?' Suzie snapped and slapped me on the chest repeatedly. She then grabbed my hand and pulled me towards the back room, then she ran over to lock the shop door once again. She was almost skipping back to me, sending her grey dress flying about, showing off some old workman boots she was wearing, just like her gran. Nothing but class.

We settled down on the well-used sofa. 'Thank you for talking to Veronica. It has saved me from having to tell any more lies,' I said, handing her the note.

'I'm sorry, she had guessed so much already. Plus we drank, and you know how that goes,' she explained and then read the note slowly. 'That's not too bad, is it?'

I shook my head. 'Could've been a lot worse.' I lay back on the sofa. 'Hopefully Veronica will come back soon. I really do like her,' I admitted and looked at Suzie who handed the note back.

'She will. Veronica loves you,' the brunette said sadly. 'We had fun, though, while it lasted, didn't we?'

I leaned over and kissed her rosy cheek. 'Yes, we did. You will always have a place in my heart, Suzie, and I will never forget you.' I took her hand and gave it a rub with my thumb. 'I'll be back, hon. We are friends, after all, forever.'

As tears wetted her cheeks, she gripped my hand even harder. 'So, what happened in France? Stuart told me the plane never came back?'

I rubbed my face with my spare hand and told her about the crash and about my own heroine Gabrielle, who I found out had been executed by the SS for helping with the assassination of ten high-ranking submariners, as well as other ranks. She was now hailed as a hero of France by the Resistance. My escape was then one death-defying action to the next. The town of Le Faouët was swarming with troops after finding a cell of Resistance.

I ran into a squad of new recruits, which the beast took over and wiped out. I took back control and semi-turned them. After that I left nothing but ash and rifles; they were found, though. It had confused them, but they still flooded the place with SS and Wehrmacht soldiers.

'Jesus, Albert, how did you get back here, then?' Suzie asked with wide eyes, her body appearing to tremble.

'I got to the coast and stole a fishing boat and somehow I made it here.' I chuckled; the sailing here was a nightmare. 'I hated the crossing to Ireland when Adrian and I went over with the army but trying to steer a trawler single-handed over the Channel was something else.'

Suzie and I embraced before she shut the door behind me. I headed home and back to my memories, with the thoughts of making new ones with Veronica.

The days and weeks passed slowly as I waited for her to return. Then a month later we buried my last friend from the past, Mickey. He'd had a good life, and his boy Stuart treated me like family. Thankfully it was old age that took him in the end with a smile on his face and a bottle in his hand; he headed off into the heavens to be with his wife, Tabatha, once again.

It was a nice service, even though a few questions were asked about the late time, but all just wanted to say goodbye to Mickey. The wake was a messy one, to the point where I carried Suzie all the way home with her passed out over my back leaving a trail of sick all the way back to my house which was closer than the shop.

I was still shaken by the loss of my last childhood friend when one day a corporal in my department who worked as the major's aide handed me an envelope. Her blue eyes looked into mine and there was sorrow on her face.

'I'm so sorry, Captain, but you asked me to keep a look out for Miss Jenkins,' she said softly before chewing her lip. 'I'm sorry, but I found her on a list.' The corporal tried to say more but her words faltered.

My mouth fell open looking at the paper held in the corporal's hands. 'It's okay, Corporal, thank you for your help with this. It…means a lot,' I said and saluted, which she returned and headed off, leaving me to open the envelope alone.

It was what I had guessed and feared. The news of Veronica's death during a raid on London, the evening of the very same day she left me in her bed. The husk of a heart I had left broke again that day as I walked home alone. I hadn't known her for a long time, but she fitted me like a glove.

Major Matterson had me carrying out local jobs for a time, despite the higher-ups pressuring him to send me back to France, but he knew I was doing a better job locally than risking his best spy catcher in occupied France.

It was on 1 June 1944 that I was parachuted back into France with orders to set the coast aflame, so that's what I did. The beast in me had fun. I cut a bloody furrow throughout the Calais area to make the Boche think that's where the invasion would come. I did a wonderful job.

After the war I moved into the shop with Suzie and we regained our love affair. She wasn't marriage material, and neither was I, but she comforted me during the bad times when the nightmares came a calling. Suzie, just like her grandmother before her, built me back up. Her family gave me back the original shop for me to run alongside Suzie who happily stood by my side. In the end everyone called us Mr and Mrs Morris, so we just went with it.

We were happy. We drank and sang and enjoyed post-war Britain. Her appetite for drink, food, me and life was unprecedented, which caused her to pass away in my arms at the age of fifty-seven in 1978. As her heart slowed and gave out, we shared a kiss. Our eyes never left each other as the life left her. I buried her in my family plot as Mrs Suzanne Morris; she would enjoy that.

Once again I was alone. Mickey's son Stuart had died in his sleep, which was sad, but for a policeman it was a good way to go, especially after some of the run-ins he'd had with gangs after the war. The influx of weapons brought back by servicemen almost swamped the police at times, but slowly they gained some control. Of course, I helped where I could.

I ran the shop on my own and was happy with my lot. The front windows and doors had a thick curtain to keep out the sun. Also, the till and counter were at the far end, so I would never be touched by the sunlight. In the early eighties I had them replaced with a reflective coating, so I would get all of the light but none of the rays. Here's to progress.

The future was interesting after the war as things moved so quickly. It's easy to keep ahead of things with the number of magazines plus television, but mostly it was the many new shops springing up selling all kinds of things for the home. Also, with later opening times I could spend my time just looking at the shelves and flow of electronics, especially from Japan. It always amused me that the countries we fought and won against now flooded our country with their goods, but that was life I guess.

It was the early nineties when my celibacy and loneliness started to weigh me down somewhat; not just that, but real company. Suzie's family had pulled away after her death, not that they blamed me, but my secret and what I had done for the family was just forgotten over time. As was the army, which I was quite happy about. But I felt the need for company again.

One Friday night I found myself perusing the shelves of the local John Lewis department store. Everybody likes new entertainment equipment, although luckily for my business there were still some people who liked a good old-fashioned pawnshop for a cheap deal. I am one of those who liked my electronic toys. With the rents from my spare properties, I had gathered a good deal of money, along with gold and silver which I took off the hands of some very aggressive criminals, allowing me to buy whatever was new and shiny.

I ghosted past the new models of home personal computers when I spied a tall redhead. She had pointed features almost like a Vulcan, and her hair reached her waist and her eyes glowed, but I couldn't tell if they were blue or silvery grey. I tracked her as she moved. She had a dancer's figure, wearing a knee-length purple dress with matching heels, but it was the way she held herself. It was impressive, like she owned the place, almost regal.

Suddenly, she stood stock-still towering over the shelf full of microwave ovens. Her eyes bored into mine, her pale face showed no emotion, but her eyes scanned over me, as I had done with her. The world had stopped for us both; we only had eyes for each other. Then she started to move, and I heard every time her heel hit the floor as she made her way towards me. Fellow patrons were cast aside like ice broken by oncoming ships. Soon she was stood in front of me. Wearing those heels, she was a couple of inches taller.

'Tracey Andrews,' she said in a tone which resembled a cat purring as it was stroked while eating cream off a freshly caught mackerel. Her long, slender fingers hung in the air as she proffered her hand like a scene from *Upstairs, Downstairs*.

I took her hand and strangely kissed the back of it. I saw the flicker of mirth on her pale face, although the smattering of light freckles across the tops of her cheeks and the bridge of her nose did seem to flare brightly.

'Good evening, Miss Andrews, my name is Albert Morris,' I replied and dipped my head slightly.

We stood unmoving for a moment still hand in hand; we were starting to gather stares from the occupants of the shop.

'May I call you Albert?' she asked formally.

I smiled politely. 'Of course, may I call you Tracey?' I asked, while inside I laughed thinking we were royalty.

Tracey nodded back with a smile breaking onto her porcelain-like face. 'We are drawing quite the crowd, Albert. Care to have a drink with me?'

We left the store without another word. Then we hit the September air, and that's when I noticed she had no heartbeat.

As we locked eyes, her lips parted showing off her lengthened incisors.

'We are the same, Albert. Now, let's drink and chat awhile,' she suggested and strode into the traffic, making me rush after her. Clearly, she had a destination in mind. When we got there, I was happy that many things couldn't kill me because this place was a shithole, to which we would seem very out of place with two posh people slumming it.

'Well, this is interesting. Come here often?' I chuckled and was then stunned when she broke her facade and brayed like a donkey.

'Oh, come on, Albert.' She laughed, making many of the rough-looking crowd stare at us some more. It seemed like the place was made of shadows. Tracey looked around and smirked. 'It is a shithole, but it's a shithole where nobody cares what you say or do.'

And she was right. My eyes could pierce the darkness to see that there was a drug deal going on in one corner, a handgun being exchanged in a booth like ours, and in the furthest corner a patron was getting orally pleasured by another, gender not sure.

'Good point,' I agreed. 'So, have you met many of us about?'

She waited for the goth waitress to drop off our gin and tonics in cloudy glasses. 'No, the only person I met was the shit who bit me,' Tracey snarled angrily.

'Bastard.' I shook my head. 'But when did you get turned?' I watched her throat as she swallowed the drink.

'1972, Bristol, went out on a date to a club, a bloke called Steve,' Tracey explained with a far-off look in her eyes. 'We were getting friendly in a corner when the fucker latched onto me and bit down. The pain was unbelievable.'

'But how did you get his blood in you? That's what you needed to change, isn't it?' I asked, pleased to have another to fact-check with.

She nodded and raised her hand to the waitress, who just rolled her eyes and muttered something to the bald-headed behemoth who pretended to be the barman. 'I'm a Bristol girl. We don't give up easy. He pushed me to the ground, but I managed to slip off my shoe and jam the heel into his throat. His blood sprayed over my face and clothes. And that was it. He did a runner out of the club. I chased him out, but after a few screams about my appearance I ran home which was just around the corner. Thankfully, my parents were out for the night as I looked a right state.' Her eyes filled with tears. I knew what would happen when she finally changed, and her parents were back, she would need to feed the beast.

The drinks were slammed onto our table, and I handed over the money. The barmaid stalked away and there was never a hint of the change coming back to me.

'I'm sorry. Did you ever see him again?' I then saw the feral grin appear on her face. 'Oh good.'

'Oh yes, I found him a year later. He had another poor woman with him, but I got to him in time before he ruined someone else's life,' she stated with a grin as music was pumped through the substandard speakers. 'So, Albert, what's your story?' Once again, she showed a crack in her stoic manner.

I took a sip. 'I was born in August 1868, and in my twenties I was attacked and turned by the one and only…Jack the Ripper.' I looked her, not a single reaction appeared on her face. Who am I kidding? She spat out her drink all over me and shouted, 'Fuck off!' and then started to once again bray like a donkey. The laughter continued until the redhead realised that I hadn't joined her.

'Shit, you're not kidding, are you?'

'Nope, I'm afraid not, Tracey. I stumbled over him as he was killing one of his victims. I tried to stop him, and—' I held my arms out wide '—TADAAAAAA!'

Her hands faintly shook at the telling of my tale. 'So, the history books are wrong, and I'm guessing he didn't get away?' she asked and waved at the now extremely pissed off waitress/dominatrix/serial killer, possibly, by the looks she was giving us.

'I bought a shop in that area, and over time I hunted him down,' I explained with an ironic chuckle, remembering how that fight could've gone either way. 'Do you think it's in our nature to kill the person who turned us?'

A thoughtful look crossed her porcelain features. 'Yes, it's such a brutal, invasive act. They can't blame us for wanting vengeance,' she surmised.

I had never thought of it before, really; but it was true, especially with the violence. Although they had never intended to turn us, we were just food to them, in the end it cost them their lives, their immortality, just for some food.

The Aileen Wuornos wannabe slammed down some more drinks. Thankfully, it was nearly closing time.

'So, Albert, would you care to have dinner with me tomorrow night?' Tracey asked politely.

Things had certainly changed in the world where a woman could ask a man out for dinner. 'Why, Miss Andrews, how deliciously scandalous of you. What would my dear papa say?' I pretended to fan my face, which brought out her donkey-like laugh again. 'Tracey, it sounds like fun. Just tell me when and where,' I said with a smile before looking around. 'Just not here…please.'

We swapped numbers, making sure I gave her my business contact number. I alternated between sleeping at the shop and my family home. I had vowed not to let anyone else into my home, it was full of my most treasured memories, and certainly not another vampire. After a hug and the now in fashion double-cheek kiss, we headed off in separate directions. With my sense now attuned to her scent, as creepy as it sounds, I knew she wasn't following me, so I headed back to the shop.

I moved like a ghost through the streets heading back to the docklands where I hunted. There was always some miscreant breaking the laws of the land. I hid in an alley as I saw a tall shaven-headed white man walk up to a car and lean in. I could hear a drug deal going down. I know it's ten a penny now, but they are still a blight on this earth.

It was a quick and easy kill as the man was sprawled upon a bench situated by a small park, which allowed him a quick escape if the Peelers ever turned up. He didn't seem to see or hear anything as I crept up behind, yanked back his head and plunged my teeth into his throat and drank. Then, with a flash of my claw, I slashed my wrist and let the change begin. As he started to twitch back to life, I thrust a fallen branch through his heart, sending ashes disappearing into the misty night thanks to a friendly breeze.

I licked my lips and tasted the drugs in his system. It was bitter, but another one done and dusted. Time for a long walk home and to think about the dinner tomorrow. I made it home without any more fun and games, and then I spent the rest of the night talking to the picture of Anna. As crazy as it sounds, it always centred me, especially after a night like tonight.

The next night I put on a new black Armani suit. For once I decided to take a black cab into the city centre because knowing my luck, I would've ended up being attacked and getting covered in claret before dinner, which I didn't think she would mind, but the maître d' would be somewhat alarmed.

I stood outside the front of the brand-new upper-class restaurant and waited, then she appeared. Her red hair was lighting up the night and the blackness of her dress seemed to drink in the shadows. Every time her matching high heels impacted the pavement, they seemed to echo throughout the world. The populous seem to skirt around her like a rock in a river.

I smiled. 'Well, don't you scrub up nice,' I quipped, bringing her godawful laugh to the fore.

'You are funny,' she said, giving my chest a playful swat. 'Shall we go in and play at being normal?' She took my hand in her pale long fingers and guided me into the glass-fronted restaurant.

When we were seated at the back I noticed that Tracey was sitting where she could take in the whole place, ever vigilant. Clearly, there was a past there. After a small amount of banter, we ordered some nice large rare steaks, with pepper sauce for a little kick.

'So, what do you do for money, Albert?' she probed.

I was honest about my pawnshop and the several houses I had bought and rented out, especial after the war when Suzie helped, who was skilful at picking out good homes and areas to buy in. 'And, of course, there is always some money to be found with the right kind of food,' I said and watched the smile appear on her face. 'And you, you don't seem to be hurting for money?'

The pale woman shrugged. 'I get by, life insurance from my parents.' Her face darkened when she said that, but it was fleeting. 'I do a bit of five-fingered shopping in jewellers, plus there is always a rich old man wanting to take me home, and who am I to deny them the pleasure.'

It was at that moment I realised we didn't have much in common, we ran on different side of the tracks, but I would not throw away this possible friendship so lightly and quickly. I had to remember that I was so much older than her, and it's hard to find friends, especially when you are immortal.

'So, I'm guessing that's why you are scanning the crowd, for your next sugar daddy, or someone you've stolen from?'

'A little from column A, and a little from column B, Albert, but tonight is about us. I'm sure you know how hard it is to make friends, especially as we don't age,' Tracey said, mirroring my own thoughts.

I raised my glass, watching the blood-red wine swill around. 'To the future, Tracey.' We toasted and the rest of the evening went well.

We ended up back at her place and her soft, plush bed. I then realised why I search for human lovers. Two cold, naked bodies in the act of lovemaking just isn't right; you need warmth and feelings to really enjoy the act.

We ate out a few more times and agreed that sleeping together was off the table for now, although we would both miss the stamina that our infliction had brought to each of us. During later years we met on the same day every year, but occasionally we saw each other out and about. Normally, she had a willing victim on her arm.

Chapter 11

London, Heathrow. November 2018

Tracey had taken me to the airport herself – well, her recent sugar daddy had paid for a limo to take us. We had previously promised never to repeat our night of passion, but the likelihood of seeing each other again was slight, so we enjoyed some fun in the limo. We had become closer than either of us had thought over the years. Together, we had found out that there was another of our kind going feral in the city of Nottingham. We found the animal scampering up the wall of an orphanage; he had killed four children before we could stop him. After that our friendship solidified. We smirked at each other as we dressed and readjusted ourselves before stepping out of the limo.

We hugged. 'Take care, Albert. You call me as soon as you are settled,' she said into my ear as we embraced.

'I will. You enjoy yourself, and thank you for all your help,' I answered as we locked eyes for the last time.

We shared a passionate yet still-lacking-something kiss before we parted. We knew that we could never be together, but our lives were intertwined, just like our bodies had been in the car. I watched the limo drive away with a hint of sadness, but somehow I felt that I would see my friend again.

While lying back in the first-class lounge for Virgin Airways, I thought about how nice it would be after all these years to experience another country, and not as a result of war. I would miss a few people, but it wasn't like the movies where I had to ask permission from the coven master to leave or anything. What coven? Wasn't that a witch thing?

It always made me laugh when I saw those films, the blokes all pale with sparkly and long, luscious hair. *Me, a boy from the streets of London, with wiry hair, who was bitten by the one and only Jack the fucking Ripper. Did he stop to teach me the ways of a vampire? Did he hell. Did I stumble into a coven who helped me…? No!* I mentally ranted. God knows why I was going over old ground again.

The flight was perfect, even though all those pulses were causing me a bit of trouble, but it was the long-legged blonde air stewardess who created the most issues. Clearly, she liked working in first class as it gave her access to the rich and famous. And I guessed if she couldn't get one of those, there was always the pilots. I was surprised Tracey hadn't become one, if only for the night flights. But then again, when her temper raged so did her Bristol accent, along with a constant flow of swear words.

Let's just say that the stewardess's hands wandered when she placed a blanket over me and along with the 'take me now' smile, it meant a troubling trouser time for little old Albert. But she also went through the same thing with every other pulse carrier in first class. Not saying I wasn't tempted, it had been a few months since I had lay with a warm-bodied woman, or, in fact, any woman – Tracey didn't count; our coupling together was one that mortals would never be able to compare – but getting caught with her in the toilet could mean trouble getting out of the airport and to my new apartment, which I had to do quickly while the sun was still in hiding.

Once the plane finally landed, I followed the sheep. Yes, my feelings towards the normal public had lessened over the year, so we went into the terminal and out to collect our baggage. Most of my keepsakes were in packing cases that would arrive in a few days. My one bag just had underwear and personal papers. Clothes, you can buy anywhere. Although most of my best Savile Row suits would be coming along with my other items.

I had arranged for a blacked-out SUV to shuttle me from the hotel to an apartment that I had rented for the year, which came with the option to buy, in midtown Manhattan on West 42nd St.

Hunger was starting to pull at me. Hopefully I could make it until sundown and then go looking for trouble. I'd hate to free up another apartment.

The driver was quiet, which I liked, so he earned himself another $50 for the courteous service. But just as we pulled up and I handed him the money, I had to ask, in my poshest accent, 'Are there any parts of the city I shouldn't wander in after dark?'

The big man shrugged. 'Everywhere can be dangerous, sir, especially off the main street – you shouldn't walk alone.' He then turned to look at me. 'I have some friends who offer one-on-one bodyguard services if you're worried, ex-military type.' He handed me a business card. 'Just in case, sir.'

I gave him a nod, grabbed my bag and headed towards the apartment building. The apartments seemed to have been washed in brushed steel and glass. It's a good job that vampires have reflections, or I would be damned. I moved towards the doorman.

'Good morning, I am Albert Morris, I have rented apartment 5c,' I said, holding out a photocopy of the lease.

'Good morning, sir,' the tall, kind-looking African American man said in reply. 'I was expecting you, sir. If I could just see some ID, then I can take you up.'

My ID was passed over. I know it was risky, but I had managed to keep my name all my life and moving here would help. He handed me back my passport, which Tracey's friends had sourced for me, and bid me to follow him. The man was a heavy drinker; I could smell the whisky leaking through his pores. One bite would get me pissed. At that thought my stomach rumbled loudly.

'Sorry, can't stand airline food,' I said, making him laugh as we entered the lift.

'Don't blame you, sir. I understand the realtor has filled your cupboards and icebox with groceries, so that should sort you right out,' he said as we travelled up to the fifth floor. When the lift doors opened, I saw that the corridor was an off-white colour. 'As I understand it, they have put some dark filters on your windows for you,' the doorman commented.

'That's good to hear. A war wound, bright light kills my eyes,' I added, and then saw him flash a US marine badge.

'Iraq or Afghanistan, if you don't mind me asking, sir?'

I shrugged as he let us into the apartment. 'A little of both, behind the lines type of thing,' I lied, thinking that World War II for assassination missions would be unbelievable.

'Hardcore, sir,' he said before showing me around.

There were plenty of now darkened windows, a nice balcony and two bedrooms for my imaginary friends. Or, as I liked to call it, my feeding room – although I ordinarily like to eat out and mainly on the dregs of humanity.

I bid the doorman goodbye and handed him twenty bucks before closing the door with a click. It was something I had read about, that a lot of the service people had low wages and used the tips to top up their wages. I sighed; I was finally here.

It was then that the darkness had started to recede, allowing the winter sun to warm the people who adore it, which wasn't me. Thankfully, the realtor had done a good job as enough light came in to light the rooms and not set me on fire. But hunger still gnawed at my bones, so I checked the refrigerator. My eyes widened and my incisors lengthened when I saw the steaks, at least half a dozen T-bones. They were torn out of the packaging, all the excess blood was poured into an empty glass, and then I used all my increased strength to squeeze the big red bastards in my hands, leaving them discoloured and destroyed.

It was old blood, but good blood. It hardly filled the glass, or me, but it would fill a gap until sundown. I checked around and saw the laptop that I had paid to be there. Luckily, over the decades I had kept up with technology, so within the hour I was set up with the apartment's broadband, and several suits and other clothes would be here tomorrow morning. So now bed.

After waking, I stood on the edge of the balcony looking at the New Yorkers and holidaymakers bustling around, all those heartbeats, all that blood pumping around their bodies. I looked up and over the way, straight into an office building. I locked eyes with a beautiful woman. She looked like a goddess with her long black hair and curvy frame. She was stunning; if I had a heartbeat, it would have been racing. I lifted up my hand and waved. All she did was give a smirk, turn around and stride off in her black business suit.

For the first time in many months, a smile appeared on my face. I turned and headed back inside. I donned my leather jacket, left the apartment and descended in the lift. It was the same guard.

'Good evening, sir,' he said.

I checked his name tag. 'Good evening, Mr Conrad, did you have a good day?' I saw him chuckle.

'Please, call me Jasper,' he said and extended his hand, which I shook. 'Jesus, your hands are cold, sir.' He chuckled again.

I barked out a small laugh. 'Bad circulation,' I lied, once again. But hey, I kill people for food, so what's a little white lie. 'And please, call me Bert.'

He looked around and smiled a massive smile. 'I sure will, Bert, but only when we are alone,' Jasper said, and I nodded and turned out. 'You be careful out there, sir – uh, Bert,' he corrected.

I pushed open the door and allowed the chilled air to waft in. 'Sure will, buddy. Did you want anything while I'm out?'

Once again he showed off his pearly whites. 'I wouldn't say no to some fried chicken, but if you can't don't worry about it,' he said.

I just held up my hand before heading into the mass of humanity following their normal routes home, to a bar or anywhere that took their fancy.

All the streets in my life blended into one, from cobbles and dirt to tarmac. But somethings never changed, it just got hidden – well, sometimes. I had done my research on New York and found out that it used to be a right den of filth. But a mayor came in and cleaned it up to bring back all the holidaymakers and their money, even after 9/11 people still flocked there. That's why these terrorists won't win. Mainly because they are hurting the public, leaving the man in power alone. Yes, they kill the poor soldiers and law enforcement, but rarely the odd senator. Like in England when the terrorists killed Lord Mountbatten, the IRA lost a lot of support and money that day. Wherever you are, there will always be a cause to fight for.

I stopped at a bar and enjoyed a medium-rare burger and fries with a couple of beers. A couple of women heard my accent and swam on over and started to chat me up. The girls were not my type, so I kissed their knuckles, we swapped numbers and I went on my way. I did notice a few angry looks from what seemed to be disgruntled locals getting wound up by the Limey getting their girls. It wouldn't have mattered if I was a Yank; they would still have been pissed off because the girls didn't want to give them their numbers. That's life.

Finally, my walk ended under the Brooklyn Bridge. The darkness enveloped me like a coat which allowed me to walk unhindered. A few girls of the night were working on either their backs or knees; some things never change. The pursuit of willing flesh has always been the driving goal, for either family or lust.

It was touching on the witching hour when I saw my goal: a tall white man covered in tattoos with a scar from eye to jaw. At this moment the human waste was slapping a blonde streetwalker to the ground. My vision narrowed and my incisors grew, then I made my move when the girl remained still on the ground. With my speed and strength, I took the man off his feet and into a stanchion for the bridge, knocking him out cold and making a gonging sound that echoed in the darkness.

In the blink of an eye, I wrenched his neck to the side, tore into his jugular and drew out the life fluid. There was a hint of narcotics, but that didn't matter as my body would filter that out. During the last beats of his heart, I released and slashed my own wrist, allowing my blood into his rotten mouth to start the change. I noticed the woman was still knocked out, so I checked the man's wallet and helped myself to his money. Waste not, want not.

I looked around as the man started to convulse. I found what I needed and plunged a piece of wood into his heart, turning him into ash. Over the years I had learnt it was better not to leave any bodies, so a little bit of my blood enabled their bodies to change from human to vampire – and once staked, no body.

The girl was still out cold, so after a brief wipe with a wet wipe (lifesaver), I picked up the girl and carried her into the light-strewn streets. It was then that she started to come to. With that, I placed her on some cold stone steps and walked away; after all, I am not a hero.

As the hour struck one a.m., I returned to the apartment block and waved at Jasper as I walked in through the front entrance. 'Here's your dinner, mate, three pieces of chicken, fries and hot wings,' I announced, holding up a bag for the gracious man.

I had bought the same for me, not sure why, but it looked good. Although, my belly was awash with rich blood.

Jasper's eyes went wide at the sight and smell. 'Aww, thanks, Bert. Did you enjoy your night?' he asked, pushing the bag under his desk.

'Not bad, got a few numbers, which annoyed some locals, but what you going to do?' I said, making us both laugh. 'Well, night, Jasper. Enjoy your food.' I waved away the money he tried to give me.

'Thanks again, Bert. Sleep well.'

I headed up to my apartment and threw all but my boxers into the washing basket before turning on the idiot box. *Buffy the*

Vampire Slayer was on, perfect. Now that was one girl who could stake me. As I watched her battle the demons of darkness, this 150-odd-year-old vampire consumed a bucket of chicken…nice.

Chapter 12

My bed called, so I placed the photos of my wife, friends and lovers in the room. The smiling Annabel, Suzie the elder swinging that sword about the shop, and then her granddaughter the drunk-looking Suzie when we played dress-up and she wore a wedding dress, and the small photo of Veronica who I lost on that damned day. I wished them goodnight and hoped for happy dreams.

Unfortunately, it didn't happen because the doorman called up saying I had a delivery. At least I would have a change of clothes tonight. The suits I bought would be collected by a local dry cleaner to get rid of the new smell, and the rest I threw into the machine to wash while I went back to bed.

After waking with a rumble of my stomach, I decided to stretch the old muscles by doing fifty push-ups – well, five, then I got bored and grabbed a bowl of cereal to try to fill the void. But, as expected, it didn't do much. The sun was dropping over the skyline, so I headed out onto the balcony in just a pair of boxers and a T-shirt while eating my Frosties. 'They're Greaaaatttttt!'

My eyes roamed the building and then stilled. Once again, the office girl across the way was looking at me laughing while shaking her head. She hugged herself and rubbed her arms as though demonstrating she was cold. That made me laugh and shake my head as I continued to eat my cereal. The woman was still laughing when she gave me the broken in the head sign before walking off, this time with a wave, but the image of her tight black dress stayed with me all evening.

I headed out as the night reclaimed the world of light. Jasper was on duty but dealing with an old couple, so we just nodded. I tried to mime a chicken and eating, which nearly made the poor man break down, but he caught on and nodded. Well, there was my shopping list for the night.

After a bit of fact-finding, a kind cabbie warned me not to go on my own to the Bronx part of town. And with a smile on my face I answered him, 'To the Bronx, good sir. I wish for adventure.' I announced this request in my best Victorian voice, but not my usual one, something from the books of Arthur Ignatius Conan Doyle. He just gave me a bat-shit crazy look and we drove off into the night.

The cabbie dropped me off at an Irish bar on Amsterdam Avenue to have a few drinks before I headed off hunting for those who would not be missed. It was a nice atmosphere and they didn't seem to hold any grudges against the Brits, and I didn't blame them for the loss of my friend Adrian. Think with your head and not your cock; that was something he paid the ultimate price for. But then again, there was a blonde at the bar who seemed to be giving the smaller of my two brains pause for thought.

And that was how I spent my time cavorting in a one-bed apartment until three a.m. with one Kelly O'Brien, who basically rode me like she had stolen me. Even my vampiric energy was pushed to its limits that night. Luckily her batteries eventually depleted, and we swapped numbers before she passed out. She was a quick-minded one, too. She called my number straight back to check it was real. But she was a stunning woman, and now a stunning snoring woman. Time to go out and feast.

Once again the darkness was like a friend and protected me. There were people's shadows everywhere, but not to me, I could see everybody. After half an hour I found a winner. An overly aggressive john who was slapping a girl after receiving some down on her knees service, and not the 'sorry, Father, for I have sinned' type. Within the ten-minute mark the man was ash and I was fifty dollars richer. Now I was on the way to get Jasper's chicken.

The next day my personal effects arrived from England, which did cheer me up a bit. I paid Jasper and his cousin Jason to help bring up the cases. Well, when I say help, I meant do it completely, and I paid for lunch, too. Pizza all round. Jasper was a good man, but I found his cousin looking through my cases when he was meant to be going to the toilet.

'You okay there, buddy? You lost something?' I asked in a friendly way.

He jolted and looked up, even though he was a big, tall bloke he looked fearful. 'Nah, sorry, Bert. I didn't mean nothing – you just got some nice stuff here,' Jason said with a bright yet false smile.

I looked into the case; it was some of the things I had salvaged from the bombing. 'Yes, I have, they were my late wife's things, keepsakes if you will, you know what I mean,' I said with cooler tones.

He must have sensed my irritation as he stepped back with his hands at chest height in a placating matter. 'I'm sorry, brother. I meant nothing by it,' he said.

The man was lucky because the beast inside would've happily torn him asunder, even though I would have had to repaint, and I do hate painting. Jasper then walked into the room sensing something was amiss.

'What's up, Bert? Jason?' he asked, looking from me to his cousin.

'Oh, nothing. Jason was just appreciating some of my late wife's personal effects as well as my own, but we're all good,' I said in slightly warmer tones, but my eyes never once left Jason's. In fact, I don't think I even blinked.

The cousins swapped a look; I could feel the tension in the room.

'Okay, then. Well, we'd better go now. I have to work later,' Jasper said and shook my hand. 'Thanks for the extra cash, buddy.'

'No worries. How about a burger tonight? I'm getting strange looks from the chicken place and they say I should be the size of a house.' We laughed, but I remained looking at Jason. Then I shook his hand and gave it a bit of the macho squeeze. Not sure if something went crack, but he did pale before heading out.

Thankfully I wasn't hungry, so I just popped out for a walk and picked up burgers for myself and a very apologetic Jasper, which of course I just shrugged off. But I had a feeling that I would be butting heads with Jason again. I also had a few ideas about my friendly business lady from across the way, whom I'd now deemed as my neighbour. I had made some purchases, so now to wait until Monday.

In the early hours of Monday morning I started to feel like I was being watched. There would be no second guessing if I was back in London; whoever it was would be tonight's dinner. But I was still vulnerable in the city that doesn't sleep. Every day I was learning about my hunting ground.

I managed to feed on a gangbanger, if you care to use the local patois, who seemed to be loitering around an intersection with a gun in his hand, and he wasn't a cop. As the ashes of his body scattered into the winter wind, I felt eyes on my back. My enhanced vision scanned the dark recesses of the street. There wasn't a thing showing up. So, in the blink of an eye, I bolted into the dark alleyways, leapt over parked cars and at one point an old homeless guy having a crap behind a dumpster – the poor guy fell back into his heap, but that's life on the streets.

Jasper was receptive to my late-night delivery of Chinese food and was still apologising about his cousin. 'Man, it's okay. He didn't really do anything wrong.' I chuckled and handed over his food. 'Now, enjoy your Chinese, and I'll see ya later, Jasper,' I said as I headed towards the lift.

'Okay, my friend, but thanks again, Bert, have a good night,' the guard called out as the doors opened and spirited me away to my new home. The thought of being watched kept my thoughts from heading back to the past, which I was grateful for. Could it be another one of my kind? Although, I had only met a few in my time – good and bad ones.

As the sun rose mockingly, I watched the early birds running about with their coffees and bagels, which did make me ponder what would happen to major cities if we had a coffee bean shortage. Yes, I live on blood, but as the Yanks say, I do like a cup of joe in the mornings. God knows where that comes from. Wikipedia, here we come.

For some strange reason I was getting excited about seeing the raven-haired beauty again, and I hoped she would get a laugh out of it. As the clock tolled six o'clock, I saw her drift into view wearing her usual black dress. I could see her scanning my darkened windows. I slowly pushed open the sliding door letting the Manhattan weather swirl around me. I could then see a small smile appear on her face. She sipped her coffee as I stepped out into view with my hands on my hips, my legs apart and my head tilted up in a heroic pose. And that's when I could see the stunning woman spray her beverage onto the window as she took in the view and crumbled out of sight in laughter.

She must have waved a few more people over who helped her up and started to take photos of me. Damn you, paparazzi. My neighbour gave me a warm smile and blew me a kiss before walking away. I gave myself a solo high five and headed back in to take off my Spiderman outfit. It was a winner.

I had been lucky so far with my real neighbours as I'd lived a reverse lifestyle compared to all of them. But tonight was doomsday. I was caught by an older white couple from two doors down. They walked out of the lift as I was trying to head out, maybe to the Irish bar again. They looked in their early forties and as though they had just fallen out of a magazine shoot. Everything they wore was a high-end brand. I nodded and hoped they would let me just enter the lift with only sharing a brief nod. But no, they stopped and both gave me an award-winning smile.

'Hi,' they both said together brightly. Then the man took over. He leaned in and shook my hand. 'You're the new tenant from 5c,' he said, still showing off his perfect set of made-to-measure teeth.

I smiled back, with my not so perfect teeth, but they looked straight enough. 'Yep, I'm Albert, Albert Morris,' I answered – and yes, they smirked at my old English name.

The woman clapped her hand to her ear. 'Jeez, I love your accent. My name is Kitty, and this big lug is Stephen, with a "ph",' Kitty said buoyantly. 'Where in England are you from?'

'London, just fancied a new start.' I let my eyes flick towards the now empty lift wantonly, but I turned back to the pair who were still talking. I knew who they were; Jasper had warned me this day was coming. They were party people.

Stephen's smile grew. 'Hey, we're having a party on Friday, you should come,' he said while his wife nodded avidly.

She took my arm. 'I heard you were here on your own. Did you want to bring a date?' Kitty said with excitement all over her sun-ruined face, these people were true sunseekers. The mention of a date made me sigh. I instantly thought about the beautiful girl from across the way. But I shook that off; I hadn't even dared to meet her yet.

'Sure, that would be lovely,' I agreed. I had already decided who I would ask. 'What time would you like us there?'

They told me to come around about eight o'clock, and then Kitty gave the typical double-cheek kiss and bid me goodnight. Finally, I could make my escape. I could see the smirk on the doorman's face. He obviously knew what had happened.

'Piss off, unless you want me to bring you back some vegan food,' I sneered.

'Awwwwww, come on now, Bert, I'm only having fun,' Jasper said, showing off those big pearly whites. He then laughed as I walked out of the front door while giving him the finger. I could still hear his laughter as the door closed to protect the man from the cold weather.

As I walked into the night, strange looks were sent my way as everyone else was wearing their winter wear, whereas I just wore my leather jacket. I took out my phone and scrolled through my numbers, making sure I didn't call anyone from England, although I was pretty sure Tracey would be up to no good. Plus, the UK is a long way to go for a pint. There she was; I saw her name appear on my contact list. The phone rang and rang, and then she picked up.

'Hello, Alby, is that you?' she asked with a slight chuckle. From the first time I told Kelly my name she changed it.

'Hey, Kelly, how's it going tonight?' I asked and waited for the tirade about her job at a major department store. We had talked several times over the phone but never managed to meet up again and relive our night of passion, which was basically down to my aversion to sunlight, and a section manager who apparently hated her.

'I'm fine, baby. Just got in, so I'm soaking my feet. You want to bring over some dinner and chill?' Kelly asked with those come-to-bed tones she had used at the bar that night.

'Yeah sure, I'd love to. I'll be right over,' I said and then heard happiness emerge in her parting words. I clicked off my phone and hailed a cab. It took a few attempts, but I was finally picked up by a friendly Indian driver call Ganesh.

'Where to, sir?' he asked respectfully in his strong accented words.

'Bronx please, mate.' I gave him Kelly's address. It was a tidy cab with the typical well-used aroma that all cabs seemed to adopt in the Big Apple.

'Are you from England, sir? I have family in Birmingham,' he asked.

I smiled. 'Yes, just moved here recently, but I grew up in London,' I stated and smiled at him through his rear-view mirror.

For the rest of the journey we just chatted about the state of the world in general. We both agreed that most people wanted to earn a good wage and be happy, but there would always be someone who wished to control and spoil it for everyone – either governments or terrorists alike.

He parked right in front of her apartment block, 1940s brick-built with an old-style iron cage elevator – even for me the trip up to the seventh floor was nerve-racking. As I pulled the cage open, I could smell Kelly already. She must have seen me step out of the lift; she loved to watch people from the spyhole in her apartment door. It opened and the tall blonde stood leaning seductively against the door wearing sweatpants and an oversized football jersey. Her clothes didn't match her sultry tones.

'Hey, baby,' she purred.

I smiled and embraced her, and then we kissed passionately. Clearly, she had just been eating some kind of chips. 'Hi, Kelly, you started dinner without me,' I joked, making her blush and slap my chest gently.

'Come on in. I guess you didn't pick anything up for us, then,' she said, playfully chiding me. She swayed her way into her tastefully decorated place. It was warm with plush carpeting and family photos littering the walls. She was part Irish; her great-grandparents came over from the Emerald Isle in the early 1900s. 'So, Alby, what food do you want, or do you want to share my funions?'

I shook my head at her. 'Order a pizza, you Yanks eat that, right?' I teased and gave her rump a playful slap. 'But no pineapple; I'm not a savage.'

Kelly poked out her tongue at me as we both remembered the large Hawaiian pizza she ordered last time. Never again.

We curled up on the sofa and chatted about her work and how tired she was of surviving rude people. 'Well, what else can you do?' I asked as I massaged her feet. Her eyes were soon fluttering enjoying my touch.

'I don't know, I've never known. Ever since school everyone asks what you want to do when you grow up. I never knew,' Kelly admitted.

I smiled at her. 'Don't worry about it. I didn't know either,' I explained. 'My dad wanted me to follow him in the trade, but I wanted more.' I took a deep breath. I had told many people about my story, although I'd had to hold back some details, like my real age, and the fact I'm a vampire. 'The family never talked to me after that day, so I never went back,' I admitted and took a sip of the water she had supplied me with. 'I'm just lucky I was left some money, so I invested it in property, but that was never planned.'

Kelly hugged me. 'Are they still alive, your parents, I mean?'

I shook my head. 'No, they died in a car crash. But not talking was down to both of us. My father and I were just as hard-headed as each other, but they are gone and I have to live with that,' I partially lied. Mother died of a heart attack in the street, I heard, and Father just died in his sleep, with his new son at his side.

We fell into silence until the buzzer for the door went. Kelly jumped up happily and grabbed the cash I had left on the table. Moments later she bounced back in with a large pizza and her blue eyes blazing.

'Here we go, Alby, half Hawaiian and half meat feast.' She put it on the coffee table with a flourish and smiled a happy grin. 'TADAAAAAA!'

'Fucking pineapple,' I grumbled, seeing that some of it had slipped onto my side of the pizza. Some gangbanger would pay for this injustice.

For someone who looked so good, Kelly packed it away with the best of them. I had a flashback to Veronica eating the roast dinner I had made her; it was a sight to behold. She had finished her half and then moved on to mine. But did she ask…? No.

'So, piglet, what you up to Friday night?' I asked and waited until she managed to swallow her overfilled mouthful of cheese and meat.

'Nothing, I have a rare weekend off. Why, baby?' she asked with hope in her eyes.

'Well, there's a party in my building and I'd like you to be my date. You can stay the night if you want,' I said and heard her squeal with happiness. I then found myself falling off the sofa with the kissing Kelly not taking any prisoners. 'I guess that's a yes, then?'

She looked down at me with remnants of my half of the pizza stuck between her teeth. 'You bet, Alby, can't wait to see your place,' she said as we continued our kiss, and then continued our travels towards the bedroom, losing clothes as we went. It was a fun night, and a gangbanger did pay the price for the wayward pineapple, although I'm sure he didn't understand my ranting as I pummelled him into unconsciousness.

Chapter 13

The days blended into one, as they do when you are immortal. I still waved at the brunette beauty across the way every evening; she looked a bit disappointed when I came out in just normal clothes with coffee in hand. I hoped that she came there every day just for me – one can dream. But could I dare to love again? Did I deserve it again? Over the years, as the world had changed, I had changed, too. Not since Suzie did I have a guiding light to keep me on the straight and narrow.

Finally, it was party night at the neighbours. I walked down to the front door to meet Kelly who was just stepping out of a cab with a holdall. She was beaming as she looked up and down at my building. I watched her walk in.

'Hey, Kelly, did you have a good week?' I asked, embracing the tall, curvy blonde.

'Hi, Alby,' she answered and gave me a brief kiss before pulling back and scanning the entrance hall. 'Damn, hon, are you minted?' She giggled like a schoolgirl as I just shrugged and took her bag, slung it over my shoulder and walked her to the elevator. It wasn't Jasper tonight; it was a new doorman who just smiled and nodded at me.

We headed up to the fifth floor with Kelly still hanging off my arm. 'Are you looking forward to the party?' I asked as we reached my level by the announcing electrical beep.

'Oh yes, I like a little dance now and then,' she said happily as we entered my abode. I watched as she ran off to look through the large window. I was nervous about the woman from the other building seeing me with my date, but I knew that her and her workmates left dead on five on a Friday. And as it was half past six I was safe. Although I didn't know why I cared so much.

I left Kelly to use the en-suite while I used the main bathroom, as two in a shower –although fun – takes longer and you tend to have to wash yourself twice.

When I entered the lounge after my shower, I noticed Kelly standing in just a towel looking at all my pictures. Any of the ones which involved me were locked away.

'Are these your family, Alby?' she asked, picking up one of Annabel on our wedding day.

'Oh yes, my great-grandmother on her wedding day,' I lied, but I saw a slight frown creep onto her face.

'But where's her husband? You have two different women getting married, but no grooms?' she pushed. She wasn't the first person to notice that. Photoshop here we come. People were not that easily swayed any more when you told them that you look like a father or grandfather.

I hugged her from behind and nipped her exposed and slightly damp shoulder, making her giggle. I could feel her pulse race. 'Mum never gave me the reason why, that's all I was left,' I explained and saw her eyes go wide at the dates written on the white border surrounding the photo. 'Time to get ready, love; time waits for no man,' I instructed and watched her walk away. Just as she turned into my bedroom, her towel fell to the ground exposing her curvy bum. The giggles I could hear were warming, but for some reason I was worried about her, and tonight.

It was time to go. We were about twenty minutes late and I could hear foot traffic still filtering down the hall to my neighbours' apartment. I wore a pair of slacks with dress shoes and a crisp white shirt with the top button undone. It seemed like the right thing to wear, but just in case I checked the other guests as they walked past my spyhole in the front door. I would blend in quite nicely; if I didn't, I could always rip out their throats.

There was a little cough, and I turned around to see Kelly wearing a red strapless gown with a small necklace of pearls and matching heels, but not too high as she was tall already. 'How do I look, Alby?' she said, sounding slightly nervous as she turned around slowly, letting the bottom of the dress flare slightly.

I walked over and took her hands in mine. 'You, Kelly, will light up the room. You are truly beautiful, and none will hold a candle to you.' I placed my lips on hers just enough to reassure her. 'Now, let's go and blow them all out of the water.' We linked arms and headed out of the apartment. That name really narked me back home, it would've been called a flat, but once again I tried to coach myself to use their unique speak, just to blend in.

Kelly was nervous as I knocked on the door, but I gave her a kiss on the cheek which seemed to quell her nerves. I couldn't fathom why she was nervous; she looked like a model.

'Albert, you made it!' screamed Kitty before embracing me. I was glad I was wearing dark colours just in case her tan wasn't real, but by the state of her skin they were real sun bunnies.

'Good evening, Kitty, this is my date, Kelly O'Brien,' I said, pushing her into the firing line. No, I didn't feel guilty at all.

I saw a flash of red as Kelly was pulled into the affray. I followed in chuckling and tried not to lip-read the curses coming from my willing cannon fodder, or date. She was soon surrounded by half a dozen ladies from Kitty's age bracket. It seemed like they were drawn to her because of the youth and tautness of her skin. *Could they be zombies?* I mused.

A beer was thrust into my hand by an overly zealous Stephen, with a 'ph'. 'Hey, buddy, how are you finding the Big Apple?'

I took a sip of the beverage; thankfully it was one I used to partake of back home. 'Not too bad, thank you. Easier than London to find your way around, thanks to your grid system layout, it's child's play.' I noticed he wasn't sure how to take that comment, but I just smiled and raised my beer to his. 'The people are friendly, though.'

He gave me a big false smile. 'Best in the world, buddy,' Stephen said, getting a few cheers from the surrounding ilk. I realised these people were upper-class arseholes. Like painting a dog turd gold, it may look shiny and nice but it was still shit.

I grabbed another beer and spirited my date away from the group of skin-admiring zombies. 'How are you doing, love?' I asked and placed the ice-cold drink into her hand, which she consumed with vigour and in a very unladylike fashion, wiping the remnants from her lips with the back of her hands. She was blessed with full red lips, so Kelly never really bothered with lipstick.

'You leave me like that again, Morris, and I will tear your balls off like a paper towel!' Kelly growled. The snarl on her lips and her nails in my arm screamed she was serious. 'Bunch of ghoulish bitches, them,' she hissed, giving the gossiping bitches a scathing look. 'They asked me what work I'd had done.'

The tanned brigade kept giving us furtive glances throughout the night. It was very disconcerting and, unfortunately, I could hear what they were saying. The men weren't too sure if I had taken the piss out of their city amongst other witty comments I had said during the night, which I had to explain to them later. And then you had the sun zombies who hated Kelly and her skin, but mainly her youth. They thought she was an escort, or a gold digger.

'Do you know what? I think it's time to leave,' I stated and saw the look of gratefulness on her face. The hosts seemed to be far away from the front door.

'C'mon, Alby, let's go,' she whispered, leaning into me and filling my nose with her scent. She turned the handle and slipped out into the dimly lit hall. She was stifling a giggle as we walked towards my front door.

I struggled to open the door as her giggling had turned into full-on laughing. We fell through the door, and that's when my lights were turned out.

Suddenly, I could hear struggling and muffled screams. My eyes shot open and I felt that my hands were tied. The room was dark, only lit by a sidelight, but I could see perfectly. Someone large, donned in black clothes and masked was struggling with

Kelly on the floor. She was gagged but her hands and legs were free.

As I allowed my senses to explore, I realised there were two others going through my bedroom and the study, which I had made out of the second bedroom because the Bronx and seedier side of the city was a 'target-rich environment', as the military say. So, no need for a killing room – until now.

I snapped the zip ties that held me like tissue paper, stepped up and put my dress shoe into the man's ribs, who was trying to rape Kelly, sending him flying. I pulled her into me. 'It's okay. Shhhh…' I said to her, seeing the panic and fear in her eyes.

I could hear someone, so I released my date and launched myself towards the man. With a punch to his stomach, I silenced him. Unfortunately, it caused him to void his stomach and bowels. A gentle punch then sent him to the land of nod.

While I was doing this, Kelly was busy kicking the potential rapist in the stomach. I moved into my room and saw that it was in turmoil. Everything I owned had been turned upside down. I could hear the muttering of the man bent over throwing things out of my cases; that's when I recognised his scent.

'Hello, Jason. Find what you are looking for?' I asked the balaclava-clad man, who jumped and spun around with wide eyes. 'You, mate, have fucked up,' I commented angrily. Then I saw a large silver pistol in his hand and what seemed to be a smile which could be seen through the mask's mouthpiece.

'Fuck you!' he snarled, and I heard the hammer clicking back ready to send the projectile towards me, but I was not there when it left the barrel. I was putting my fist against his jaw, dislocating it and knocking him out.

I headed back into the lounge and found many people standing there. Kelly was being held by Kitty when a man from the party walked up to me.

'Mr Morris, my name is Captain Ray Hughes. Can you tell me what happened?' the tall and broad policeman asked firmly.

'We were tired, so we left the party early. Then as we came into the apartment I was hit on the head,' I stated and rubbed the back of my head, which didn't hurt any more. I then explained how they tied me up, but not well enough, and how the one on the floor still groaning had been attacking Kelly, which made her sob even harder. 'I hit one over there,' I explained, pointing. 'Then I saw another intruder in my bedroom going through my things; he turned and took a shot at me.'

Kelly pulled away from Kitty and ran to me continuously whispering, 'Thank you.'

It was then that the first responders arrived and all the other guests were moved away. We were both checked over by paramedics and given the okay. The bruised and battered criminals were taken straight to hospital. Some of the party guests thought I had been overly aggressive with them, but the captain and most of police thought I should've done more.

They took Kelly and I back to her apartment, where we spent the whole of the morning shacked up in bed just sleeping and not much of anything else. When we started to move around the place I could feel that something was different between us, so without even a hug I headed home to clean up. Jasper wasn't on the door that night, so at least I didn't have to tell him about his cousin, and hopefully they wouldn't paint him with the same brush.

Once home, the doorman said the owners were horrified something like that would happen in their property and they would be in contact. He handed me some new door keys as the detective had told the owners that the perpetrator, Jason, had copied my keys while helping me move. My place was a mess, but it didn't take me long to get it all back together again. Thankfully, all my photos had been left alone.

I popped down to the local police precinct just after the sun had gone down to sign some paperwork. They had all pled guilty, but what else could they do since they were caught red-handed? That's when I learnt that Kelly had gone down alone to the precinct earlier in the day to give her statement. Clearly, we were now done. And that final nail was driven home by a text thanking me for our time together, and for saving her, but every time she thought of me, she would be reminded of that night, so it was goodbye and she was sorry.

Feeling a bit down, I headed out onto my balcony hoping to see my neighbour, but of course this is me we are talking about, so not a dicky bird was seen. I thought it being Monday she would be there…but no.

I decided to hunt, so I put on some old clothes and headed downstairs. I saw Jasper was on duty as the lift opened in the foyer. 'Hey, Jasper, how are you?' I said brightly when I saw him standing at his station, but he looked tired and withdrawn.

The tall man dipped his head slightly. 'Evening, Mr Morris. I'm glad to see you're okay,' he said apologetically. 'I don't have the words to say how sorry I am.'

I held up my hands to stop his misplaced apology. 'Hey, unless you put the keys in his hands it's not your fault,' I stated forcefully. 'It hasn't affected your job, has it?'

He shook his head. 'It was close. If it wasn't for you and other residents they would've canned my ass. Plus, he admitted to taking imprints the day we helped you move,' Jasper explained while wringing his hands together. 'Stupid idiot, leaving his wife and daughter all alone now.'

I didn't know what to say. Yes, I felt bad for them, but in the end it was his own fault. 'Well, I am sorry for his family, Jasper, but it was all down to him,' I stated and started to head towards the door. 'Want me to pick you something up, Jasp?' I asked, looking over my shoulder as I pulled on the door letting the fresh air in, which made the man at the desk shiver.

'Dealers choice, Bert. I will never say no to food.' He smiled, albeit with less life than he usually had.

I barked out a laugh. 'And you're still so skinny. You're a lucky man, Jasp. See ya later, mate,' I said before heading out into the cold night.

People were just heading home. I shot a quick look to my mystery girl's window, and there she was with her hair shining thanks to the light above her. I could see her searching for me, or at least that's what I thought anyway.

It was getting late, so I decided to continue into the underbelly of the city, maybe under Brooklyn Bridge again. With thoughts of the brunette and which outfits I would surprise her with, hoping for the exact same coffee spraying reaction as last time, I didn't see the two 'man-mountains' standing in my way.

'*Ooofffff!* What the...? Sorry, mate, my mind was somewhere else,' I said apologetically with a smile on my face, trying not to piss off the walking steroids.

'Mr Morris, the Blood Coven wish to invite you for a meeting...now!' boomed the mountain on the left, with no emotion at all.

I frowned. 'Coven? Is that a thing here, then?' I asked the walking boulder, who nodded. 'Shit, I got that wrong,' I added, watching a limo turn up and Lurch open the rear door. I had two options: fight in front of everyone or go to see these people... 'Shit.' I got in and sighed as the vehicle drove away into the traffic.

Chapter 14

I had no idea where we were going. The driver didn't answer any of my questions, but we were clearly no longer in Manhattan as there were trees everywhere. After a time, we drove through a stone archway which had black wrought-iron gates. The gravel driveway was covered by a canopy of trees, and thanks to my eyesight I could see a large, old mansion which made anything Mary Shelley could write look like children's playtime.

'Well, that's imposing.' I chuckled and watched the driver's eyes twinkle with mirth.

An old, grey-haired man walked out of the huge building and opened the door just as the wheels stopped turning.

'Good evening, Mr Morris. Please follow me,' the butler said and walked off slowly through some heavy oak doors.

'Are you expecting the peasants to attack us, Jeeves?' I joked, trying to relieve my rising stress levels.

The old man looked back. 'Very droll. My name is Graves, sir.' He carried on his slow journey through this very bleak house.

All of the wooden interior was stained like alabaster, and the carpets and drapes were blood-red – they really were trying too hard to do the whole gothic horror bit. We walked into a room with a roaring fire and large impressive portraits hanging on the walls.

'Please take a seat, sir. Master Sebastian will be with you in a moment.' Graves bowed and left.

I will be the first to admit it, I didn't like this place. It stank of other vamps and wealth. I then heard footsteps on the plush carpeting.

'Ah, Mr Morris, glad you could join us,' came a voice. I turned and saw a man in his sixties with dyed black hair wearing a tuxedo. Everything was thin from his lips to his arms and legs; he looked like he was made from a matchstick.

'Not that I had any choice,' I responded with light tones, remembering the two burly men who had collected me. I took the man's proffered hand. 'Nice place you have here. I'm sure Dracula would love it.'

The smile never left the man's face. 'Oh, shucks. Yes, the twins are a bit imposing, aren't they, but no harm done,' said the lipless man. 'Anyway, my name is Samuel Sebastian III, and welcome to Blood Manor.' He opened his mouth to reveal his fangs.

'Cheers, two first names, that's fun for you,' I said, trying not to let my old accent come into play, but I didn't like this man.

His fangs bared again, but with anger this time. 'My family have called this home for two centuries,' he said, throwing his toys, but he did relax when I held up my hands to placate him.

'I'm sorry, Samuel. I was just joking. Your home, it's very nice.' I looked around pretending to admire the ugly décor.

'Thank you, yes, indeed. I let the coven use it for our meetings, and some of them live here too,' he said as we slowly made our way down the hallway.

I nodded while pretending I cared. Tracey and I found out that we couldn't be together long term, so how did this lot do it? 'So, how big is your coven?'

'We will have time for that, Albert. They are waiting for us,' he said urgently. We came to a pair of ornate double doors; he placed his hand on both door handles and smiled at me creepily. 'Welcome to the Blood Coven,' he said and pushed open both doors to reveal a large round table with large wooden throne-like chairs. There were thirteen in total with two spaces. Unlucky for me, I guess. 'Ladies and gentlemen, Albert Morris has arrived,' and he escorted me to one of the free chairs.

I looked around and saw that with my escort it was an equal split of men and women. All the men wore the same clothing as Sebastian, and the ladies wore gowns from the time I was born.

By the looks of them, my jeans and a button-down shirt was not appropriate for such meetings.

'Well, hello,' I said, giving them a little wave.

'Mr Morris, may I ask why you didn't seek us out when you arrived?' demanded a woman, who looked like she was in the twilight of her years, and maybe other people's, too.

'Well, firstly, I didn't know you existed, so that's why, I guess,' I answered, after which they looked at each other confused. 'And, secondly, we don't have a coven in England,' I added.

Once again they muttered, but I couldn't be bothered to listen. A man next to the woman opened a file. 'Well, Mr Morris, that is untrue,' he said with a sigh. 'They have been tracking you for some time. They just chose not to induct you, due to your habit of spending time with the humans.'

I managed to hide my shock and disbelief as they told me I was being spied upon by this so-called coven, but the anger was palpable as I thought about these people acting like they were in charge. *Who do they think they are?* I had better tell Tracey; she might want to kick their arses. She's a bit touchy about being followed, touched and even breathed on unwantedly.

'They didn't even want to say hello. Ah, well,' I said dismissively and smiled at the dead-faced crowd. 'And may I ask to whom I am speaking?'

They just sat there like a bunch of statues, then the man looked up. 'In here you may call me number three,' he said and flicked through my file.

A laugh escaped. I was thinking we were in a James Bond movie. 'Okay, so what can I do for you? Clearly, I'm not coven material.' It was good to see them nodding in agreement.

'Mr Morris, you are right about that, but whatever you do impacts on us,' said another unknown face. 'It seems you have brought your habits to our land. The police have informed us that you and a human partner were attacked in your home, and that you let the attackers live?'

I leaned back in my chair and steepled my fingers like any good Bond villain. 'If I was on my own they would've been food, but my date was there. Then before I knew it my neighbours poured in, including one of your bloody Peelers.' That caused them to look confused again. 'Your cops, that's what I meant,' I clarified.

'Be as it may, Mr Morris, you should limit your time with humans just for feeding time. And if you mend your ways, we will happily induct you into the Blood Coven,' a woman my age said coldly, but a smile belied her tone. She was pretty, had long dark hair and with what you would say a noble standing about her.

'Also, I see in your file that you killed your sire, is that true?' No. 3 stated. This brought one or two sneers from the Council of Blood, which I imagined was the name they had given themselves.

I had to stifle a yawn – not because I was tired, but because I was tired of this shit. 'Yes, it turned out I had stumbled upon Jack the Ripper when he was torturing his latest victim. He was savaging her when he then attacked me – and he meant to kill me, not turn me,' I snapped at them. 'He was torturing humans in my area, and I thought he might come back to finish the job, so I got to him first,' I explained, which brought nods from over half of the council.

'We are aware of that and other instances in Britain,' a faceless voice stated.

'Their coven does seem to be very lax with their members, I must say,' said a woman who was dressed like Queen Victoria. 'Also, Mr Morris, the report says here that you worked with the British armed forces during the war, is that right?'

'Yes, it was a world war after all, and who says I wouldn't have been killed during one of those godawful air raids that took so many?' I speculated with visions of Veronica flashing through my mind. 'I had every right to fight back!'

No. 3 leaned forward. 'But your coven declared themselves neutral,' he said and went to continue, but I stopped him dead.

'They are not my fucking coven. I was turned over a hundred years ago, and not once did they approach me. So they obviously didn't want me to follow their bloody rules… Did they?' My temper had allowed my accent to come to the fore, and these snotty vampires did not approve of my language. God help them if they ever met Tracey; she made sailors blush. 'I kill only when I have to, and then only those who deserve it. I like being with humans; they are fun.'

Queen Victoria knocked on the polished table. 'But it's not our way. We have staff to deal with the cattle,' she scoffed.

I stood up. 'Those are your rules, not mine,' I growled and made to leave, but the woman who was my age motioned for me to sit down.

I did as instructed but the mood of the room remained uneasy. I didn't think they were used to people standing up to them. 'So, you don't like what I do, and if I don't change my ways… What? What's going to happen?'

'Nothing…yet,' came a different female voice from the shadows. 'We, Mr Morris, have a lot of power in this city, and we can't have you running around upsetting the status quo. If you change your ways you can join us, which gives you a certain amount of protection, safe houses in the city, though none of us have used them, and many willing cattle to be bled.'

I let out big sigh. 'I'm not trying to disrespect you or your ways, but I have found that vampires shouldn't be around each other too much. I have tried it and sleeping next to another cold body is no fun at all for me. Well, all bar the stamina,' I said, and gave them a roguish grin and a wink, which only one returned, and she was the vampire my age, visually speaking, that is.

'Humans are nice and warm, so it's nice to feel that and let it take me back to when I was human.'

The room went quiet apart from the staff walking about and the wall-mounted torches flickering. They obviously didn't like the modern era.

No. 3 closed the file in front of him. 'You shall be watched, Mr Morris. Please don't do anything which will bring trouble to our door. The driver will take you back now,' he said, and suddenly the table cleared and I was left alone.

At this moment in time all I wanted to do was set the whole place on fire. *Who the hell do they think they are?*

'Mr Morris, the car is waiting for you,' Graves the butler said with a respectful bow.

I looked up at the man and pushed back the old heavy chair. 'Thank you, Jeeves, lead the way.'

'The name is Graves...sir,' he said with a tired and bored look on his face.

'That's right, lead on, Macduff,' I joked back, but he didn't smile. He took his job very seriously.

I followed the man, passing a few of the council looking on from the dark recesses of the manor. All I did was wave and smile to acknowledge their presence. The butler led me to the front door and opened the door to the limo.

'Thanks, Graves, look after yourself,' I said, sitting in the back seat.

Before the butler closed the door, he leaned in. 'A word of warning, sir. Don't push them on this – they are quite stringent about their rules, sir.'

I shook the man's hand. 'Thanks, Graves, I'll think about it,' and within minutes I was being driven back to Manhattan. I leaned forward and spoke to the driver. 'Any chance we can pick up some fried chicken; my doorman loves it.' To my surprise the man did, although I'm pretty sure he regretted it the next day as the whole car smelt of fat-drenched chicken.

I walked into my apartment building foyer and watched Jasper hurriedly hugging himself as the cold air filtered into the spacious area. His face soon cracked a wide smile as he saw two buckets of Colonel Sanders' best fried chicken, and it was then that he saw the limo outside just pulling away.

'Hell, KFC is going upmarket, delivered by stretched limo. Bert, you shouldn't have.' He beamed as I handed over the plastic bag.

'When in Rome, mate. It is New York, after all,' I said happily and headed off to the lift. 'Have a good shift.' I pressed the button to call the lift and looked back to see his hand waving in the air as his face and other hand were rooting around for his favourite pieces of chicken. He looked like a child at Christmas.

I made my way into my empty apartment, flicked the switch and bathed the place in light. The way the night had gone left me agitated, so I kicked off my shoes and turned on the idiot box. I ate some 'fat food' knowing that it could not kill me. A man has to do what a vampire has to do! I decided to wait until later to phone Tracey, knowing what kind of fallout there would be when she found out we were followed by this so-called coven.

The early hours flittered away. Even Anna didn't have any ideas for what I should do. Although, the bottle of Scotch I had finished off came up with some great ideas; such as stumble about, shout at a lamp, and the best one was passing out in the bathroom and cracking my skull open on the bath. It takes a lot to get me drunk to the point where I pass out, but I guess I had reached it.

I woke up with a banging head, although it wasn't real pain. It was more memory pain from before my change, but it was a novelty to wake up covered in my own blood and not someone else's. I guess I was living in interesting times and starting to experience new things in the Big Apple.

I stood by my balcony windows as people started to rush to work. I closed my eyes and remembered living in London with my friends and running through the small streets of Whitechapel. I barked out a laugh remembering the lanky redhead Adrian swearing at our local copper and making off while still gesturing to the Peeler, then running straight into a lamp post, which caused the rest of us to stop running because we were laughing so hard. Happy days.

Sleep didn't come to me that day, not that I really needed it, but it was good to rest the mind and body from time to time, so daytime TV it was. It amazed me the number of adverts they had over here, although they have their reasons, and it was even getting like that back home. I decided a nice long email to Tracey was called for. My head wasn't up to her losing her temper. It must be a redhead thing, because when her temper blew the language that came from her delicate mouth would make a squaddie run home and tell his mummy. Somehow, I think the UK coven was going to have their arses ripped open.

Finally, it was time for my neighbour to show up on her balcony. She appeared there last night, hopefully she would do it again, so I ran off to get ready. No joke this time, something smart that showed I had embraced the American way of life.

It was time. There she stood at the window in her typical black business suit with black tights, but this time her black hair was pulled back in a loose ponytail. I saw her eyes widen when I stepped out onto the balcony as the sun had disappeared over the New York skyline.

I stood on a chair and placed my other foot on the balcony ledge. With my chin held high and my fist on my hips, I knew I had nailed the look I wanted. My eyes flicked towards her; she was wiping tears from her eyes. Clearly, I had hit her patriotic side. I think it was the cape that clinched it. She blew me a kiss and walked away laughing, then a couple of things happened.

I noticed many people in the same building with her taking photos of me posing in my Superman outfit, but that I didn't mind. The other thing was the limo outside my building and the woman from the coven who seemed to be of my age staring up at me sporting a quizzical look. I waved down at her, trying to lighten the situation, but she was gone.

'Crap,' I muttered as I heard the buzzer go on the apartment intercom. Leaving my audience to their laughter, I ran indoors and picked up the phone. 'Hello?'

'Mr Morris, I have a young lady here to see you,' stated the doorman, whose voice I didn't recognise.

'Hmmmmm, and does this lady have a name?' I heard a muffled conversation before he came back on the line.

'The lady said you know who she is, so stop playing games and let her up…sir.'

That made me laugh, and I told him to let her up. It was then that I remembered my outfit, which I speedily swapped for some comfy shorts and a polo shirt.

There was a knock at the door, so I quickly put on some slip-on trainers, jogged to the door and put my left eye to the peephole. I was right; it was the dark-haired woman from the Blood Coven.

'Now, now, Mr Morris. Are you going to leave a lady on your doorstep all night?' she said with only a slight hint of an accent.

I opened the door and gave her a smile, which turned into a look of amazement. The woman was wearing a red ballgown with a tight corset, which nearly made her pale breasts spill out of the gown, and around her neck was a diamond necklace with a large emerald that happily nestled in a wonderful place.

'My apologies. Please come in.' I moved out of her way as she glided in as though on air. 'Please, take a seat.' I pointed to my sofa, although her outfit would have been more suited to a throne.

'Thank you, Mr Morris,' she said and settled down with such grace like someone from Henry V's court. 'Now, please take a seat. May I call you Albert?'

'Of course, would you like a drink…Miss…?'

'No thank you. I won't be here long, and my name is Anastasia,' she said happily. 'I thought I would come and see you about the meeting, but I guess you didn't take it to heart, especially after what I saw when I arrived, Mr Superman.'

Fair play to the woman, there was only a faint sign of mirth on her lips. But it was her face – I recognised it.

'Well, I don't take kindly to people I don't know suddenly telling me how I should live my life,' I said sternly, but I still had a lingering feeling I knew her.

Anastasia sighed. 'I'm not surprised, they are a bit set in their ways, and you have obviously moved with the times, whereas they have insisted on staying in the past,' she answered sadly. 'But that is by the by. Tonight we are going to a dance. So, go and put your best suit on, then we can hit the road, as the humans like to say.'

'What, a dance, with me…? Why?'

She put her gloved hand over her mouth to giggle but recovered quickly. 'My apologies, Albert. Well, it's easy. You interest me and, like you said, you want to live your life by your rules, and you're a breath of fresh air to me. This ball will get you seen by the powerful. And as you will be seen on my arm, they will accept you, knowing that I am from the coven.'

I frowned and stared at her; the ghost of a smile still adorned her lips. 'I don't like to be used either, Anastasia, so no thank you.' I looked directly into her eyes, which sparkled much like the diamonds around her thin neck.

'Oh, don't be silly, Albert. We are going to have a night of dancing and getting to know each other. No offence, but there is nothing from you that I want or need, apart from your company,' she said happily, waving her hand at me. 'So hurry up; time is ticking.' She spoke with such a tone that I felt my body moving under its own steam. Her voice was one that expected to be listened to and obeyed.

Half an hour later we were taking the lift down. I was wearing my Hugo Boss tuxedo with a crisp white shirt and a bow tie that she had brought in her clutch purse which matched her dress perfectly.

The doors parted and we strode out like the King and Queen of New York, even Jasper who had come on duty gave me a mock bow with a big shit-eating grin on his face. *Yep, tofu burgers for you tomorrow, buddy*, I thought. He must have read my mind because his face dropped as I smiled at him when I held the door open for my now date.

We travelled slowly through the Manhattan traffic in the limo which had brought Anastasia. We sat in silence for a while, but it was starting to nark me. 'So, what's this dance about?'

She cast her superior eye at me. 'It's the Policeman's Ball. The coven is a very good donor to their charities, and with that it allows us a bit of leeway when things get messy,' Anastasia said with a smile, allowing her incisors grow. She took my hand in hers, the long white silk glove kept the chill out of her touch, especially when dealing with the mortals, it stops it from being a topic of conversation.

'Ah, so we are playing nicely with the local Peelers.' I chuckled as the beauty on my arm looked confused as hell. 'The bobbies, coppers, the police,' I explained, using my best London boy accent, making her laugh along with me. 'So, how come you're allowed to play with the cattle, as one of your friends called them, and I cannot?'

She stared daggers at me. 'One thing, they are not my friends. It is a committee, and they asked me to join, which I did,' Anastasia stated, lightly crushing my hand. 'Which allows me to carry on with a certain lifestyle. And this is committee work tonight. You will learn if you play the game. Life won't change for you…much.'

'I understand what you are saying, but it's not my thing really,' I admitted and watched the people outside bustling about. 'I had that from my father and the army. I do what I want to do now. It's a long life and I want to enjoy it.' I carried on people watching.

I felt her squeeze my hand, which made me look at her. 'I can't blame you for that, but there are a few members who don't like you or where you come from.'

That made me chuckle. 'Because I'm British?'

She nodded. 'Yes, some are very old and lived through King George's reign and the revolution. They still hold grudges.' That did make me laugh.

'Jesus, I'm not that old. How can they blame that on me?' I asked while still laughing at the pettiness of some people.

Anastasia shook her head. 'No, they were loyalist. When the English were kicked out they lost everything, and they expected you countrymen to come back and overthrow the revolutionaries, so they hate all the British,' she stated as the car started to slow down.

'Why invite me, then? Why demand that I change my ways so I can join them?'

'There was a vote, and they lost,' she said happily as the driver got out of the front of the limo. 'They wanted you killed for disrespecting the coven.'

My door was then opened. I was stunned at her words as I got out. I proffered my hand for her to step out, and we walked together up the carpet towards the front door. I leaned in. 'They really want me dead?'

'Yes, but we shall talk about it later. Now we show our public face,' she instructed as we walked into the large room.

I handed her a champagne flute and took one for myself from the pretty waitress. We mingled and were introduced to a few couples and older men, who all flirted with us, which was very disconcerting.

'See, Albert, you're a natural, the others are so stuffy.'

Soon the orchestra started to play, and she guided me onto the polished wooden dance floor.

'I'm not much of a dancer, I'm afraid,' I admitted. The last time was on my date with Veronica.

'I have danced all my life. Let me lead and just relax and let's enjoy ourselves,' Anastasia said.

And that's what I did as we twirled around the dance floor. She was perfection; her footwork and posture were correct.

'You are amazing! Where did you learn to dance like this?' I panted slightly – it was hard work all this spinning around.

'I had lessons continuously as a child. My sisters and I loved to dance, but my brother not so much.' Tears glistened in her eyes momentarily, but with a shake of her head her composure returned.

I looked around the ornate building built with light stone; it was quite nice. I saw the policeman who was a guest at the neighbours' party. He nodded his head when he saw me. *So that's who told them about what happened*, I thought. The music stopped.

'Would you care to sit and talk awhile?' I asked Anastasia.

'Yes please, I just need to visit the ladies' room, so I will find you in a moment,' she said, placing a soft kiss on my cheek before gliding away into the mass of bodies.

I watched her move through the crowd effortlessly before turning and claiming two more flutes of the very nice champagne. I spied a small table in the far corner of the room, which I headed to. Most people wanted to be seen at these functions, but not this kid. A table in the deepest depths for this vampire. With an old man's groan, I sat down and let my body relax – well, until a shadow appeared over me.

'Good evening, Mr Morris. How are you?'

I looked up and saw the policeman I knew. I stood up and shook his hand. 'Ah, Captain Hughes, it's good to see you again. I am well, thank you. And yourself?'

We both sat down. Damn that third seat. 'Please call me Ray, and I am doing well, thank you,' he replied. The policeman was a tall, broad man with salt and pepper hair and a strong jaw. He looked at me intently. 'How did it go with the coven the other night? They said they were interested in you?'

'So, it was you who told them about the break-in.' I frowned.

He held up his hands to placate me. 'Hey, man, just doing my job. The higher-ups give me a job to do, so I do it,' said Ray, which seemed to be the truth.

'You know about us, then? Doesn't it worry you?' I asked, but the man just shrugged.

'Nah, there's not many of you, and it's not like you are killing hundreds.' He chuckled and leaned in closer. 'I know the old boys of the coven don't like what you are doing, but the bosses and I appreciate you culling the scumbags. Wish you would all do it.'

I nodded. 'I learnt that years ago. Innocents are always hunted by evil – beast and man. So, I turned the tables, especially as no one really misses the bad ones.' It was then that I saw Anastasia walking back with a smile on her face. 'Ah, my date is coming back.'

He nodded and stood up. 'Then I shall leave you be. What happened to that girl you were with that night? She was a peach.'

'That night shook her. When she thought of me it brought it all back. So, bye bye baby,' I said sadly.

He put a hand on my shoulder. 'Sorry to hear that, buddy, happens way too often. Well, enjoy your night, Albert.' With a dip of his head to my date, he then said, 'Hello, Anastasia,' and kissed her proffered hand.

'Ray,' she said, albeit a bit abruptly.

Maybe some background there, I thought and watched her sit down and take a sip of champagne.

'Watch that man, despite his amiable manner he makes people disappear for the coven,' she said coldly after he'd walked away.

I couldn't say I was surprised by her admission. Anyone who worked for a third party when they themselves were paid to enforce the laws of the land was dodgy straight away. 'Sounds like I'm in big trouble?'

'All depends on whether you bend to the will of the coven or dress up as superheroes to flirt with humans,' she replied quickly and laughed into her glass.

The captain was still looking over at times, which was starting to irk me. 'So, may I ask about your history? You look familiar to me, but I can't quite put my finger on it,' I said, trying to sound sincere and not just nosey.

She stared at me for a second, then lowered the flute back onto the table and made sure it was settled on the coaster. 'I'm sure once I tell you my full name it will come to you,' Anastasia expressed.

I smiled, intrigued. 'We shall see. So, milady, who are you?'

The young woman straightened her back, placed her hands together on her lap and looked at me. 'My name is Anastasia Nikolaevna Romanov.'

Chapter 15

I sat stunned. 'Holy shit. I read about what happened to your family, and there were always rumours that you had got away,' I recalled, remembering the uproar about the Russian royal family's murder at the hands of the Bolsheviks. 'I'm so sorry about what happened to your family,' I said, although I felt foolish saying it, especially after so long.

'Thank you, Albert. I was lucky to get away. There was so much smoke from the gunfire in the cellar. We had corsets with diamonds sewn into the lining, which stopped some of the bullets,' she said and lowered her head.

I could see tears dripping onto her gown, so I handed her a napkin. 'I'm sorry, Anastasia, I didn't mean to bring it up again. Please forgive me,' I apologised, but she just waved it off and dabbed at her eyes.

'Please call me Sia. It's what my little brother, Alexei, used to call me,' she said and took quite a large draught of the bubbly drink. 'The bastard Yakov Yurovsky, may he rot in hell. When he realised not all of us were dead, they started to club and bayonet us. But I was lucky…ish.'

I moved closer to her. 'How so, Sia?'

That brought a warm smile to her face. 'One of our maids was with us, Natalya, a kind, fun girl with a sharp wit. Mother didn't like her, of course, but all of us girls did.' She chuckled remembering the young maid, but then her face straightened again as she continued her story. 'She was already dead, so in the smoke and confusion I placed my rings on her fingers. At that point in time our clothes weren't any better than the servants. When the killer moved in to get our other maid, Anna Demidova, who was still alive at the back, I snuck out through the door and stole one of the men's coats and made my escape. Some loyal guards helped and smuggled me away.'

'Wow, you were so lucky. How did you get turned?'

The Duchess Romanov waved down another waitress and took two chilled glasses. After taking a sip, she placed it back down onto the table. 'Just a random act. I was walking one night in Sweden. I was attacked and dragged into a dark alley and bitten. I always carried a dagger since the attack on my family, so I fought back. As with you, his blood got into my mouth and I was changed.'

'Did your sire die?' I asked.

She nodded. 'Yes, on my third strike I struck his heart, and the silver-plated dagger finished him off.'

We moved on to better subjects: the places she had lived and loved or hated, thanks to the loyal guards who had smuggled her out. They had also managed to collect a lot of family heirlooms whilst the country was torn apart by the revolution, which allowed her to have family photos and also the money for those who saved her to live in comfort. She couldn't blame them for keeping some of the gold. The corset of diamonds alone meant she never had to work again, although she could not bear to sell the item that saved her life.

As the evening came to a close, we once again found ourselves in the limo. Sia was curled up next to me resting her head on my shoulder. 'I came to New York in 1952, and once the coven found out who I was they almost demanded that I join them, so I did,' she said in sleepy tones.

'I still don't understand why they are being so bossy with me; I'm just trying to live the life I was dealt,' I stated, but I never received an answer. Dragging up her past had obviously tired her both emotionally and physically. I pressed the button on the door panel to notify the driver.

He looked in the mirror after the divide had dropped. 'Yes, sir?'

'The lady has fallen asleep. If you could drop me off back at home and make sure she gets home safely?' I asked politely.

'Of course, sir. We are ten minutes away from your abode,' he said and moved the limo into another lane. 'Oh, and Lady Romanov informed me to pick up some fast food for you. I have four-foot-long Subs in the trunk. She said you have a piquancy for such foods.'

I barked out a laugh that made Sia grumble and mutter something about disciplining bad pillows. 'Thank you, my friend, and thank the lady when she wakes up, too,' I replied as the limo coasted to a stop outside my building.

I moved Anastasia over and rested her head so she wouldn't slide around too much on the leather seats. With a final look back at her, I stepped out. As I did I heard the click of the boot release popping open to reveal sandwich goodness.

Even from the sidewalk I could see Jasper's eyes piercing the darkness searching for food, then his teeth came out to play as he saw the bag in my hand. The limo pulled away as soon as the boot was quietly closed so as not to wake up the sleeping duchess. Who'd have seen that coming? And I couldn't tell a soul.

'Hey, Jasper, how's tricks?' I called out as I walked in through the glass double doors. 'I got foooooood,' I announced and smiled at him.

'Subs. Thanks, Bert. I could get used to this – being served from a limo.' He chuckled and picked a couple of the Subs from the bag, leaving two for my own late-night consumption. 'But thank you. My night has been quiet. How was yours?'

I looked at the doorman who was trying to kill himself by sandwich. 'I was taken to the Policeman's Ball. It was nice, and she was great company – Russian,' I said and winked at him. I had to wait until he'd finished his mouthful for a reply; he had bitten off more than he could chew.

'She sure was a looker. You're a lucky man, Bert,' he said while still gazing at the sandwich. Obviously, they were in love and I was interrupting their time together. 'Has your date been here long or is she a newbie like you?' Jasper was quick, and now he had forced the Sub into his way too small mouth.

'Yeah, she has, grew up here,' I lied and decided to leave the young lovers to their food dance. 'Night, Jasper, enjoy.' With a wave of his hand and the slap of a rogue slice of tomato hitting his workstation, I headed back to my domicile to rest and think about the night's events.

The next day was just a good old-fashioned duvet day. My hunger grew as the hours ticked by and the beast that normally lay in slumber was restless again, so I knew I had to go out tonight to feed, but it was only going to be a quick run out.

The thing with the coven had got to me slightly, so I sent another email to Tracey giving her more info. The reply to my first one had vindicated my decision to contact her by email because the language my friend had used even made me blush – and as my blood doesn't circulate, that was an amazing thing to happen.

Soon it was time to see if my neighbour was out and about. As the sun started to disappear over the skyline, I headed outside holding a nice steaming cup of tea wearing sweats and a T-shirt. As I closed the glass door behind me, my eyes flicked up to see the raven-haired woman. We shared a smile and both lifted our coffee cups.

Both of us just drank our beverages and smiled at each other, but then she surprised me by pointing at me, then herself and then pretending to drink. I broke into a bigger smile and nodded. The girl bounced on her toes excitedly, held up her index finger and trotted off back to where I assumed she worked. The happiness I felt again managed to quell the beast of its murderous thoughts, but I'm sure it would soon rise once again. Just then, the girl came back with a large pad of paper. She held it up so I could see it. It read: *Tomorrow 6:30pm, downstairs, Rose*.

I put my thumb up to her and nodded. Again, she beamed a winning smile and waved before making her way back inside. As she walked away, her head kept on flicking my way with a faint pink tinge to her cheeks and a warm smile on her face.

Once she disappeared out of sight I looked down onto the busy street, and just like yesterday there sat a limo. Standing next to it was the one and only Anastasia, who was dressed quite conservatively in jeans, knee-length brown riding boots and a black coat, for fashion not warmth. I noticed she was looking from me to the window where my neighbour had been standing. Then just like that she walked into my building, and I knew this would be trouble.

This time Sia just made her way up to my apartment. I thought the doorman would've stopped her and rung up to me. *But no*, I thought as the doorbell rang. I was mistaken, which I didn't mind since it wasn't the first time and it wouldn't be the last. The bell rang again, so off I went to my doom. The peephole confirmed who I knew it was.

'Evening Anastasia, sleep well?' I asked as I opened the door wide. She just walked in, barging me aside. 'No, please, come on in,' I said quickly with sarcasm.

The woman threw her coat onto the chair and then threw herself onto the sofa. 'Albert, you are causing some shit, you know that,' she growled with anger flashing in her eyes.

I leaned against the wall and shrugged. 'What do you mean, pray tell?'

'Well, firstly, you left me in a limo all alone. That pissed off the old boys at the coven,' Sia stated. 'It is not the correct way to treat a lady, they said.' She waved her hands about in frustration. 'And you are continuing to flirt with that human opposite despite the fact that I have told you they are watching you.'

That pissed me off. 'Yes, and I told them I don't care. None of the coven lot have cared about me for over a hundred years, so why start now?' I snapped angrily before moving across the lounge to retrieve her coat and hang it on one of the coat pegs by the door so I had a place to sit.

Anastasia ran her long fingers through her hair. 'We are going around in circles, Albert. They won't stop. They are bored old vampires who do not wish change, and I believe that you scare them.'

I sat in the chair and dragged the palm of my hand down the front of my face in frustration. 'Is that why they sent you here, to calm me down or spy on me?' I asked.

'Neither. I came here of my own accord. But what you have to understand about the old duffers at the coven is that they have all lived for a long time, and they have got used to people listening and doing exactly what they are told. And when someone slights them…' she said.

'An English someone,' I pointed out helpfully.

A smile did ghost her lips briefly, but it was soon taken away. 'Yes, that doesn't help much. When I left they were in a meeting with Detective Hughes. All I know is that they were discussing you,' Sia explained as she fiddled with her fingers.

I was calming down a little, appreciating that Sia was genuinely trying to help me. I realised that I had forgotten my manners. 'Would you like a drink, some wine or tea?'

'Wine would be nice, thank you,' she answered.

I stood up and took a bottle of red from the wine rack. It was one of my last bottles from the 1800s. 'So, what do you think they are going to do? Fine me or just go for a spanking?' I pulled out the cork and let the wine breathe. It was the aroma of wine that pulled me back to memories of happier times, when we had shared family dinners. I repressed a laugh when I thought of my wife's annoyance, especially when Emma, our daughter in all but blood, had got drunk and attempted to drink all the remaining gravy from its receptacle as our boy, Stanley, cheered her on while Anna and I were in the kitchen tidying up. It brought a warmth to me deep down.

Anastasia shook her perfect hair. 'Nothing at the moment. I think they just want Hughes to keep an eye on you,' she explained. 'Including that girlfriend of yours across the way,' she added.

At the mention of her, my eyes blackened and my incisors had an airing. 'She has nothing to do with them; she knows nothing about us,' I growled. I knew her caring words were a warning about the future and that there would be blood if I carried on the way I was going.

Sia raised her hands and smiled. 'I'm on your side, Albert. I have championed your cause within the coven. Just watch yourself,' she advised before taking the wine glass I had offered. I felt the wine was ready; breathing is highly overrated for people and wine.

This time I sat on the sofa with her but at the other end. 'Why does life have to be so difficult? I thought moving to this city would make a nice change for me. And it did for a while, but it was short-lived.' I sighed and closed my eyes in frustration, then I felt her hand slip into mine. My eyes opened and I saw her smiling at me.

'I'm glad you are here; it's been too long since I've met someone genuine. I'd like to be your friend, Albert. I want you to trust me,' she said with a sad smile as tears began to fill her eyes, making them glisten like the Romanov diamonds that saved her life and paved her way to safety away from the revolution and the Bolsheviks.

'Thank you, I'd like to be friends,' I said with a smile, 'but I don't like to be controlled. So, if this is some trick by the coven, you can leave now, with no hard feelings,' I said firmly, to which she nodded.

'It isn't, this is just me, Sia, your friend,' she said before leaning back into the sofa and looking out of the window. 'You have a nice place here, so much better than the dark manor. They love the whole gothic genre; that's why we were wearing all the old dresses. I had enough of that at the royal palace.'

I laughed and drank. 'I was lucky. Just a working-class boy from London who went to the army to travel the world, which didn't work out as we only got to Ireland,' I said, making us both laugh. I checked my watch and realised my hunger was building. 'Now, I need to feed, so it's time to go for a wander around town.'

'At the coven we have thralls who come to get bled. They enjoy the whole vampire genre – plus they get paid for their service,' Sia explained. She must have thought about actually hunting like the predator she was, as she then asked, 'May I come with you? It would be nice to hunt.'

I watched her for a second, then gave a curt nod. 'I'll go and get changed, then we'll go out,' I said and headed to my room. 'Oh, you'd better send your limo away. It won't really blend in where we are going.'

As I changed my clothes I could hear her talking on her phone telling the driver to go back to the mansion and that she would call him later if needed, which made me think she had more plans on her mind than just hunting – maybe I was the victim.

Within ten minutes we had passed the doorman, whom I didn't know, and arm in arm we walked out into the cold dark streets heading for the Bronx.

Her heels seemed to echo down the street. Whenever I walked alone in the city, people always did their best to avoid me or have any kind of eye contact. Something in their hearts was telling them that I brought hurt with me and they should fear me. It's like walking into a dark room and something in your heart tells you not to – unless you're a blonde woman in a movie, then you walk in blindly and call out, 'Hello, anyone there?'

'So, what do you normally do, Albert?' Sia asked, referring to the killing process.

'Well, it's quite easy really, head to the bad parts of the city, keep to the shadows and wait for a drug dealer, pimp or some other degenerate to turn up, then chow down,' I explained. We continued walking, crossing street after street. 'But don't kill them,' I warned. 'Feed them a bit of your blood, just enough to start the change and then—'

That surprised her. She stopped walking and stood completely still, interrupting my instructions. 'You change them? Are you mad, Albert? The coven will stake you straight away if you have been siring willy-nilly,' she spat angrily, grabbing my arm and turning me to face her. 'I knew you were reckless, but this is the worst thing possible!'

I grabbed her shoulder. 'Calm down, I start the change so I can turn them to dust. You can't just leave bodies around with no blood in them.' With that, her breathing started to ease. 'I would never sire anyone; you know this life is a curse.'

Sia gave me a sad smile. 'It is what you make of it, Albert, that's why we don't mix with the humans unless we have to. Mixing with other vampires, you have company for life, albeit a bit boring at times,' she said as we linked arms again and continued our journey.

'But humans have a warmth about them which I desire and crave,' I admitted. This seemed to kill the argument as we walked silently through the street hoping to see some prey. We passed a bar, so I decided to pull her in with me. 'Let's have a drink and go fishing,' I announced, and once again a frown adorned her pretty face. As we walked into the establishment, I knew I had picked correctly; this was a true dive bar where the locals ruled the roost. *Perfect*, I thought as we took a booth in a dark corner.

A very 'second-hand' looking waitress walked over. I wasn't sure if she had two belly buttons or if one was a bullet wound. But, fair play, she did try to provide the whole service with a smile, showing off her gleaming white teeth, all four of them.

Her look screamed meth addict, but her badge said waitress, which was what we wanted at this time.

'Two beers, please, import if you have them?' I asked, and she walked away trying to sway her body seductively, although it looked more like she had bad hips.

A panic-stricken Anastasia looked pointedly at me. 'What are we doing here? I thought we were going to feed!'

'We are. We are fishing, and you are the bait,' I answered happily.

She tutted. 'And what makes you think I want to be the bait?' she stated with a raised eyebrow.

I gave her a knowing look and scanned the scummy bar. The leather seats were faded and scuffed, and the pool table had beer stains amongst other fluids if my sense of smell was anything to go by, but as I suspected quite a few of the dozen male occupants had libidinous looks in their eyes aimed at my guest.

'Because if you went for a walk outside to take a phone call, I reckon you could eat your fill.'

The waitress, who now seemed to be shaking from withdrawal, gave us two Stella lagers with glasses which last seemed to have been cleaned when I was a baby.

'Thanks, hon,' I said and gave her a twenty-dollar note. 'Keep the change.' I smiled, showing all of my teeth, which more than tripled hers.

'You're not from around here, British?' the waitress asked.

'Yes, and this lovely lady is Russian. We are having our own cold war,' I joked, making Sia chuckle as she drank from her bottle.

'Whaaaaat!' the waitress drawled, clearly not understanding the joke. She left even more confused than before.

The men at the bar were getting interested in us, but mainly Sia, of course, and some of their pulses were racing. 'So, want to play, or shall we just move on?'

Anastasia took another draught from her cold lager. 'I'll play, but if any more than two follow me, you'd better come out and help,' she said sternly, which matched her black eyes. The Russian woman then stood up, took her phone from her bag and said something to me in her national language before heading outside. It was only later she told me that she had called me a floppy horse's cock.

After a couple of minutes, two guys who were chatting in a booth against the other wall both stood up and ambled out with lust in their eyes and a purpose on their minds. They had flicked their eyes to the barman, who very quickly gave a brief nod and then looked over at me. Then another two men walked to the back of the bar seemingly following the signs to go to the toilet, but with my hearing I heard the fire exit open and then close.

It had gone wrong already, and she wouldn't let me forget it either. I went to stand up when I found myself very popular with three large beer guts hovering over my table and stopping the majority of light whilst adding to the bad smell.

'Can I help you, gentlemen? I was just about to find my friend,' I said with a smile, smelling the aggression exuding from them, along with body odour.

'Hiya, buddy. Now, why would you like to leave? We can all have a beer together. I'm sure your pretty friend will be back in a bit,' said a man with one gold front tooth and wearing a John Deere hat. Strange really, as we were in the city.

Another man gave a guttural laugh. 'Yeah, but she may not be so pretty.' That comment made the other men give dirty laughs.

'Well, I don't think so, my friend. Now, move away, or you will have to explain to the next five-dollar hooker you go to why you only have one *nut*.' I spat out the last word and flexed my fist. Suddenly, I could hear a fight going on outside. I knew I had to go.

The third man, who didn't seem to have a neck, prodded me in the chest with his podgy, hairy digit. 'You are staying here, little man. If you do, you might get out of this place in one piece,' he growled.

That was it for me. I grabbed his finger and with a quick flick of my wrist it was pointing to the heavens, making the man stagger back screaming as his bone felt fresh air for the first time. Then I quickly solidified my promise to John Deere by punching him in his junk, which appeared to rupture his left goose egg, sending him to the ground out cold. The second man threw a punch at me. With a dip of my head I let it connect just above my forehead, which shattered two knuckles. With my right fist I then collapsed his nose, but not into his brain.

I stood up quickly and dodged the haymaker from a random man who had joined the scuffle. I kicked out with my foot, scoring a hit against the side of his knee, tearing tendons and cartilage as I did so, and flooding the night with shouts and curses. I made my way out of pub and followed the noises of another scuffle. I soon saw the epicentre of all the trouble. One man was down on the ground and another was on all fours vomiting with one hand cradling his testicles. They may have needed to be renamed after this action.

A thug with tattoos running down his neck was holding Sia's body down while a ginger-haired man held down her legs, but they were stuck what to do next. To use her as they wished, one of them had to let go to get her clothes off.

I picked up a plank of wood which had been cast aside and swung it at the ginger's head, sending him to lullaby land. This panicked the other man to see his three friends either knocked out or crying for their mummy.

I locked eyes with the cold green eyes of the attempted rapist. In a split second he jumped up and ran. He was just about to reach the corner when half a brick caught up with him and possibly sent him back to second grade.

'You okay, Sia?' I said, rushing over to her.

She slapped my hands away. 'I'm fine, they hit me with a plank,' she snapped, jumping to her feet and giving the man crying about his nuts a kick in the face. 'I thought you were going to help me if there were more than two of them.' She started to rearrange her clothes and brush off the dirt.

'Well, yes, I did say that, but the three lumps of meat inside hindered me a little. I'm sorry,' I exclaimed and watched her now with hands on hips.

Her incisors grew. 'Fine, which one is mine?'

The men were still out for the count as I went through their wallets and plucked out the driving licences for a little visit later on. I can't abide men like these. If it hadn't been Anastasia, it could've been someone else who wanted a drink or just to sit in the warm. This world was now perilous for the weak and innocent.

I wandered back to Sia and linked her arm with mine. 'We can't, too many people now. I'm guessing the police will be on their way and they will claim we attacked them. We will be held until the sun comes up,' I said as we disappeared into the shadows.

'Damn it, I'm really hungry now,' the Russian duchess admitted with her teeth still on show for the world to see. 'I need to feed.' Clearly, the fight had drained her reserves because her Russian accent had slipped in.

I held onto her tighter. 'It won't be long, I promise. The gangs will be out and about in a bit, but maybe we can find one to share,' I stated.

As I said that I saw a long beaten-up car with six gang members cruising down the road. They stopped by an intersection even though the lights were green. A tall Hispanic man wearing a parka jacket walked from the shadows, leaned into the car and then turned retreating back into darkness. The streetlights enabled such clandestine things.

'Here we go,' I commented.

As we walked closer, I could see the man in the dark leaning against the wall. His face was illuminated by his phone. Then another man walked up and they palmed something to each other, payment then drugs, and they parted.

'Is he dinner, Albert?' Sia whispered.

I smiled at her. 'He's the starter.' I handed her a rolled-up pile of dollar bills and crossed the road away from his eyeline. 'Mess up your hair, hunch down a bit and make sure he can see the money. We want him away from the wall, okay?' I advised.

With a wink and a scarily toothy grin, she limped away while messing up her hair. The limp was a nice touch. I followed against the wall so close that I could hear the fibres of my jacket catching on the imperfections of the stonework.

Sia stopped in front of the man. 'You holding?' she asked with a Russian twang she had allowed in.

I saw the feral grin appear on the well-rounded man's face as he pulled his hood back to show off some facial gang tattoos and a blue bandana. 'Hey, Mama. I haven't seen you before,' he said as he pawed at his groin. 'We can trade a blow for some blow,' he suggested, and then laughed at his own wit.

Sia took a step back, making him sneer. 'I just want some ice, that's all. You got it?' she asked, taking another step into the street illumination.

Finally, he stepped forward angrily. 'Yes, bitch, I got it. If you got da green, it's all yours, but I want a show first. Show me those blouse bunnies you got hiding there,' he demanded.

He didn't see me walk up behind him and wrench his head back.

Sia stepped forward with fangs bared, leapt onto him and sank her fangs into his pulsing jugular.

I dug in from the other side, but the helpings were meagre. After a mouthful, I slit my wrist and drenched his mouth with my blood. 'Sia, off,' I growled.

She lifted her face showing a blood-smeared mask, eyes like coals and fangs dripping.

'He's going to start to change,' I warned.

Her eyes returned to normal as she understood my meaning. He started to convulse and when he stilled, I took a silver-bladed flick knife I had made especially for this job from my inside pocket and plunged it into the man's chest. With a flash he was gone.

The ex-duchess leapt into my arms, wrapped her legs around me and kissed me furiously, smearing blood all over the place as we shared the kiss. She leaned back. 'That was amazing and tasted so much better than those cattle that plod through our doors,' she exclaimed and kissed me again. I couldn't help it with the beast awake. We were drawn to each other, with the blood of the kill pumping.

'C'mon, I still need to feed properly,' I said, letting her back down. Then from my other pocket I handed her a wet wipe and we both cleaned each other up. I could still see her smiling in the darkness. I just hoped I hadn't created a monster. We heard a car engine far off, so throwing the wipes into a nearby trash can along with the drugs that didn't burn up we walked off arm in arm keeping to the shadows.

We made it to the Bronx, which wasn't that bad a place, but when you walked into the bad spots you knew about it. The two of us walking arm in arm together brought a lot of looks our way.

'Albert, what was that tang in his blood? I haven't tasted it before,' said the Russian girl while picking some flesh from her teeth.

'Drugs, probably meth. Don't worry, though, our bodies don't react to it,' I reassured her as we walked into what the locals called the Badlands.

We were walking into an old derelict industrial park, which was a popular meeting place for women of the night and their willing customers. I then saw a big pimp shoving his little white hooker/employee about. They were hanging around a piece of waste ground that looked like it had once been used as a car park for the surrounding companies. Now left to decay, nature was trying to reclaim it with wild grass shooting up from the cracks in the asphalt. There were a few cars in the darkness, and I'm sure all of the occupants received their money's worth.

Sia stood silently with me as we watched another car pull up and converse with the tall dark pimp, which ended with him pushing his employee into the car and taking a few bills in return before the car drove off into the scrubland.

'What do you think, Albert?'

I assessed the scene. We were stood in the doorway of an old carpet factory staring out at the moonlit wasteland. I scanned and saw that all the parked cars seemed to be moving in a rhythmical nature. 'Okay, wait here,' I said. She nodded as I crouched and moved off as quickly as I dared.

I headed towards the pimp. He was resting lazily against his own car, seemingly bored and not paying attention. I continued to move towards him using whatever shadow and cover I could find. I negotiated the twenty feet quickly enough, leaving the last five which I could do in the blink of an eye. I was now so close to the man that I could hear the tinny emissions from his iPod earphones. I crept closer. It must have been a sixth sense because when I was within three feet, he turned around and went for his gun.

'Fuck you, motherfu—' he spat until my fist took him off his feet and into sweet Morpheus. The gun he was holding flew away into the darkness, but it seemed all his girls and punters were still busy exchanging services. I heaved the tall man onto my shoulder and carried him back towards Sia. 'Dinner is served!'

Her teeth glinted in the darkness. 'Bloody hell, that was quick, but you first, Albert,' she said.

So I plunged my fangs into his jugular. Strangely, his blood was clean and tasted like a drink from a fresh cold stream. I felt my stomach awash with his blood, so I pulled away and let Anastasia drink the rest. It didn't take long for Sia to be full, so then once again I fed the pimp my blood.

We sat together in the disused factory waiting for our victim to turn. Shouts had started to come from around the pimp's car; one of his working girls must have come back and panicked when he wasn't there. In the other cars the grunts and groans kept on coming. When the time came and the pimp turned, I plunged my knife into the man's heart to disappear him from this earth forever. Nobody will weep for him, and later I saw all his girls going through his car before driving off with it.

The last thing I remembered was Sia lunging at me and kissing me furiously. And I don't know how we got home, but I do know that we shed our clothes from the front door of my apartment to the bedroom. Our beasts had taken control of us after being allowed out to play during the kills. Blood flowed in the bed using teeth, tongue and claws until sunshine filtered through the curtained windows making shadows on the wall. By that time our lust and beasts were sated, so we could rest.

Chapter 16

It was midday and we were laid up in my bed; we had a slight chuckle about the situation. 'Well, that got out of hand,' she said with a smile on her face.

'Yep, maybe that's why I hunt alone,' I replied and kissed her hair as she cuddled up resting her head on my shoulder.

She nodded with the bedsheet covering her modesty. 'I kind of understand the human thing now. Don't get me wrong, last night was great, but our bodies, cold on cold, does give an uneasy feeling,' Sia admitted.

'My friend Tracey, we have the odd night together, but we know it won't work. We aren't designed to be together. It's a shame as it would've been ideal. I believe we are solitary animals; we hunt alone and live alone. I think that's why the coven is so strict on other people. Mainly because they are struggling being together, so they deflect by picking on other vampires' actions,' I lectured. The little bitch then bit my nipple, which caused her arse to be slapped.

'I think you are right, Albert,' she mused and traced my body with her nails. 'Maybe I should get a place of my own. Although, the old duffers will kick off and blame you.' She allowed a smirk to appear on her lips.

I slammed my head back onto the pillow. 'Shit, and the hits just keep on coming.' I chuckled and closed my eyes.

'So, did your friend Tracey talk to the UK coven yet?' she asked, still playing let's irritate Albert with nails and questions.

The woman just wasn't going to leave me be, so I picked up my phone and checked for messages. 'Ah, we have a message from her. Oh, crap!'

'What's up?'

'Tracey said she noticed, and these are her words, some nosey, needle-dicked prick following her, and she punched him. And it turns out he was working for the coven, like Ray the

Dick,' I told Anastasia and then texted Tracey back. 'She has a meeting with them soon. God knows how that's going to go,' I said.

'Why, do you think they will hurt her?' she asked, looking concerned.

I rubbed my forehead. 'Well, I'm not sure. As you know I have never met them, but Tracey can be a bit feisty. And if they push her, it might go badly.'

Anastasia smiled and sat up, letting her body free to the world. 'Well, come on. Let's give it another go in a nice hot shower. Better safe than sorry.' She bounced happily towards my bathroom.

I felt bad as I was going on a date later with a girl I had been pining for, but then again Sia was royalty, and I am but a servant, so I gave chase. Who knew duchesses squeal just like us commoners?

8 p.m. Notting Hill, London

Tracey Andrews was incensed. Not only were these coven pricks pissing off her friend Albert about him going out with nice, warm and normal women, but now they were following her, too.

She strode to the address of the little rat bastard who was following her last night. He had spoilt her date with a football player from Chelsea. She could've milked that for days, possibly more. *But nooo*, she had to pick the only footballer who didn't like to see his women punch out a four-eyed sneaky twat. Tracey stomped down the pathway to number 48 and punched the overly large black wooden door. It was a nice white stone town house, so the coven was clearly minted.

She impatiently tapped her new Louboutin Iriza shoes in navy blue, not her favourite colour but they matched her dress, and waited for the door to be answered. It was a good job that vampires healed quickly because her feet were killing her. She chuckled to herself when she remembered how she had accidentally skewered Albert's thigh with a different pair of stilettos during a night of playing Drunken Horny Redhead versus Albert.

The door creaked open and there stood an old man. 'Hello, I was told to come here,' she said dismissively.

He dipped his head. 'Ah, Miss Andrews, please come in, our members are waiting.' He moved aside.

Tracey took off her Armani coat and handed it to the man who looked at it, shrugged and hung it on a coat hook. 'Well, where is this coven, then?' she said with more than a hint of impatience. There was a large mirror in the hallway, so she checked her make-up and smoothed down her brand-new Roland Mouret navy crepe dress. It cost her nearly £2000. Tracey hoped that they would appreciate it. She checked her phone for any messages but there were none so far. She placed it back in her Gucci Dionysus bag.

'My name is Alfred Masterson, coven master,' the old man said, smoothing down his own Savile Row suit. 'This way, miss. The others are waiting for us.'

Tracey silently chuckled to herself that she had given the great coven master her coat. 'Nice place you have here,' she said, letting her Bristolian accent come to the fore, but he didn't reply. He just dipped his head politely and opened a large white door at the end of the hallway.

She walked into the dark room which had a large polished wooden table. Her eyes flitted around, it had thirteen chairs and two were empty. 'Unlucky for me,' she whispered while being directed to an empty chair. 'Cheers, Al.' She chuckled inwardly as Albert mentioned that vampires in the USA get a bit pissy if you mispronounce their names. Tracey looked around and saw what looked like the cast of a docudrama about the rise and fall of Henry VIII. They were split fifty-fifty men and women with Alfred but not including my fine ass.

'Alfred, if you please, Miss Andrews,' he said coldly as he took his seat opposite her and started to read through the file in front of him. 'Right, to business. You are Tracey Daphne Andrews, born in Bristol to John and Alison Andrews, whom you fed upon on the night of your turning, along with your siblings,' he read out and looked up at her.

Her nails had dug into the polished wood of the chair. 'What the fuck is wrong with you? How dare you talk about them like that!' Tracey almost screamed, her eyes now coal black, but these freaks didn't even flinch. 'I loved my family, and that bastard turned me into this animal!'

Alfred nodded. 'Indeed, and you killed him – and now you have embarrassed the lifestyle,' he said in a monotone-like voice which any office worker had perfected over years of service.

'Well, it's either that or death. And I prefer life and fun,' she replied, looking around at the cold, emotionless faces. No wonder Albert had kicked off at the USA coven, bloody busybodies. 'So, I do my best to keep under the radar, and survive.'

'Yes, we know, dear, that's why you are here,' said an old crow who was wearing the newest fashion of Henry VIII's court.

Tracey looked at them. 'You have been spying on me. That's not something friends do. So, why do you want me, and why wait so long?'

They all seemed to laugh, although clearly they were out of practice as it sounded like the death throes of seals.

'We don't just let anyone in,' said a man who looked like Alan Sugar. 'We chose you because you treat the humans as a vampire should: for money and food.'

Then it clicked – they wanted her to keep away from Albert. 'So, this is really about my friend Albert. I heard that he got called in by the local coven, and they didn't like his lifestyle,' Tracey said pointedly.

Another woman who appeared to come from the depths of the Tudor years cleared her dusty throat. 'Yes, lying with and marrying the cattle, he is quite the embarrassment, and we don't believe someone like you should sully yourself with such company, young lady,' she criticised.

The redhead bristled. 'He loved all those women, and he fought for this country when you fuckers most probably stayed hiding in your bloody crypts.' Her accent had now gone back to broad Bristolian. 'He's a good man and just wants to be left alone!'

The same woman leaned forward sporting a wispy top lip and too much make-up and jewellery, but her fangs were prominent. 'The problems with humans are just that – their problems. He allowed his nature to be known and used. And that could've impacted all of us,' she snarled.

Tracey's fist bounced off the table. 'Then maybe you should've talked to him. But no, you just watch and criticise instead of guiding and teaching,' she retorted, struggling to remain calm. Albert always said her fiery red-headed temper would get her into trouble.

It was Masterson who intervened. 'Calm yourselves, ladies. Mr Morris's failings are not why we are here. The reason for this meeting is to ask you, Miss Andrews, if you'd like to join our coven?' he asked calmly, making Wispy Lip sit back, but Tracey was still stamping mad.

'How many are in this coven?'

Alfred gestured to those around the table. 'This is the coven, the best of the best over the centuries,' he said with pride. 'And we wish you to join our numbers.' They all tried to smile, apart the woman Tracey had clashed with.

'And I suppose I would live here and follow your rules?' Tracey asked, and the coven head nodded. 'And what if I don't want to?'

'Well, we shall continue to watch you, to make sure you don't do anything that we don't like. And if you break the rules, then you would be punished,' he explained like a schoolteacher.

Tracey scanned them all angrily. 'What will they do to Albert? And if I joined your little club, could my friend see me here when he comes for a long visit?' She gave them all a feral grin.

A man who hadn't said a word so far gave a dark chuckle. 'Mr Morris is not allowed back in these lands. The Yanks will make sure of that. Their punishments are harsher than ours,' he said.

The redhead saw the old woman smile who had gobbed off about her friend, which proved that their punishment would be finite. She had to do something about this. They thought they could control people because they were old and perceived themselves superior, even though they just sat in their ivory tower and played lords and ladies. *Fuck 'em*, she thought. 'Can I think about it, please?' she asked.

They all looked at each other and agreed, all bar the bitch. Tracey knew that was going to happen. Alfred led her out down the hall and back to the front door. After she collected her coat, he opened the door.

'Please consider our offer, Tracey. It would make your life easier and bring some young blood into our group,' he said calmly.

'I'll think about it, Alfred, I truly will,' she replied, pulling off an Academy Award winning fake smile. 'How long do I have to decide?'

The old man's face was thoughtful. 'You have one week. Come back this time next week, and don't let Victoria upset you. She really is quite nice…deep down.' With that, the door was closed and the redhead disappeared into the night, needing to rip some poor person apart, and then plan.

Manhattan, New York

I was finally ready for my date. Anastasia had left early as the sun's rays had disappeared enough for her to escape to her waiting limo and back to the probably aggravated coven. It had been years since I had felt nerves like this as I put on one of my many branded suits with a dark purple tie.

My watch told me I had ten minutes, so with a last look around my apartment I headed out, making sure that I had locked the front door. I didn't want to come back to another surprise, especially with that shit Hughes on my case, and a drawer full of potential rapists' driving licences, who shall receive a visit from me sooner or later.

The tall and ever-happy Jasper was on the door tonight. 'Evening, Bert. Date tonight?'

'Yep, with a girl from the office opposite,' I admitted and saw his grin widen. I held up my hand to stop any typical man-to-man sexual references. 'I think you'll have to manage with your sandwiches tonight, mate, unless I am really unlucky.'

The tall man showed off his pearly whites. 'Well, a man's got to suffer sometimes, don't we. Have a good night, Bert.' He gave me a wink and another knowing smile.

I smiled back. 'See ya, mate. I hear there's a new vegetarian takeaway place opening, might try it,' I shouted back.

As I started to cross the road I could still hear the doorman's pleas for mercy, and that he was a carnivore. The traffic was busy, but that made it easier to jaywalk, and there she was all wrapped up to protect herself from the harsh winter winds. I stopped a couple of feet away from her and smiled, which she returned making the world feel that little bit warmer.

'Well, it's nice to finally meet you. I must admit I am quite thankful that you're not dressed as one of your alter egos,' Rose said, her dark brown eyes twinkling with mirth. Then she held out her small dainty hand. 'Rose Sanders, parents named me Rosalyn, but if you call me that I will beat you to death with your own spleen. And you are?'

I shook her hand gently. 'Albert Morris, and that's what my parents called me, amongst other things,' I said. Her smile warmed the shell of my body even more.

'Ah, you're a Brit. Well, at least you don't sound like those men off *Downton Abbey* and expect this girl from the colonies to swoon, Mr Morris,' she teased, and then winked.

I knew straight away that I liked her.

'Aren't you cold?' she asked.

I laughed. 'Nah, I'm a London boy. If I was in that show though, I would be cleaning the boots or the toilets,' I said, which made her laugh. 'Nope. I'm a cold-blooded man like all British men as we plot to overthrow our old territories.'

She linked her arm with mine and pulled me down the street. 'Well, I am freezing my ass off, Berty. Do you mind if I call you Berty?'

She was looking up at me as we walked through the crowds. Anna used to call me that; it had been so long. 'No, that's fine, Rose. Where are we going?'

'That's for me to know, and you to find out,' she stated, steering me through the throngs, using me as a battering ram. 'It's not a well-known place, nice and quiet so I can pump you for information.' Her face blushed when she said that. 'Errrrr, not in the sexual sense either. I'm a good girl. No conquering Brit is getting over my ramparts on the first date.'

She was a talkative little thing. 'On my honour as an Englishman, your colonial virginity is safe with me,' I replied, to which she guffawed.

'I wouldn't go that far, Berty. And about your honour, I've read history books. Your words aren't to be trusted in our young nation. But you're cute and I like your accent, so I will trust you…for now,' Rose said with a chuckle before pulling me into a side road.

I raised my eyebrows. 'I didn't take you for a back-alley girl, in the non-hooker sense of course.'

She shot me a look and playfully thumped me in the stomach. 'Berty, your mouth is digging a hole that only a night of Martinis can fill. So, Sir Morris, I hope your wallet is brimming over,' the small and curvy motormouth said before pulling me through a dark doorway, which had thick contoured glass filling the door. It didn't even look like a pub or bar. I expected to feel a gun to my head with a shout of, 'Let's get this done!'

My arm was released as Rose bounced over to a dark wooden bar, which seemed to be a throwback to my youth, although it didn't have sawdust or wood chippings on the floor to soak up the drips off the slaughter-housemen.

'Hiya, Sammy. Martini for me and whatever Lord Lucan wants – and he, for his smart mouth, is paying,' Rose said brightly and spun around pointing at me. 'I will be over there. When you pay for the drinks you can deliver them over yonder.' She pointed to a fairly well-lit booth compared to others.

I watched Rose walk away waving at others as she slid off her coat and sat down on the leather seat.

I turned to the barman who was waiting for my order with a grin on his face. 'Okay, milord,' the barman said with a grin. 'What is it you want, pink gin?'

I sighed. 'No thanks, mate. I'll have a beer, imported if you have one.'

'Well, well, Rose has found Lord Lucan. Michelob okay?' the pierced man asked.

I nodded and watched as he popped the cap off and slid it over. 'You want a tab, buddy? She looks in the mood to party. You're in for an expensive and talkative night, my lord.'

Rose smiled and waved at me. 'Yeah, let's tab it,' I agreed. 'It looks like a fun night. I'm Albert, by the way.' I offered the man my hand.

He took it. It was firm but fair. 'Sam, nice to meet ya.' He looked up and laughed. 'You'd better hurry, buddy, she's getting antsy.' He handed me the drinks.

I turned to see her waving me to her and mouthing, 'Come on.' So that's what I did. The old wooden floorboards creaked as I made my way to her. 'About time, slow poke,' she chided me and grabbed her glass. She started to down it, then even before I had sat down she was gesturing to Sam the barman for another round.

'Thirsty much?' I asked, surprised.

'It's been a long day, Berty. What do you do for a living, are you really a superhero?' She chuckled and drained her glass as Sam replaced it with a fresh one. He didn't bother with me as my glass was full and still had condensation on it. 'Cheers, Sammy,' she said.

'Slow it down, Rose. I'm not carrying you to the sidewalk again,' Sam said, and then received the middle finger in return.

The brunette only took a sip of her next drink and seemed to relax. 'So, where were we?'

'What I do for a living. Actually, I'm just resting on my laurels at the moment, cashed in some investments and decided to head across the pond,' I explained happily and took a draught from the cold beer. It was nice. 'And I'm afraid I'm just a normal man…ish.'

'Rich boy, eh, can't blame you for that. What about friends and family?' she asked while still leaving her drink in place, which meant she wasn't a lush. She played with her long hair that shone in the lamplight. It was so dark it looked like she was being covered in darkness.

I took another gulp. 'Family have passed, friends not too many, always preferred a small group.' She nodded in agreement, which I wasn't quite sure about as she did seem like a party girl. 'So, what about you?'

'Well, I work at the lawyers' office opposite your apartment, but you knew that anyway.' She smiled brightly. 'I'm a copywriter and I enjoy it. My parents live in Anchorage in Alaska, where they split their time between there and a small ranch property in the middle of nowhere. It's lovely and quiet out there.'

'Sounds nice, and what I've seen on the TV looks fantastic, especially the winter,' I said.

'I thought you weren't a sun bunny. Those windows you have don't show anything.' Then she blushed furiously as I raised a quizzical eyebrow. 'Errrrr, not that I was looking, much.' She took a gulp of her drink. 'So, what gives with the shades? Not a mass murderer are you?'

'Well, not a mass one. It's more a hobby than a vocation,' I joked, making her giggle. 'I had a stint in the army and my eyes were damaged in a bomb blast, to the point where sunlight could blind me, so I daren't not have shades – too much of a risk.'

Rose looked all soulful. 'I'm sorry, Berty, that explains why I only see you once the sun goes down,' she said and received a corresponding nod. 'It's a good job I'm a night owl, then. And in the city you're lucky to have direct sunlight anyway.'

I waved to Sammy for another round. 'So, any brothers and sisters?' I asked her.

'Nope, they gave up when they had me. Once you've reached perfection, you only have downwards to go.' She chuckled but it was forced, so clearly there was more, but that was for a later date, hopefully. 'I have friends around here, but no besties, just never seemed to like people for that attachment.'

The conversation died for a moment as Sammy delivered the drinks and took the empties away. 'So, this is your local, then?'

'For work it is, then there's another one in Queens where I live. I share with another girl called Sharon; luckily she's just as untidy as me,' she said with a guffaw. 'Is it just you in that big apartment, or do you have a harem with you, Berty?'

She did have a wicked and quick sense of humour. 'Nope, just Mr Agoraphobic here. Me and my carnivore doorman,' I said and then told her about the chat before our date, and the threat of a veggie burger.

'Oh, you are evil, Berty. I like it.' She laughed and then her demeanour shifted. 'I know it's not my business, but our security guards told me that you had the police at your apartment one weekend?'

I rested back in the seat, stretched out my arms and sighed. 'There was a party in my building, a lot of bronzed people loving themselves, and I was painted into a corner, so I went and took a girl I knew as a date. They didn't like me, and the Botox brigade hated Kelly.'

'Bit of a hotty was she?'

'Yeah, you could call her that. We left early and interrupted a burglary. I was knocked out, and when I regained consciousness they were attacking Kelly,' I said, after which Rose gasped and grabbed my hand. 'I managed to get free and stop them in time, but the damage was done between us. The perpetrators all pleaded guilty, so they will go down.'

It went silent again. 'Did you like her?' she probed.

'Yeah, we were still just friends really, you know, seeing how we fitted into each other's lives. That situation was something that couldn't be overcome, and I feel bad for her, but I couldn't even comfort her.' I sighed and took another pull from my drink. 'But we move on; life is hard.' I gave her a weak smile which never reached my eyes.

She clapped her hands together. 'Right, let's get a cab to mine. I can change, then we can go and have a burger and drinks at my other local. You in?' Rose asked, now full of life again.

'Do I have a choice? I am paying, after all,' I joked.

'That's the spirit, my old mucker,' she replied in her best East End accent. She had obviously seen too many *Only Fools and Horses* reruns.

I shook my head and finished off my drink. 'Okay, treacle. You go to the bathroom, and I'll go and settle up, okay?'

Rose looked confused and trotted off. She was wearing her typical black business suit with a white blouse.

I headed up to the bar. 'Can I pay the tab, Sam?'

'Sure.' He worked at the till and then handed me the bill. 'There you go. Oh, you do know she will kick your ass when she finds out what "treacle" means,' he added and gave me a wry smile.

'Does everybody watch English TV around here?' I chuckled and put several bills on the counter which covered the tab plus ten for a tip.

He just shrugged and chuckled to himself as he put the money in the till. 'It makes a change from the mainstream. It's all good,' he said, and I turned around as Rose arrived pulling on her coat. 'Well, have fun, you two.' He smiled and started to wipe down the bar as we bid farewell. 'Have fun, treacle,' he added, giving her a wink.

I shot him a look as I held the door open for her; he was really enjoying himself.

'Berty, what does "treacle" mean?' Rose asked from outside, and that's when Sammy lost it.

'I'm not sure. Sammy told me to say it,' I replied loudly and watched Sam still and his face straighten. With an air of victory, I showed him the finger. Life was good.

Chapter 17

'SHARON…MAN IN THE HOUSE!' Rose shouted out as we walked into her apartment. She looked over her shoulder. 'She'll be about somewhere.'

'HEY, GIRLFRIEND, IS HE CUTE…? CAN I BORROW HIM?' a voice filtered through the clutter-filled apartment, then a brown-haired girl came running out of a bathroom with a towel wrapped around her body and one on her head. 'Oh, he is cute. Can *I* borrow him?'

Rose clamped her arm around my waist. 'Nope, hands off. Albert, this is my roommate Sharon.'

'Hi, nice to meet you, Sharon,' I said and shook her slightly wet hand.

Sharon's eyes went wide and then she shot her friend a look. 'You got yourself a Brit! Awesome!' she said and then just walked off to her room. 'Well, I have to fly. This baby has got to go to work!'

'Right, take a seat, Lucan, I'm going to change,' Rose announced before giving me a wink and walking off. She then stopped and opened her friend's bedroom door to ask, 'Hey, what do Brits mean on TV when they call someone "treacle"?'

Shit! I prayed to any god who was willing to hear, even though I was a soulless beast from the underworld – well, London, but close.

The air stilled. 'I'm not sure,' Sharon said, after which my heart almost started to beat for the first time in over a hundred years. 'Oh, the Net says it's short for "treacle tart". It's something called cockney slang from London, which means "tart", a woman of loose morals… Why?'

Rose, with a face like marble, turned towards me. 'No reason. I just heard it at a bar,' she said, her eyes never leaving mine. She closed her friend's bedroom door and walked back towards me. 'Well, looks like you will be paying for a second date,' she said firmly while poking me in the chest. 'If there is another one, that is.' She then turned on her heel and stalked away. 'And I have expensive tastes,' she added over her shoulder.

I am cold-blooded, but the temperature in the apartment seemed to have dipped unnaturally, which made me fear for Sharon who was still wearing a towel and misted with beads of water from her shower. Or that's the way my mind went.

A door opened and then I felt a presence over my shoulder. 'Let's go…treacle,' Rose whispered with her lips so close that they tickled the minuscule hairs inside my ear.

I turned to see the biggest shit-eating grin on this bloody continent.

'C'mon, Berty, I'm hungry,' she said and started to make her way to the front door. 'Later, girl. Have a good night at work,' she called to Sharon.

I followed her out after not hearing a reply from her roommate, who was singing what sounded like a song from *Cats*, in a feline voice. It even made her friend of three years wince. 'Sharon likes to sing, then.' I chuckled.

'She does. Our fellow tenants, not so much.' Rose laughed as she led me out of the building and into the chilly Queen's air. Once again she hooked my arm with hers. 'C'mon. It's not too far,' she said, dragging me along with her.

This time she took me to a bar which didn't look as bad as the last one. It was themed to look like the quintessential ye olde English pub, and it looked clean.

We wandered through the perfectly polished door into a light setting. It looked as though it had just been refurbished as all the brown leather seats were in good condition. 'Looks nice,' I said looking around the place.

'Nice doesn't cut it, buddy boy. Now, let's get our order in and grab a booth before it gets too busy,' she said and pushed me towards the bar with a petite, shaven-headed barmaid. 'Hiya,

Kirsty. A dirty Martini for me, and I'm guessing an imported beer for Prince William.' She laughed at her own joke.

'You drunk already, Rose?' Kirsty teased, which my date just waved off, and then the barmaid looked at me. 'Stella okay?'

I nodded. 'Sounds good, thanks. Could we run a tab, please? I have a penance to pay for.' This made the girl laugh, along with my date.

'Run your mouth off, did you, my lord?' She shot me a wink.

I shrugged. 'Maybe, but who am I to say?' I said and took my drink. Rose had already departed to find a booth. 'We'll be ordering some food too at some point.'

Kirsty handed over the dirty Martini, which looked awful to me. 'Sure, what's your name, then, unless it's William?'

I just shook my head and handed over one of my old business cards I used for the shop.

'Nice to meet you, Albert. Just wave when you want a waitress.'

I took two menus. 'Cheers, and have a drink on me,' I said, but she just waved it off. Most probably because Rose was going to fleece me. I arrived at our booth, pushed the drink into her open hand and offered her the menu.

The night went well and we chatted about this and that and about her job, which I didn't have a clue about. We ordered some burgers that were very nice. Mine was as rare as could be, which did its job.

I received a couple of texts from the duchess asking how the night was going and telling me that the coven was kicking off about her wanting to move out and into the city. But what did surprise me was a text from Tracey telling me about her meeting with the UK coven. The fact that it was all in capital letters didn't bode well for the coven.

'You're popular tonight,' Rose half-joked.

'I'm sorry. A friend just wanted to know if I had ballsed up yet, and my friend Tracey in the UK is just having a bit of trouble.' I sent Tracey a quick reply telling her to keep her temper and not to do anything to jeopardise her safety.

My date did actually look worried. 'Will she be okay? Do you need to call her?'

I had to laugh at that. 'I'm more worried about the other people. When she loses her temper the world moves aside.' We both laughed, then Rose yawned.

'Sorry, Berty. It's time for me to head to dreamland. Some of us have work to go to in the morning,' she said and started to put on her coat. 'But I'd like to do this again sometime?'

I smiled at her. 'Me too. How about you come to mine for dinner? I might even cook.'

'Won't your doorman get jealous?' She giggled. Clearly, the Martinis had left their mark.

'Well, we agreed to see other people, and he will just have to respect my wishes,' I said and winked. She gave another drunken giggle. 'But I will take him a burger and fries from this place; he'll love it.'

Rose fastened up her coat slowly and methodically doing each button one by one while the tip of her tongue protruded from her lips as a sign of her inebriation and concentration. 'Well, Berty, you can place your order, pay the tab, you lucky man, and then you can walk this princess back to her castle... Whoops,' she said as she staggered sideways and rebounded off a photo of Frank Sinatra on the wall.

'Good plan. You lean against this lovely wall, and I'll be back,' I told her and received a very messy salute in response. I went to place my takeout order and pay the tab, which made Kirsty look at Rose with worry. 'I'm walking her home, then I'll be right back.'

She raised a very thin eyebrow. 'Not looking for a goodnight kiss then, milord?' she asked and handed back my card and receipt, which I traded for a twenty-dollar tip.

'Nope, first date. Plus, she's tipsy. Not my style, young lady,' I responded and put the card back into my wallet. 'But feel free to phone her after I come back – talking of which, could you order me a taxi for when my order is ready.'

She looked at me carefully and nodded. 'Hurry back, the chef doesn't hang about,' Kirsty stated.

'No worries.' I headed back to my swaying date who clung to my arm straight away. 'You okay?'

Rose looked at me with a drunken grin. 'Did you know the room is spinning?'

I walked her out of the door and held on tightly as the frigid air hit her, making Rose slump against me. She was surprisingly heavy for a woman, although those words would never pass my lips, not after Suzie's granddaughter asked me if she was putting on weight one day in bed. Apparently 'only a bit' wasn't an acceptable answer. The speed in which that naked woman bolted into the shop to retrieve a horsewhip was out of this world. And then came a painful conversation about women's feelings and a question about whether I wanted to carry on living with skin.

With my strength it didn't take long to walk her to the door of her apartment building. The stairs were tricky, but we managed it as she sang some Lady Gaga for me, which was nice, and she managed to get her key in the door first time.

'Well, this is me, Berty. Thank you for a wonderful night, and I'll call you about Saturday,' she slurred slightly and pulled me into a hug before giving my cheek a smooch. 'Stay, Mr Morris, and try to warm your cold ass up.' With a smile she turned and walked into her apartment.

'Chat soon, Rose,' I replied and waved at her just as the door closed. I heard her kicking off her shoes. 'Night, treacle,' I shouted, and then smirked hearing her swearing and running for the door, but I was gone as expletives chased me down the stairs.

I received my takeout order and a respectful nod from a chuckling Kirsty back at the pub who was on the phone to Rose.

Kirsty happily informed me once the call had finished that Rose was swearing like a sailor about me taking the piss again, but my taxi arrived before I could defend my actions. So, I bid farewell to the bald-headed barmaid and jumped in the yellow cab to take me home and to a very happy-looking Jasper. The one thing I wasn't so happy about was the car following behind me with Captain Hughes in it.

As I walked into the building I knew Jasper could smell the meat and fries even before the bag came into sight.

'Bert, you didn't, you were on a date?'

I shrugged. 'This way I keep you loyal. Anytime we get into a shootout with the cops, you'll have my back?' I used my hand as a gun to shoot him.

He laughed heartily and even winked. 'Sorry, my man, cops and people of my colour don't get on. They will just light me up in passing. When they come for you, my black ass is running out the door the other way.'

We laughed, and then I headed off to my apartment just as the phone was ringing. It turned out to be the man who was not willing to take a bullet for me, but eager to take all the food stuff I had brought forth to feed him. All he wanted was to ask where I had bought such foods of the gods and declared his fealty and love to my banner. In real terms, he just wanted to know when I was going back to get some more. The pig.

In the early hours I texted Tracey to ask what she was going to do about the coven in London. What worried me most was the fact that she texted back a simple reply: don't worry, I'll deal with it and a smile emoji with a kiss at the end. It was just like the scientist working on the Manhattan Project saying the bomb would be loud when asked to describe how powerful it would be. But at least I was a continent away, so the fallout for me would be at a minimum.

As the morning crept on I decided to join the mortals in the act of sleep, and I promised myself that I would tell Annabel and

Veronica about Rose and the upcoming date. No doubt they were rolling about upstairs laughing at me, especially if both Suzie's had got in on the act from heaven.

Rose did text me from work mid-morning saying how much she enjoyed last night and how the bathtub featured as her bed for the first few hours of sleep, and I had to promise not to try and get her drunk again. I wanted to point out the fact that it was all her own doing – but, as she stated, women are never wrong, so deal with it. But we agreed that she would come over on Saturday night for a meal, although she insisted that it wouldn't turn into a sleepover as Sharon's parents were in town and her wonderful personality was needed.

I hunted the next night, which was a quick and easy one. It was always nice when they attempted to take your wallet at knifepoint. I guess he wouldn't be going home to his wife and six kids that he declared having and who were awaiting his return. I doubted what he said was true, but people say some funny things when they are about to die.

Friday night came and I headed out to the shops to pick up some fresh steaks, and some blood which I claimed was for making black pudding, or blood pudding in some places, but it was really just a quick snack.

I kept a lookout for that coven rent boy Ray Hughes. I didn't detect him, but that didn't mean he or another lackey weren't in the crowds. I got home, unpacked my groceries, grabbed a wine glass of blood and settled down in front of the old idiot box to appease myself with Walter White and Jesse making meth for the populous. But just as the aforementioned Jesse said the word 'bitch' for the first time, there was a knock on my door. I knew it wasn't my party-going neighbours as Jasper had told me that his fellow doormen had heard I was not their type of person, which took a weight off my mind. I was sure I could handle the disappointment of losing such tanned people.

I instantly knew who it was, so I opened the door. 'Hey, Sia, come on in,' I said and moved aside to allow the posh frock-wearing, once Russian duchess to waltz her way in. 'You okay?'

'Da, I'm okay, just wanted to get away from the mansion.' With all the grace of her previous station in life, she sat down and picked up my glass and sniffed it. '*Net*, are you drinking the blood of beasts?'

I slammed my arse down next to her. 'Yes, and what's with all the Russian? You spoke like a New Yorker last time. What gives?' I snatched my glass back in good humour and took a sip. Yes, it was cold and not a patch on the two-legged kind, but it saved going out.

She folded her arms like a petulant child. 'I told the coven that I wanted to move out and live alone like you. But they all came together and forbade me from leaving and refused to give me my money to buy a place,' Anastasia spat angrily along with some Russian swearwords I didn't understand, which I was happy about.

As we shared the drink in silence, I allowed her to cuddle up to me. 'So, I'm guessing your money isn't in a bank or anything?' I surmised and chuckled as the once Romanov royal stuck out her bottom lip.

'No, they have a vault in the bottom of the manor. Samuel distributes the funds when needed,' she mumbled. Her face was going red as she tried not to cry. It was a sight to behold. 'How is your girlfriend? Rose, is it?'

I gave her the glass, although she did pull a face when she drank the viscous fluid. I took out my hip flask and poured the rum that reminded me of home and good times into the glass, which made the old animal blood go down easier. 'She's okay thanks, coming over for dinner tomorrow night. Did the coven say anything?'

Sia huffed a little, but that was due to the fact that she wanted me to bed her, which of course I wouldn't as Rose and I were together. We had discussed this previously on a late-night text session. 'I heard Hughes and Sebastian talking. They just said that you were at it again, nothing else, but would I watch you for them.' She rested her head on my shoulder.

'Thank you. Now what are we going to do about your money? I can lend you some, but not enough to buy a property,' I offered. I did have enough, but I was hoping to buy this place at a later date.

Her head moved and she looked at me strangely. 'You would do that for me, lend me some money?'

'Of course, imagine the interest I can earn. We could live forever.' After which I received several painful slaps. 'All right, all right. Damn woman, the huge solid stones on your rings hurt.'

She gave a sad sigh and downed the rest of her drink before standing up. Then without a word she walked into my kitchen and took a bottle of wine from the rack, grabbed two glasses and came back and sat down. In silence she poured us full glasses, these were not small ones either, and then took a sip.

'Simple,' she said suddenly, breaking the silence. 'We either ask them again nicely, or we rob them.' She then burst into fits of giggles.

And that was how the night went: drink and plans, each one more ludicrous than the first. We did end up in bed together, but as agreed Mr and Mrs Genitals did not shake hands. She didn't want to go back home, and I didn't want to try kicking out an unhappy Anastasia in the early hours.

'Albert, can I ask you something?' she whispered with her head on my chest.

It was three a.m. and she wanted to chat. This didn't bode well. 'Of course, but I don't have to answer if I don't want to, okay?'

She huffed again. 'What did your wife say when you told her that you were a vampire?' She gazed up at me with her caring eyes.

'She called me a monster and refused to see me again. I didn't see her for over a year,' I said, giving her the partial truth. The real story was bad enough to live through the first time let alone reliving it all now. Some feelings never lessen over time.

She leaned in and kissed me, pressing her lips onto mine, but this time as a friend not a lover. 'That must have been hard but also amazing when she came around to see sense. You're a great guy, even for a commoner.' She was then tickled into submission.

We allowed sleep to claim us and let the accursed sun do its morning warm-up while we hid.

Midday arrived and Anastasia helped me to prepare dinner, and also to carry out a general clean-up, including the knickers she had left last time. I insisted that she take them home with her just in case Rose was nosey and had a look around. A used red thong in my washing basket would bring an unwanted conversation my way, and I think she still had some mileage on the whole 'treacle' debacle. Who knew the Yanks were avid watchers of classic British comedies?

The sun had finally pissed off and the limo had pulled up to collect Anastasia. We had a hug and a politically correct kiss and she hoped that the night would go well. But before she went, Sia pulled me in close.

'Albert, I know you love them, but hide your photos. When you tell her the truth, then you can share them. There are enough lies we have to tell anyway, so don't increase it by having them on show,' she advised and cupped my cheek. 'Don't sabotage yourself even before this has time to grow with Rose.'

As I watched the limo drive away I knew she was right, so that's what I did. I kissed my Anna goodbye, along with Veronica and the two Suzie's, of whom the world would never know the likes again. All their pictures were wrapped in a nice linen tablecloth that my wife had embroidered as we sat together and watched the world go by.

Everything was ready, I even had candles flickering away causing shadows to dance across my lounge, then there was a knock on the door. I had asked Jasper to let her straight up with a promise of more burgers to come from the bar near her place.

I opened the door and there she stood with a larger-than-life smile and her shiny black hair hanging loose down her back. She was wearing a plum-coloured wrap-around dress with matching heels, but not aggressively high. We embraced and did the European kiss on both cheeks.

'Hiya, please come in,' I said, struggling not to utter the words that could cause me pain but loitered in my mind anyway: '*Hello, treacle.*'

Rose eyed me carefully. 'I see you are learning, Berty,' she said and stepped into my apartment. 'Holy fuck, have you been robbed?'

I chuckled. 'No, I just like it neat and not looking like it's been hit by a whirlwind.' I received a slap; she does seem to be a violent person. 'Would you like a tour?' She nodded quickly and took my hand as I showed her the apartment.

'Jesus, Berty, are you rich?' she asked and then immediately slapped her hand against her mouth. 'I'm so sorry. I didn't mean to say that out loud. It's none of my business.' Her cheeks almost matched her dress.

I pulled her into a warm hug. Well, she was warm and I was room temperature, which was always a fun conversation when it came up. Even today it weirds me out that we still digest things and use the bathroom, all without our heart beating.

'Hey, don't worry about it. And no, I am not rich. I'm just fairly comfortable,' I explained as we made our way into the kitchen where I had a bottle of French red wine breathing away happily.

'So, what have you made me today, Mr I Am Comfortable?' she said, giving me a wink.

I handed her a glass of red wine. 'Just a simple bolognaise with tagliatelle and freshly made garlic bread, or I can cut up some French bread instead, depends on you?' I asked.

'Unlike other women, my lord, I love garlic. It's only when you start firing from your ass cannon that it gets a bit stinky. But as I am a lady, that won't be a problem for me. You, I'm not so hopeful about.' She chuckled and leaned against the marble work surface as I finished preparing the food. 'Well, I'll leave you to it while I look out of your balcony at all the poor people dragging themselves back to their hovels.' She walked away with her nose in the air and a perfect posture, which showed off her figure perfectly.

And just like all the women I have known in my life, she ate the dinner like it was a competition. Rose wasn't messy, but there was no conversation, just an easy silence as we ate. She wiped her mouth with a napkin.

'That, Berty, was awesome. Good looking, comfortable and a cook – I might just keep you.' She chuckled.

'Would you like dessert? It's chocolate mousse,' I asked.

She shook her head. 'Oh no, I've overdone it, I'm afraid.' She lifted up the napkin to disguise the little belch that escaped from her mouth. 'Better out than in.'

I stood up and cleared away the things to the kitchen where the greatest invention of our age would clean the dishes overnight. I walked back from the kitchen and saw Rose sitting on the sofa gazing into the real-gas effect fireplace. She turned to me with a smile as the flames reflected in her eyes.

'Everything done, or do you have staff coming in the morning?' She grinned.

I sat down next to her and picked up my refilled wine glass. 'Staff are nowhere to be seen in this house. So, how was Sharon? Did she grill you much after our date?' I asked.

'Nope, just jealous as hell. She's always had a thing for you Limeys. But you're my first foreigner, and I like it,' she said softly, picking up the remote control and flicking through the channels.

'Now, I will tell you this once,' I advised sternly. 'If you put on *Downton Abbey*, I will have you thrown out by my doorman,' I growled when her channel hopping lingered too long on the show.

'What about *Jane Eyre*?' she said and started to pretend to fan herself. 'Papa, I have the vapers.' She placed her hand to her forehead and pretended to faint.

I leaned forward and rested my face in my palms. 'Jesus, kill me now,' I groaned, and then felt her hug me from the side.

'Oh, cheer up. Let's watch *Die Hard*, it's always a laugh,' she said and started the movie. If I was honest and I was John McClane, I would've hidden, or just cried like a baby. But that's just me. We chatted through the movie about her week, but soon the chat lessened as a tall German terrorist was angry about his brother being killed by Bruce. By the end of the film I had a small bit of drool on my shoulder as tiredness and a full belly had overcome her.

I kissed her on the forehead as the credits started to roll. 'Rose, wake up, love. It's way past eleven,' I said just loud enough to drag her from her slumber.

'Aww, but you are so comfy,' she murmured into my wet shoulder.

'But you have that thing tomorrow with Sharon, or did you want to crash here?' I asked, and her eyes locked with mine.

She sat up and wiped her mouth and blushed slightly at the damp spot on my shirt. 'Sorry about that. Oh, are you trying to seduce me, Mr Morris, because I'll have you know that I am a lady.' Somehow, she managed to hold in the laugh that was creeping up.

'Of course not. I would never dare to tarnish such a reputation as your good lady,' I said as I stood up and smoothed out my crinkled and now dribbled on shirt. She took my proffered hand, stood up and placed her lips on mine.

'Not tonight, but maybe I can stay over in the week, eat out and enjoy ourselves, just not too much,' she said softly, sporting a demure look. I nodded, and then she slammed her body against mine. 'Cool, now get your butler to call me a cab, and I will see you…Wednesday?'

I headed over and dialled for Jasper. 'Sounds good to me,' I said, and then the phone connected. 'Hey, mate, can you get a cab for my date to Queens?'

'No problem, Bert. Will it be bringing back a burger?' Jasper probed.

'No, no burger. Jesus, do you have tapeworms or something?' I rolled my eyes at Rose, who was frowning as she could only hear my side of the conversation. 'Just eat your sandwiches, or I have some leftover bolognaise with tagliatelle?'

I could hear his leather-like skin creak as he smiled. He never said a word, but he knew his silence was wearing me down. He must have been a voodoo priest in a previous life or something. Finally, he broke his vow of silence. 'I do like Italian food.'

'Fine, I'll heat some up and bring it down when the cab arrives,' I grumbled, knowing that he had beaten me again.

'You're a good man, Mr Morris.' Jasper chuckled as the line went dead.

Rosie was now giggling as she knew about my and Jasper's history.

'Somehow I have adopted a large doorman who gets pissy when he's not fed on time,' I said in mock exasperation as I started to gather up the leftovers. The devil inside pushed to scrape the remains off our plates into the offering, but I ignored the fun suggestion.

'Aww, but it's cute. I just have a homeless person I caught trying to bang a dead pigeon the other week, so consider yourself lucky, Berty,' she said with mirth.

The phone blipped telling us that the cab was downstairs. She gathered her coat and bag, and I carried a steaming bowl of food and some garlic bread. The man I delivered it to had a smile so big that it wouldn't surprise me if ivory hunters were after him.

Rose and I embraced and fell into a deep and sensual kiss before I opened the taxi door. I watched her get in before closing the door. We waved goodbye to each other through the back window of the departing yellow taxi. I then felt something that I hadn't felt in a while: I felt alone.

Jasper saw my dark mood as I entered the well-laid out reception, so all we did was nod. I headed back to my empty apartment and sat there with a tumbler of Napoleon brandy. I then sent some texts to Tracey and Anastasia just to touch base.

Tracey said she was fine and that she was set up with a gunrunner who was in town on some business for the week, but she wasn't worried about the coven as her new beau's security guards beat up the snooping little shit who had been tracking her for them. Her words, not mine.

Sia was another thing. The coven had voted and decided again to refuse her access to her funds and she was now under house arrest. I felt bad things were going to happen to these covens, and soon.

Chapter 18

I found my mood of late dark. On several of my jaunts out to feed and also to provide food for my adopted love child Jasper, I had spotted the coven crotch sniffer Captain Ray Hughes. I saw pain in that man's future. The only thing that held me back was not knowing how far up the New York Police Department's chain of command the coven's influence went, so making him disappear would be tricky and could bring a lot of trouble my way.

Not only that irritant, but Tracey had gone quiet. Her phone was now dead. That concerned me; her phone was her life. It did make me wonder if she had pushed the UK chapter of the coven. Okay, that makes it sound like a B-movie. Or perhaps the flavour of the week had tired of her company, but if that had happened it would normally go either of two ways: They part on good terms, they kiss and at some point Tracey empties his bank account by stealing all his information as he sleeps. Or they fight and he gets someone to make her disappear – in that case, the man in question and his minions would be torn limb by limb. But there was nothing I could do from the other side of the pond.

Anastasia was my main concern because they had withdrawn all limo privileges and her phone. It was only because I had told her to always have a spare phone hidden, as you never knew when you might need it, which was the case now, that she had one.

Sia had phoned almost begging me to come and get her. They were worried that I was brainwashing her to split from the coven. All they seemed to care about was her link, although long since dead, to the Russian royal family.

I took a cab past the entrance and saw armed guards standing by the gate, and once again the bastard captain had followed me. There was no way to get inside and leave with Sia. At some point the coven would decide what they were going to do with me. The fact that I was in America and alone would make things easier for them. One plus point was the constant contact with Rose; a simple word from her cleared away all my worries.

Finally, it was Wednesday, and once again I was waiting outside her work on the sidewalk. The door of her office building opened and there stood Rose sporting her radiant smile. She slammed her body into mind, smashing our lips together.

'Miss me?' she asked excitedly, looking deeply into my eyes.

I brushed her dark hair away from her face. 'More than I can say, Rosie. Shall we go?' I asked and took her overnight bag from her. I groaned at the weight. 'How long are you staying?'

She pulled me along to the pub. 'Just tonight, any more than that and I'll need a ring and commitment,' she said, winking back at me.

We parted the crowds easily enough, entered the pub and then saw a different barman, which I thanked God for, but my date had guessed.

'Still not off the hook, buddy boy. Now, buy this treacle a drink and bring the menu,' she instructed before taking off her coat to reveal her usual black business attire, but this time it was just a bit tighter. That said, Rose could wear a shapeless sack and still look amazing. 'Oi, quit perving. Drinky, *por favor*,' she demanded with a big grin on her perfect face as she sat down in the same booth as last time. And just like that I started a tab, carried over the drinks and ordered another Martini to follow in five minutes along with a menu.

'There you go, Rose. The menu and your next one are on their way,' I said, making her blush.

She fluttered her mascara-adorned eyelashes at me. 'You know me so well.' She smiled before downing her drink and waving her hand at the bar as the last drops of Martini hit her tongue. 'But we will not be drinking all night, milord. Some of us have work in the morning.'

I moved my hand like I was controlling a puppet. 'Blah, blah. Cry me a river, baby. You're just jealous.' I moved quickly to dodge the five-fingered slap of justice. 'I'll work again…one day.'

Her drink had been replaced and now she was perusing the menu intently. 'You, sir, are a shit, and I don't think a job would suit you. You need to be an owner,' she said as she twirled a strand of her long hair. 'As you told me, you've owned a store before. You're a leader not a follower.' Then she squeaked with excitement. 'How about a bar? You can live above it and if I can still put up with you, I can do the books – once I do some classes, that is.' She beamed a dazzling smile.

'You in a bar? Isn't that risky?' I replied. This time, despite my vampire quickness, her hand connected with my head.

We were both silent while musing the idea, or maybe she was thinking about how to get her revenge on me, but time would tell on that one.

'It's an idea, Berty. You do look restless,' she said in her loving tone.

I could see the concern in her eyes, even though we had only known each other for a short time, and I knew she was right. But to move forward I needed to tell her about my past, which for now was not something I wished to do.

'Sounds like an idea. Not sure I'm rich enough to buy in Manhattan, though, but your idea does have some merit,' I stated, after which her lips turned upwards slightly.

With our food orders taken and another round of drinks ordered, Rose told me about her week so far, which as you can imagine wasn't that amazing as an office worker. Then she started to probe about my friend in trouble.

'So, no contact at all from the Brit? And Anastasia is having family problems?' she asked with a funny look on her face. 'Not a lot of details, Berty. What's really going on?'

I sighed. 'I'm sorry, not my business to share, I promised.'

That seemed to placate her, for now. But if I knew anything about women it would go to seed in her mind and she would dwell on it. We chatted about the bar idea, and even dragged the barman into the conversation. He agreed about the prices in Manhattan, but the outlying boroughs were still manageable, it just depended on the crowd you wanted to attract.

We ate our meals, just a simple burger and fries. Jasper wasn't at work today, so I didn't have to play provider for the ex-soldier. I hefted her bag after paying the tab and led her to my home.

'Rose, I have a question?' I said and saw her raise a quizzical eyebrow.

'Okay, lay it on me, Berty?' Her face straightened wondering where this was leading.

We crossed the street and headed towards my building. 'Do you actually earn money at your job, or do they pay you in shiny objects?' I asked, and then let slip a small chuckle.

'Mr Funny Man, they pay well enough, thank you. And when you act your age you might see some of it. But the way you're going, I'll be able to buy a car with all the money I'm saving.' She punched me on the arm so hard I thought it had also bruised my other one.

We linked arms and headed into the building where we received a brief nod from the doorman, Gerald I think his name was, who strangely didn't need to be fed by me, which made a nice change.

As soon as we stepped into the lift, Rose kissed me while running her fingers through my hair. Within minutes of the lift doors reopening, we were in my apartment with fire in our eyes and passion pouring from us.

She placed a hand on my chest. 'Give me ten minutes, lover.' With a chuckle she ran to the bedroom kicking off her shoes as she did.

If my heart worked it would have been going 100 miles an hour. There were some things about vampire physiology that had always intrigued me, such as not needing to take a breath, but we did to fit in, it was really just muscle memory. But as our hearts didn't work to push blood around the body, how did Mr Happy join the party?

'ARE YOU LISTENING? I'M READY!' Rose shouted out, clearly wanting to keep my neighbours up to date.

I walked towards my bedroom door, but I had to stop to tidy her shoes, the messy cow. I entered my room and saw a vision of beauty, which was my Rose, sat on the bed wearing a knee-length black silk nightie which matched her hair, both glistened in the room's sidelight.

'Wow, you look stunning,' I muttered and walked over to the bed, joining Rose in more ways than one.

It had been many years since I had felt whole. Of course, all the time before being bitten by that cursed monster, and when Annabel and I were together, the brief period with Veronica and little Suzie, and now with Rose.

We made love into the night until our bodies called it quits way before our passion abated, but it was such a glorious coupling that it would have made the gods who judged us jealous.

We sat at the breakfast table drinking coffee and eating croissants. Our eyes were locked on each other with playful smiles on our faces. Questions had been asked throughout the night about my stamina and the quietness of my heart as she lay her head on my chest. All I said was that it had always been like that. Not a good answer, but it stopped the conversation, thankfully.

We embraced by the front door as goodbyes were said along with kisses and touches. 'Thank you for last night. It was…amazing.' She cupped my cheek. 'Will call you later, okay.'

'Perfect. I'll miss you,' I said, hoping I wasn't being too soppy. I knew she wasn't that type of girl, which was one of the reasons I liked her so much.

She slapped me on the chest. 'Prat, but I'll miss you, too.' She kissed me again. 'See you Friday.' After a wink, she waved from the lift as the doors closed.

I closed my own door and leaned my head against the wood smiling to myself as I tried to hold onto the feeling of being happy. I still had her smell on me from the shower we had shared; it was bliss in its purist form.

For the next two weeks nothing changed as Tracey was still missing. Whereas Anastasia had managed to get a call out to me on her hidden mobile. She was still on lockdown because she wouldn't bow down to the coven. They wanted the Duchess Romanov, and that's what they received. She simply told them that a Romanov did not bend on knee to anyone, especially the likes of them.

After that phone call it had gone quiet, but I received a text from the butler, Graves, telling me to watch my back. The coven were concerned about the hold I had over Anastasia, and they were discussing how to sever the ties between us, which I didn't like, at all. Also, she had been moved into the dungeons, or 'the cellar' as they called it, and they had found the spare phone, so the captain had been called.

The relationship between Rose and I grew and grew. She stayed over midweek and Friday nights, which were the days I yearned for. This weekend, though, things had changed. Things were out of my control and once again my life would start to unravel.

Rose stayed Friday and also Saturday night as a treat. We had a meal out and a trip to the cinema on the Saturday just like other couples. I was happy. We said our goodbyes at midday on the Sunday still with childish smirks on our faces like we had been caught doing something wrong.

As the sun finally decided to do a disappearing act, I relaxed into my chair and gazed out over my balcony through the vast window holding a chilled glass of blood with a dash of Scottish single malt whisky. Then there was a knock on the door, which was strange. Either it was the doorman or a neighbour.

'Please be the doorman,' I muttered as I made my way to the door. I stopped dead as I realised that it wasn't a human on the other side. I closed my eyes, reached out with my senses and threw open the door. 'TRACEY!' I exclaimed, and then felt her slender figure glide into mine. 'Where have you been?' I whispered into her ear as I moved her into my apartment. I released her and picked up her suitcase.

'Blood and booze. I like it,' the stunning redhead said, licking her lips. She stood in front of me draining my glass wearing a red dress with matching coat and heels. Never scruffy this one. She passed me her coat and kicked off her shoes before making sure they were neat and together.

I walked over to the sofa where she had made herself comfortable and poured her another half-and-half mix, which I'd prepared after Rose had left. 'So, is there a story here, Tracey, or did you just fancy a visit?' I asked, pouring myself a drink before sitting down alongside and turning to face her. 'Never known a room to be quiet with you in it,' I commented, which did bring a smile to her face.

She took another sip. 'Nice place you have here, Albert. And I like your new girlfriend, really pretty,' Tracey said, making me sit up straighter. But before I could ask, she grabbed my hand. 'It was that fucking coven. They showed me pictures of you both. I suppose they were trying to make me jealous, and they thought I would be so thankful that I would turn my back on you, my only true friend, and join them in thanks.'

'Fuckers,' I said, frowning. 'I tried to contact you for weeks. What happened?'

She downed her drink, which I refilled. Tracey nodded her thanks. 'Well, you know what I'm like, plan for the worst and hope for the best,' she said, and chuckled as I nodded. 'It started two days before the meeting.' Then she started to tell me what had happened…

Chelsea, London, United Kingdom

Tracey strode through the streets of the city of London on a mission. She was wearing what she called her 'arse-kicking gear' in all black, which was a big change for her: leather jacket and tank top, black Lycra leggings and knee-length leather boots with block heels – no spikey fun ones tonight.

She was angry because she had been given an A4 brown envelope by a bicycle courier who rode off as soon as her fingers made the envelope crackle. Her first thought was a possible spouse trying to drag her into another messy divorce saying how she was the other woman. That sort of thing never bothered her; the men were used then thrown away, and obviously Tracey never made it to the court hearings. She would've gone just for the laugh as she explained all their perverse sexual kinks for the wife and court to hear, but they always held the hearings during daylight hours.

She tore open the envelope. Her smile faded seeing the glossy photos of her friend Albert arm in arm with a beautiful brunette. He was looking happier than she had ever seen him. 'Good on you, Berty,' she said, knowing that this name was used by one of his true loves. She sadly thought that he hadn't set himself up to be hurt but falling in love with humans would only end in tragedy. Yet she had vowed to always be there for him, either as a friend or occasional lover.

Looking again at the envelope and its contents, she knew instantly who had sent it to her. The coven was trying to provoke her by using her friend, and that's why she was storming through the streets. Tracey had just torn apart a mugger who thought he would try his luck and steal her phone – that wasn't a problem. But when she snapped his wrist, the idiot dropped the phone and it had broken. In a second her eyes went black and her demon stretched its legs. Picking up the man by his throat, she drove him into the shadows of a nearby alley before ripping him asunder. In the end you couldn't even call what was left a human, but the demon and her hunger were now sated.

Tracey ended up at a three-story house in Mulberry Walk, Chelsea. She banged on the door until a large man, at least six foot six with skin dark as midnight, although his eyes were like stars, answered.

She hugged him. 'Freddie, long time no see. Is Tony in?'

The big man barked a booming laugh and in a baritone voice he answered, 'Trace, you're a sight for sore eyes,' and he held her tight. 'Yeah, he's in, but he might not want to see you. You know, after the episode with his now ex-wife.'

She rolled her eyes. 'That was ages ago. And she took a swipe at me, the bitch.'

The big man laughed. 'You were wearing her dress, Trace, and her shoes.' Freddie chuckled. 'Then you said she was too old and fat to wear it anyway.'

'I tell the truth and I'm hated for it. It truly is a harsh world, Freddie.' The redhead laughed. 'Now go and ask Baldy if I can have a quick word.'

The man nodded and allowed her to squeeze past him.

'You're losing weight love,' she commented while patting his stomach, which just made him laugh even louder.

The man pulled out his mobile and dialled and then had a whispered conversation with someone. He clicked off and silently nodded. 'He's in the office. Play nice…okay?' he boomed.

Tracey winked. 'Sure thing, Slim, you can trust me.' She skipped up the carpeted stairs. It looked like something from the

1950s with all the flowery wallpaper; his mum had obviously decorated it. She knocked on the door and was beckoned in from a past lover of just two weeks ago. 'Wotcha, Tony, how tricks?'

The thin man with a bald head and piercing grey eyes pointed to the chair. 'What do want now?' he asked wearily. 'You've caused me enough shit, babe,' he snapped and held up his hand. 'I know I was cheating on her, but still, the things you said to her were bang out of order.'

She sagged. 'Sorry, Tony. You know I'm a gobby bird with a potty mouth,' Tracey answered in softer than normal tones. 'But I need your help; I'm in the shit.'

The man laughed, showing off several gold teeth. 'But you're a vampire. Not much can kill you, Trace. What can shake you?' Tony asked.

They locked eyes. He was the only person who knew she was tainted with the vampiric gene when he found her feeding on a hitman who had come for him in the night.

'It's a coven of the fuckers. They are threatening a friend of mine in the States, then they will come for me.'

'What d'you want me to do? My boys won't last against you let alone a whole load of your lot,' he stated.

'I wanna kill them, all of the old bastards that threatened me and my friend,' she sneered, letting her incisors lengthen.

Tony leaned back in his leather office chair and tapped his fingers one at a time repeatedly. 'Okay, but put those fucking teeth away, they scare the shit out of me.' He chuckled. 'How can I help you?'

Tracey smiled; her lengthened incisors now gone. 'I can't believe that Tony the Hammer is scared of little old me,' she said with a dark chuckle and giving her eyelashes a flutter. Then she started looking through her rucksack and pulled out a jet-black bottle with a wax-sealed top. 'I need you to empty this and then refill it with a surprise, amongst other things.'

He frowned and looked at the bottle. 'What is it? There's no label on it?' Tony asked, turning the bottle in his large, calloused hands. 'Can I open it?'

She nodded and watched the man delve into his desk drawer and bring out a corkscrew.

Within seconds the cork was withdrawn with a pop; he sniffed at the mouth of the bottle. 'Holy shit, that's rum and it's potent,' he exclaimed, obviously impressed.

'Indeed, it is. When my friend packed up to leave these shores, he found this in a drawer with a letter from his friend's granddaughter. She had found it in her grandma's things after she passed away. She knew that the bottle had originated from him, so left it for him with a heartfelt note before she died,' Tracey said, remembering the day Albert found it. If she hadn't been there he would've taken a lethal walk in the sun.

'Damn, poor bloke. This must be old?' Tony asked, scanning the bottle.

Tracey nodded. 'It's from Admiral Nelson's ship the *Victory* at the Battle of Trafalgar.'

His eyes widened and he instantly grabbed two tumblers and poured out two fingers of the dark liquid. They savoured it together. She watched him pour the rest into a crystal decanter and place it back on the ornate silver tray where it belonged.

'You have a deal,' he announced. 'What else do you need?' he asked, making Tracey smile and pull out a list which she handed to him.

'Well, we have two days, then I need to get the hell out of the country, and quick,' she replied.

The bald man nodded.

The Meeting, Notting Hill

The tall redhead arrived at the coven house looking high-class as ever. Wearing head-to-toe Chanel, a calf-length dress, which mirrored the outfits that Chanel thought Egyptian women would wear, with low strappy heels and a large shiny black bag along with her gift for the coven.

Tony, bless him, had a car waiting around the corner to take her straight to Dover, then France before making her way to America to find Albert. Not only that, he had a group of men in a removal van to clean out the house. If it all worked out as it should, Tony would sell all the items from the coven's house and send Tracey's half of the profits to Albert's address. Obviously, if it didn't go well and Tracey didn't make it, there would be a lot of ash, and he would have it all.

'Ah, good evening, Miss Andrews. Please come in,' Alfred Masterson said and moved away from the door. 'I hope you are well?'

'I've been better, especially after seeing what Albert is up to,' she said and saw a twitch of a smile on the man's face. 'But I am here to give you my answer.'

The old man smiled. 'Perfect. My apologies for the way things were handled, but your Mr Morris is causing a lot of waves in our old colonies and they aren't happy,' he explained as he took her coat but left her with her bag.

'What will they do to Albert? I wouldn't want him hurt,' she said meekly, playing the concerned jilted ex-lover and friend.

The old man turned to her. 'That, I'm afraid, is out of our hands,' he said and continued down the corridor. 'He has a corrupting influence on all those around him. Mr Sebastian will have to take steps soon, whether he wants to or not.'

They entered the dark room again and she saw the same familiar faces again, all stuck back in the centuries when they were turned. Tracey hated them with a passion.

'Good evening, ladies and gentlemen, thank you for welcoming me back,' she said with a humble smile, putting on a false front for all to see as Alfred made her comfy on her chair.

There were both smiles and sneers from the coven, the latter from the rotten carcasses called women.

'Hmm… We'll see if you are good fit, girl. Your boyfriend in the States will be ash if he's not too careful,' one of the females cackled.

Tracey bit her lip. 'And you are?' she asked politely.

The old woman smiled. 'Emily DeWitt, and to my left is Edith Grey, and to my right is Jeremiah Heaver.' The named people nodded and grimaced.

Alfred then stood up. 'My apologies. Let me make the introductions, especially as you may be making our coven up to a baker's dozen.' He laughed.

In turn each person stood up as they were introduced: Albert Andrews; Tarn Walker, who had a nose that pointed to the ceiling; Esme Whitworth, who allowed her cleavage to be on show, which was vast enough to conceal a watermelon; Maude Guppy; Jesse Turner; Jack Sanderson; Arthur Honeybottom, which nearly made Tracey giggle like she did at school years ago; and finally Isaiah Faulks.

'Jesus, looks like the world's worst football team,' Tracey muttered, chuckling at her own wit.

Albert settled down in his chair whilst shaking his head. Clearly, she was failing to win them over. Oh well.

'I have a gift. It's a bottle of rum from Nelson's ship,' Tracey announced, retrieving the bottle from her bag and placing it in the middle of the large polished wooden table. All eyes were locked on it.

'Oh goodness, that is very gracious,' said Jeremiah. 'Forgive me for asking, but how did you come to have ownership of this?'

Tracey placed her bag on the ground and smiled. 'Albert Morris,' she replied and then saw their stunned faces. 'I have a corkscrew somewhere.' She knelt down under the table as if to search in her bag. Instead, she pressed a car alarm fob. With a soft beep it activated the surprise.

The explosion was a dull thump sending wood and death into the air; ash filled the atmosphere making the redhead cough. She pulled two silenced .22 pistols out of her bag and stood up. Amongst the smoke and ash, she could see that the majority of the coven had already gone to hell.

There were only three left: Edith, whose eyes were gone; the bitch DeWitt; and, of course, Alfred. He must have been reaching for the bottle and was thrown backwards, missing what was inside the bottle, but he was hit by something, maybe the glass because he had no lower jaw and only one arm.

DeWitt stared at Tracey angrily although she was peppered with wood fragments from the previously pristine table. Without losing the staring contest, Tracey levelled the gun at Alfred's head. With a gentle squeeze of the trigger she sent a silver-tipped bullet into his brain, and then a second shot into the man's heart, causing him to turn to ash.

'You fucking bitch,' DeWitt cursed and then flinched as her long-term friend and confidant Edith followed Alfred in the long-awaited afterlife.

Tracey moved her pistol to DeWitt's face. 'Takes one to know one,' she said happily.

'Why? We are vampires. We welcomed you in,' Emily DeWitt said, who had been turned by her young lover, although she was sixty, but she did love the strong, young boys. He was bitten by a noble after coming back from France with Henry V's army, and she was to be ended by this bitch.

'Simple, you threatened me and the man I care about – and for that alone I would torch the world,' Tracey said and squeezed the trigger so Emily could follow the young lover that she herself had killed after finding him with her friend Edith. Ironically, they as then would turn to each other for company and torment for the rest of their unnaturally long lives.

With that she placed the gun in her bag, dusted herself down and walked out, opening the door wide to let in the large men and Tony. No words were exchanged, just a kiss on his bald head, and she made her exit to the car heading for France and then America. She drove off with a smile on her face and hope for a better future alongside Albert as he chased love once more. This time she would be there to help him pick up the pieces when his love undoubtedly passed into memory, again.

Chapter 19

The apartment was silent after Tracey had finished her tale.
'Jesus, Tracey, you wiped out the whole coven! What was in that
bomb?' I asked, looking at the now relaxed woman.

'Ah yes, I had a bit of luck there. One of Tony's boys used to
be in bomb disposal for the army. He was in Iraq and
Afghanistan taking apart IEDs. What that man didn't know about
bombs could be written on the head of a pin,' she said excitedly.
'He caught the man who had killed a few of his friends with a
bomb. Simon was caught with his hand on a detonator switch
and a shaped charge of C-4 rammed up the terrorist's ass. He
was arrested and kicked out of the army. They hushed it all up,
of course, but they never found all the bits of the man.' She gave
a dark chuckle. 'But I digress…lead in the bottom, a small
amount of C-4 and a shitload of silver – boom.'

I just shook my head in amazement. I knew she mixed in
some shady circles, but this was crazy. 'So why did it take you
so long to get here?'

Tracey took another drink. 'I wasn't sure what forces they
might have watching for me, so I went to Calais, then was
bundled in a container for a long, lonely trip across the Atlantic –
my clothes were ruined.' Her eyes went black.

'I'll buy you some new clothes. Just promise not to bankrupt
me.'

She raised her hand. 'I can promise nothing, Albert, but now,
I will use your shower,' she announced, to which I pointed to the
main bathroom and watched as she undressed on the way letting
her red dress fall to the floor. 'Care to wash my back?' she
shouted back at me, giggling to herself.

An hour later I was nervously playing with my phone. Rose
hadn't texted to say she was home, and that worried me. But then
again Sharon, her roommate, could sometimes make her forget
with some drama or another.

Tracey walked in wearing silk pyjamas that she had brought in her case. Her wet red hair draped over her shoulder as she lazily rubbed it with a towel. I handed her the last of my blood/alcohol mix, which brought a smile to her face.

'So, where's your hotty? You told her yet?'

I shook my head. 'She went home earlier, but she hasn't answered any of my texts,' I replied, and we looked at each other. 'It might be nothing, unless the coven had been tipped off that you were coming here.'

'It's possible, but why take a human? It doesn't make sense,' she stated.

'What about any of their decisions making sense? They are all in their own little worlds,' I growled, my phone creaking as I gripped it too tightly. 'And no, I haven't told her.'

There was a bang on the door, making us both jump.

I threw open the door. 'Jasper, what are you doing here? You're not meant to be working tonight?'

The tall doorman's dark skin shone with sweat. 'Bert, can I come in?' he asked with wide eyes and a look of worry. He walked in and stopped suddenly when he saw Tracey. 'Damn, it's raining beautiful women.' He looked me up and down. 'I dunno how you do it, my man.'

I pushed him to a chair while Tracey laughed and drank up the compliments as she always did. 'This is my friend Tracey from England. This is Jasper, he's a good man and works on the door of this building,' I explained. They greeted each other kindly. 'So, what's up?' I asked the panic-stricken man.

'I had a call from my buddy Stefan who's working on the door downstairs tonight. He was contacted by the taxi company that took your guest home. They told him they couldn't make contact with the cab driver, so they were concerned. They asked Stefan what time the cab picked up the fare and left, but while Stefan was answering them, they had a call from the cab driver's wife. It turns out that he was arrested and only released an hour ago,' Jasper explained, and then he saw my face go paler than it had ever done before. 'The charge was bullshit, and the passenger was taken away by a plain-clothes cop.'

My head dropped. 'Did they get the name of this cop?' I asked sternly.

'Captain Hughes. Isn't that the prick you'd said about before?' Jasper asked, to which I gave a curt nod in response.

Tracey was bored as Jasper and I had our important discussion. She just took all the information on board as our emotions started to rise. My eyes flicked to her, and she held a smirk as she deemed this an appropriate moment to play Candy Crush on my phone.

I then stood up and started to pace before stopping to look out of my window as I made my decision. I lifted my phone, scanned the texts and found the one I wanted. I tapped to call the recipient, lifted the phone to my ear and waited for it to connect, which it did in five rings.

'Mr Morris, I was expecting your call. It seems as though the coven may have acted rashly, yes?' Graves the butler said calmly, answering questions before I had even asked them.

'What are they playing at? Where is Rose? Is she safe?' I demanded to know and started to pace while my friends watched on.

'Calm yourself, sir, they have received some disturbing news from London. A week ago the coven in London went dark just after they had met with a person of your acquaintance. Then your red-headed friend was seen entering America via a seaport, and they panicked as they thought you were together and planning their destruction,' he explained in his matter-of-fact tone. 'And yes, she is safe. I put her with Miss Romanov and they are getting on well.'

I sighed with relief because at least she was safe, but God knows what they were talking to each other about. I knew how playful the girls were, and it didn't bode well for me at any rate. 'May I ask why you are being so open with me, Graves?'

'Simple, I am the butler of the house, not of the people here. They merely have a long-term rental agreement with the owners. But they have asked that I be the mediator between yourself and the coven,' he said, and then I could hear some whispering at his end. 'Would you come for a meeting, Mr Morris? I promise your safety.'

So much for the master of the coven's family being there for centuries, then, I thought. 'Yes, I will, and I know you believe that. But the coven cannot be trusted, especially the captain,' I answered.

'Indeed, sir. I shall send the car for you, but you will notice that we have armed guards, on the front gates only, for your safety as well as theirs,' he clarified and clicked off the phone.

Tracey stood up and walked over to me. 'What did they say, Berty?' she asked, then she seemed to realise that her choice of name was only used by those who held a special place in my heart. A look of worry attacked her perfect features.

There was a tug on my dead heart. I shrugged it off and gave her a hug and a kiss on the cheek. I couldn't blame her as our emotions were running high. 'It was the butler of the coven house – they have Rose, but she's safe. As we thought, one of their people saw you at the port, and they're scared you're here to destroy them with my help,' I explained, making her shake her head and laugh, her arms still draped over my shoulders. 'Graves, he put Rose with Anastasia in the cellar. So, she is safe, for now.'

A cough came from the chair. 'So, what's the plan, Bert, and what can I do to help?' Jasper asked pointedly, his army training and conditioning coming to the forefront – protect the weak and help your friends.

'I don't think you can. This isn't your fight. There are things at play here that you don't know, and I won't risk you!' I replied firmly.

All he did was smile in reaction, which made me frown. 'Now, put each other down for a moment and sit your asses down,' he instructed, pointing to the sofa.

We both sat down like two naughty children and looked at a new side to this ordinarily quiet man.

'I have seen some shit during my time in the marines, but nothing has compared to you, Bert. You only appear when the sun goes down, and you come back in the a.m. with jet-black eyes and blood spots on your clothing. Then the thing with my cousin – his friend hits you with an iron bar, which he said was hard enough to kill you, but you get up and snap your zip ties. Then my cousin tries to shoot you, and he said you moved quicker than light,' he finished, taking a breath as if to continue.

'I've never known you talk so much, unless it has to do with food,' I replied. We all laughed nervously. I was still astounded at how observant he had been. *Damn you, Marine Corps.* 'So, what is it you think you know, Jasper?' I asked wearily.

He shrugged. 'Well, you and Red over there are vampires, or something like that. But you're a good one. It hasn't gone unnoticed that a lot of gang activity in the Bronx and other shady areas has dwindled to almost nothing. You have the gangbangers running scared, and they are calling you the Shadow of Death,' Jasper said with a laugh.

'Shit, so much for being stealthy. I was always crap at it.' I chuckled and looked across at Tracey, who was clearly enthralled with the story being told.

He focused a glare at me. 'Were you ever in the armed forces or was that a lie?' he asked with a look of hurt and betrayal etched on his face.

I smiled at him. 'I was in the London regiment for some years in Ireland, then I was with the British SOE, spy hunting, plus other not so fun stuff against Hitler. So, I was in the forces, just a different time and place than I could admit to,' I explained.

Tracey and Jasper looked upon me in awe. I had never really talked about that with her. Only the closest of people were told, but I just stopped after Suzie passed.

'You're right about the rest. I went through some dark times when I was first turned, and killed some innocents, but I conquered my demon and focused on those who broke the law. I made some friends with the coppers that way,' I continued.

Jasper frowned at my terminology.

'Police, Jasper. I made friends in law enforcement.'

Tracey jumped in, 'When you first get bitten, you can be feral and feed on anything. Some vampires never change and just kill for the sheer pleasure of it. But Berty and I managed to adjust.' A dark shadow came over her face. 'When my boyfriend bit me, I killed my whole family that night. If I close my eyes, I can still see their faces as I tore them apart. I didn't know I was doing it. I just woke up bathed in my loved ones' blood,' she recalled sadly with tears rolling down her pale cheeks. She moved closer to me. 'It physically and mentally broke me.'

Jasper looked at me. 'So, who bit you, then?' He looked surprised when I smiled.

'He was bitten by Jack the fucking Ripper,' Tracey cut in excitedly, pulling herself from her haunting thoughts.

'Oi, that was my story,' I barked and gave the redhead a sour look. 'But, yes, and I killed the fucker too.' I saw Jasper's eyes go wide and his mouth fall open.

The doorman was shaking his head. 'Nah, I can't believe it. You were bitten by the one and only Jack the motherfucking Ripper?' He had come to terms with his guesses about us, but for it all to be true, along with the back stories, his mind was blown. 'Fuck!' he exclaimed, still shaking his head. 'What we gonna do about Rose?' he asked, dragging us back on topic.

I rubbed my face. 'Graves knew he was being listened to. But what he did say was that there are only armed guards on the front gates, but we can't necessarily trust that,' I advised, watching Tracey walk off and come back with her bag. 'What have you got?' I asked.

The redhead flicked her long hair over her shoulder as she delved into her bag and pulled out three small padded bags. 'A gift from my friend: Ruger SR22, semi-auto, small calibre, which means less noise and kick. And ten rounds of magazines, all silver-tipped – one in the head stops them and gives them something to worry about, then one in the pumper turns them to dust,' she said with excitement.

And that's why Tracey is a wanderer, I thought. Life was just too boring for her after a while.

Jasper checked them over with a practiced eye and hand, pulling back the action to check the workings. 'I thought you Brits didn't like guns?' he asked.

Tracey smiled. 'They are just hard to get after some loonies went crazy, but let's say I run in some less than law-abiding circles.'

The doorman smiled knowingly. 'They look good. Any more ammo?'

'Another clip of each, but that's all of the special ones,' she explained and pulled out a box. 'These are normal bullets,' she said and then pulled out a small make-up bag. 'I also have two suppressors; it was either a third one or my hairbrush. You know what happened there,' she added casually before starting to brush her long, fine hair.

'Well, Bert won't need a suppressor as he will be inside,' Jasper added.

I picked up a pistol and mirrored his actions. 'Yep, plus with our hearing it won't matter. It's for the neighbours,' I explained, and he nodded. 'What about the guards, they will be human?'

Tracey smiled. 'Leave that to me. I have an idea. But do we want them dead or just out?'

Jasper chewed a nail. 'We can't have witnesses, especially with their links to the cops.'

'Okay,' Tracey told Jasper. 'Leave that to me. It'll take some time, though, so you grab their radio and monitor things.'

Then I explained the layout of the rooms I had seen, which wasn't much help, and I described the butler, so they knew to leave the man be, unless he showed hostility. 'There is no mobile signal there, so, Jasper, find the landline and kill it.'

The plans were outlined as much as possible, although it was risky, and Jasper had a friend's car which could be declared stolen if it all went bent. I put on my suit and placed the pistol in the small of my back tucked into my trouser waistband, which was uncomfortable as hell. I also placed a spare clip in my jacket inside pocket. It wouldn't matter if they searched me.

Tracey walked out in her arse-kicking gear, which made our mouths drop. 'Deadly and beautiful – what a mixture,' she purred as she placed her gun in a holster.

Jasper and I scanned over her tight black clothing like two dirty old men watching a yoga class.

The phone then buzzed telling me the limo was here.

'Good luck, everyone. If it goes to shit, just go, get out of there and run,' I instructed. I shook Jasper's hand, then I hugged Tracey, maybe too much. 'Good luck, Trace,' I said and kissed her quickly, but she pulled me in for a longer one.

'You, too, Berty. I'm always here for you. Stay safe,' she said lovingly. As we parted, I nodded and headed off to my doom.

The chauffer opened the door and said a generic greeting before whisking me away into the darkness. As the limo drove into the night, I had time to think about how far Tracey had come. At first we were just fleeting acquaintances, then friends, and then lovers for a time. We both knew it would never work full-time; she was too flighty and vamps shouldn't hang out with others of their ilk. How the coven did it was beyond me.

I was thankful to Tracey for standing by me through this whole coven business, and I knew she would have my back. But I also knew that when this was over, despite how much her head told her to stay, she would be like the wind, off to new places for fun and excitement.

The armed guards opened the gates. Again, thanks to my sight, I could see them clearly. They were huge with Kevlar vests and sporting semi-automatic rifles along with a pistol on their belts. I was right: they were humans. *Have a nice afterlife, boys*, I thought as we continued towards the house. I held no bad feelings towards the men; they had just picked the wrong side. I could see Graves standing at the front of the house.

He opened the car door. 'Evening, Mr Morris. I would say good, but that would be a lie,' the grey-haired butler said dryly. He then showed me into the house. 'The coven is ready and waiting for you.'

'Anastasia?' I asked, holding the old man's arm and pulling him back.

A brief look of annoyance flashed over his features, which quickly disappeared. He gave a brief shake of his head. 'You have no friends in that room, sir, and they have a new member too.' He pulled his arm from my grip.

The hall was empty as we headed towards the meeting room that I had visited before. We stopped outside the meeting room doors where the members were gathering inside.

Graves briefly looked at me and mouthed, 'Good luck,' before opening the doors. That's when I saw the new member.

'HUGHES, WHERE IS ROSE?' I shouted, losing my cool instantly, causing some of the group to sneer, or jump. I heard the click of the door as it was closed behind me.

The cop smiled at me, showing off his newly lengthened incisors, but it wasn't him who talked first.

'Calm yourself, Mr Morris, your friend is safe enough,' Samuel Sebastian, the thin-lipped bastard and coven master said, but I couldn't fail to notice his look of worry.

'For now,' the once ex-captain and ex-human being added snidely, making a few of them roll their eyes at the childish man's behaviour. So, he didn't have the backing of the whole coven.

'Now, now, Ray, do not exacerbate the situation, please,' Samuel chided the man, who didn't seem happy about it.

We all sat in our respective chairs around the table.

'Albert, after our last meeting we had great hopes that you would change your ways.' Samuel sighed. 'But yet again you have seemed to negate our instructions and started to court this Rose girl. Is that true?'

I looked at him. 'You should know, you have been following me and sending photos of me to my friend in London,' I stated with ire.

'Yes, well, that was done without my knowledge,' the master said, looking at several of his coven members, who didn't seem to be bothered about the chastising. 'But talking of London, do you know what happened to them? Communications have gone dark and it seems your friend who has recently entered our country was involved.'

I shrugged. 'I wasn't there. She texted me about the photos and how they were gathering information on my friend and I – at your bidding, no less.' I shot him a glare.

'Enough of this shit. Give up chasing the human blood sacks, and we'll let you go, and maybe your friend…after a while,' Hughes said perversely.

Samuel slammed his fist onto the table. 'Know your place, Ray. You are new-born compared to us, so SILENCE!'

The ex-law enforcement seemed to swell with anger at the man's words.

'So, Albert, have you seen Miss Andrews at all?'

I shook my head. 'No, I've been trying to get in touch with her for a couple of weeks,' I answered, and then looked at the captain. 'I didn't want to be part of this bloody thing. The coven wasn't interested in me for over a century, so I shall continue to do as I want.' I looked around the table. 'And you can stay in your rented ivory tower, lording it over nobody.'

Angry rumblings filtered around the room. 'Samuel, I think this man is more trouble than he's worth. Just a commoner. Let him go or kill him,' said a man I didn't know.

'Algeron, please, we don't kill people just for disagreeing with us, despite what some believe,' Samuel replied, shooting a look at a few of the coven.

I smiled. 'Trouble in paradise, Sam. I hear Anastasia wanted to leave, but you locked her up, and also refused to give her back her money?' I asked, looking around and seeing the occupants shift uncomfortably in the dimly lit room. 'Or are you using her funds to live here?' I added, after which they stilled. I seemed to have hit a sore point.

'It's Samuel, Mr Morris, if you please. Miss Romanov is just smitten with you. Once you are gone, she will see sense and stay where she is cared for. We are her family now,' the coven master stated, but he only received a few nods.

'Bullshit,' I said, mocking them and their coven.

They looked back at me with anger, but then the doors were kicked open, bathing us in bright light.

'TAKE THIS, MOTHERFUCKERS!'

Tracey and Jasper

Meanwhile, a little earlier…

'What the hell is this thing, it's embarrassing?' Tracey chided the big man as she picked at the frayed upholstery in the vehicle.

With a huff, he replied, 'I wanted to blend in; it's a Honda Civic.' He kept his eyes on the red dots in the distance. There were no lights on this road and the trees flashed by illuminated by his substandard headlights.

'They are getting away. This piece of shit can't even keep up with a fucking limo,' Tracey shot back using her earthy language, which seemed to embarrass the ex-gang member and ex-marine.

The steering wheel creaked as he tightened his grip. How could somebody be so hot yet so foul-mouthed? He decided to change the subject. 'So, what can kill vamps? Stakes through the heart?'

'That kills everyone,' she scoffed, making him grind his teeth.

He shot her a look. 'Fire?'

'Again, if I set you on fire it would fuck you up, right?' She raised an eyebrow giving him an 'I'm with stupid' look, which he read straight away.

'What about crucifixes, can they kill or just hurt you?' Jasper asked, grasping onto the hope that she would take this seriously.

She brought her slender fingers up to her chin in a thoughtful pose. 'Hmmm, that's a good question. I'll tell you what, we'll get two crosses, I thump you with one, then—' That's as far as she got before he gave up.

'Fine, I give up, how does Albert put up with you, honestly,' he grumbled and regained his concentration on the limo's red lights.

She smiled like an Academy Award winner. 'Because I'm a delight to be with, Jasper, and I rock his world in the sack, and he does likewise,' Tracey said with a faraway look in her eyes. 'One time I swear I lost a filling when…'

Jasper turned the radio on loud to drown out her five-minute diatribe of a weekend in Brighton. His eyes nearly bled straining to focus on the limo when Tracey started to use hand gestures while the Eagles sang about 'Hotel California'.

After twenty minutes he turned off the radio; thankfully she had stopped and was just gazing into nothingness. There was a slight smile on her face.

'They are slowing down. What should I do?' he asked.

'Just drive by. Don't change speed or look over at the gate,' Tracey answered as they caught up with the black stretch limo. 'Wish I was in that. I could've been his date,' she said and pouted before looking back at Jasper. 'You ever shagged in a limo?'

'Jesus, woman, do you hear yourself? If you were with him, he wouldn't have this problem,' he borderline shouted. 'And no, I haven't.'

Tracey shot him a look. 'You should,' she replied, cuddling herself and smiling at the memory. 'Anyway, pull in here,' she said quickly, and pointed to a small track into the woods which was rutted but hadn't seen traffic in a few days. 'And yes, we would have the same trouble. I killed the UK coven before I came here.' She smirked seeing Jasper's face, which looked as though he had just seen his upcoming death. He watched her jump out of the car as they stopped, then she ducked her head back in. 'Come on, slow poke, did you want to live forever?' she teased with a wink.

Jasper turned off the engine which made a tingling noise as it cooled down. The ex-soldier felt the coldness surrounding him like a death shroud. He wished he had phoned Albert instead and just stayed at home and ordered some chicken and gravy.

'You're a dead man, Jasp,' he muttered to himself as he felt the car rocking and saw the smiling assassin bouncing the car while laughing. 'Shit.'

They walked back to the main road. It took a few minutes until they could see the large guards. 'Those vests, how much do they cover?' Tracey whispered.

'Just the important organs,' he said and showed her by sketching over his body.

She nodded and pulled her gun and clicked off the safety catch. 'Follow me. I'll knock them down and then take the one on the right. You thump the one on the left, then we swap. Okay?'

Before he could nod, the redhead was up and walking quickly. Then in a burst of speed that he had never witnessed before, the woman ran forwards with gun raised. The men only just heard her boots hitting the tarmac as a bullet shattered the first man's right shoulder, making him drop his weapon which swung uselessly on its strap. The second small calibre bullet had the same effect on his other shoulder.

The man on the left gave a shriek in fright as he saw the carnage. He raised his weapon but was stopped with a bullet to the shoulder where the butt of his rifle was heading yet would never reach. Her last shot was to his kneecap, sending him down, and then Jasper's fist sent him into darkness from which he would never return.

The vampire leapt and sank her teeth into the neck of the first victim. After a couple of mouthfuls, she slit her wrist letting some drops of blood into his mouth, which was opening and closing like a panicking goldfish. Tracey then repeated the act with the other guard.

'Jesus, you don't mess around, girl,' he whispered, screwing up his face in horror.

'Can't – if you move slowly, your mistakes catch up with you. Now get a stake to kill these fuckers with… Or have you got a crucifix?' she asked with a smirk.

'Bitch,' was the audible muttered retort.

Soon Tracey had staked the men, leaving the guns in place. With a gleeful look on his face, Jasper checked the weapons and slung them over his shoulder. He almost skipped like a child at Christmas as he followed the crouching and running redhead. But his eyes kept betraying him. Instead of looking for dangers, he was casting an admiring glance at the pinnacle of womanhood in Lycra. That's when he noticed her hand behind her back showing off the middle finger.

She then stopped and raised her hand. 'Wait here,' Tracey whispered. Her eyes pierced the night to see two men standing by the large, intimidating all oak and black iron studded front door. One man was old and grey, the other younger by a decade and wearing a driver's hat. There was no noise apart from the wind in the trees, but she still managed to creep up behind them and press her pistol to the nape of the hat-wearer's neck. 'Morning, gents. Nice night isn't it?' she said, making both men jump.

The older man turned slowly. 'Ah, Miss Andrews, my name is Graves. Bernard here and I are not any danger to you,' he said calmly holding up his hands, which was mirrored by his colleague.

'Yes, Berty did say you were helping him. How's it going in there?' she asked, lowering the gun and slipping it back into its holster.

'When I left, Albert was shouting at them, but the stroke of good luck we do have is that they have now turned the police captain, so the police won't be coming today,' Graves stated.

Tracey walked into the open and whistled for Jasper to come up. 'So, how many are in there? Where is Rose and Lady Muck?' Tracey asked with mirth.

'We don't have staff at this time of the night. It's just me and the driver,' Graves said and waved at the house. 'Walk straight ahead and just follow the voices.' He gave a low chuckle. 'The cellar is straight ahead, the door with a large ornate ring on it, ugly thing but they seem to like it.'

Jasper turned up panting. 'What's going on, who are these guys?' he managed to say before bending down to take a deep breath. Maybe he should have more salad on his burgers from now on.

'Too late, *One Lung*, we gotta move,' she replied before taking out her gun to replace the magazine. 'We're going in. Follow me, and when we enter I'll head right, you go left, shoot anyone there. Man, woman, doesn't matter – they are all vamps. Got it?'

'What about the phone line? I haven't cut it yet,' the Manhattan doorman admitted.

Graves smiled. 'I have unplugged the phones for tonight's activities. We do not want any other gate crashers tonight, do we?' he said dryly with a cold smile.

Tracey placed a kiss on the older man's cheek. 'Thank you. Now let's go before Berty pisses them off too much.'

Jasper nodded and readied his own pistol by clicking off the safety.

'Errr, could you try and keep on target – the furniture and wooden panelling are quite expensive, you know,' Graves added, making Tracey roll her eyes.

Tracey walked off and put her hand on the door. 'We'll do our best. C'mon, Jasp, let's get our boy,' she said whilst opening the door and following the voices as instructed.

Knowing how dark and dingy the last coven's meeting room was, she guessed this would be similar, so Tracey and Jasper turned on all the lights as they walked and then stood in front of the meeting room doors. She raised her three fingers and looked at him. 'Ready, calm and professional,' Tracey said.

'Oorah!' he said, quoting the well-known US Marines' war cry, and then kicked the door in. 'TAKE THIS, MOTHERFUCKERS!'

Back to the present…

Tracey shot Jasper a look and then started to fire, unleashing hell on her fellow soulless creatures to send them back to the underworld.

As the door was kicked open, I grabbed at the pistol lodged in my waistband against my lower back, it had shifted but I managed to pull it free. Bullets flew past my head. I could hear and feel them pushing their way through the air. I saw Jasper moving to my left with gun in hand and flashes from the barrel illuminating the whole place, and then the flash of ash and red hair as Samuel Sebastian was erased from this astral plain thanks to Tracey's deadly and well-placed shots. He was right about her after all.

I knew my target – the fucking captain, but he was bolting for another door. I couldn't get a bead on him as there were too many things moving. The whole coven was on the move, there was lace and velvet all over the place as they tried to get out of the aim of the angry doorman and crazy redhead. I went to run after Hughes, but one of the coven stood in front of me holding a brass fire poker.

'You're going to pay for your treachery, Morris,' Algeron cursed with eyes like coals. So I planted a bullet in his heart, turning him to ash.

The funny thing was that as the silver-pointed invitation to the netherworld entered his body, both our eyes followed my ejected bullet casing as it spun away into the carnage. He really did look surprised.

'After him, Berty!' Tracey shouted with a smile on her face as she punched a woman who looked like Queen Elizabeth, and then she shot an older man trying to gut Jasper. 'Go, baby!' she still had time to shout before throwing the queen into the roaring fire, sending piercing screams and ash into the air along with Tracey's cackles of laughter. The woman from Bristol was enjoying herself way too much.

I nodded and ran out through the open door. Then I saw a glimpse of a leg disappearing through another door further down the hallway, which was instantly slammed shut. The out of place iron ring handle swung. Once I kicked it open, I was thrown back as three holes appeared in the wood sending splinters flying at me, and one of bullets taking me high in the shoulder. *Owwww!*

'Damned bastard!' I shouted angrily and kicked open the door, firing as I moved in. Sparks appeared as the slugs impacted the stone wall at the bottom of the cellar steps. I heard the sound of screams and the impacts of fist on flesh.

The demon inside was willing me on and panting for vengeance and blood. The world fell away as I slipped down the last two wooden steps – who polishes cellar steps for Christ's sake? I quickly got up, then there were the sounds of a fight and another scream and the thump of a body hitting the floor. 'Rose, Sia, are you here!' I shouted into the dimly lit place.

'BERTY…HELP!' screamed Rose, not in panic but frustration.

She moved forward into view revealing Ray Hughes with his arm wrapped around her neck and a gun in his other hand pressed to her skull. 'Wow, you look like shit,' she said.

'Thanks, love,' I replied before searching over both their shoulders. 'Where the fuck is Anastasia?'

The twat gestured to the cell where he had drugged his hostage. 'She is sleeping. The bitch got a bit gobby.' He grinned demonically showing off his fangs.

I gave the ex-copper a sneer, then locked eyes with my Rosie. 'Did they hurt you at all?'

'Who? The coven of fucking VAMPIRES? What the shit!' she spat angrily while I saw the dick of an ex-captain laughing at me. 'All this time you were *Twilighting* me?'

'No, nothing like that. I really like you and I was trying to tell you the truth, but these pricks got in the bloody way,' I growled, 'all because I fell in love with you. And they want me to be cold and miserable like they are.'

Rose locked eyes with me. 'Wait, you love me? How? When?' Tears filled her eyes.

Oh shit, did I say that out loud? I sighed. 'Since the first day I saw you. Then I made you laugh, and once I saw that I was hooked,' I recalled, and then groaned as my bullet wound started to knit together. Luckily, no one saw the crushed bullet pop out and fall down my shirt.

'Enough of this lovey-dovey bullshit. One move, Morris, and she'll be deader than Elvis!' Hughes snapped and made Rose squeak in pain as he shoved the gun in harder.

I shook my head. 'What is it you want? Money? Gold? I have both?' I offered, but he shook his head. 'What then? You want me dead? Then kill me, just let her go first. Don't hurt her, please.'

'Aww, so noble. Yes, I want you dead, but then I want her to be with me, forever,' Hughes said and sniffed at her hair.

Rosie grimaced and her eyes widened; she knew what 'forever' meant to the man holding her.

I pleaded with him, 'No, please, kill me and let her go. This is no life for anyone. You chose this, but most of us were forced into it. And I can assure you the first thing she would do is kill you, as I did for the bastard who turned me into this monster.' I stopped talking and then sagged as the battle noise continued upstairs. They were really burning through their rounds. 'I've watched too many loved ones die in my time as this thing, and I swore I would rather die than turn anyone into a monster like us.'

Tears were now flowing down Rosie's cheeks.

'Well, tough shit. I LOVE THIS SHIT, THE POWER I FEEL, LIKE I'M A GOD!' he ranted with spittle flying. He moved his gun over her shoulder and took aim at my head. 'Say goodbye, dickhead.'

'Rosie, close your eyes, love. Don't watch this, please,' I said softly. As her beautiful eyes closed, I heard the click of his trigger, then the hammer hitting the bullet, the powder igniting, and the last sound I heard was the bullet cutting through the air.

Chapter 20

I turned my head at the last millisecond, which caused the bullet to leave a bloody gash along the left side of my head, like a demonic farmer ploughing a furrow. The next shot missed as I lunged at the pair, knocking them to the ground. I heard the scream and exhalation of breath from the soft and lovely form of Rose, who was now the filling in between two black-eyed and fang-baring snarling vampires.

In his panic, Hughes had dropped his gun; but instead of using his teeth or claws, he furiously struggled to reclaim it from where it had landed.

I pushed Rose from us. Unfortunately, she rebounded off the wall with a grunt. I heard my friends calling out as they stomped down the stairs. I jumped on the back of the scurrying man, digging my claws into his fleshy back and making him scream like the bitch he was.

'JASPER, GET ROSE OUT OF HERE…NOW!' I shouted and received a backhanded slap from my enemy, which rattled my eyes like I was in a cartoon. I fell off him, but before he could once again try to reclaim his service revolver, I resumed clawing at his back.

'BERTY, GET OFF HIM! LET ME SHOOT HIM!' Tracey shouted.

I turned the monster onto his back and started to hail blows into his face, tearing flesh and shattering bone. My knuckles bled and finally broke because of the punishment they had dealt. I realised I was screaming as my attack continued, and then a calm, angelic voice cut through the fog of my rage.

'Berty, get off him, please.' I turned to see a red-faced Rose standing there with a gun. Tears were still streaming down her face, but her voice and hand were calm. 'Do it now, Berty!'

I saw it was Tracey's gun that Rose was holding. The redhead was standing behind her nervously, probably worried that the brunette would shoot me. I rolled off the now twitching animal who no longer had a face, but I knew he could come back even though it would take some time.

BANG. BANG. BANG. BANG. The noise was deafening as the ex-policeman, ex-vampire and now ex-alive was turned into ash when the silver-tipped bullets tore his immortality away.

There was another bang as the gun hit the old wooden floorboards, and that's when my eyes met Rose's. I went to talk, but the girl I had fallen for just shook her head.

'Nothing, Albert, please. You can't say or do anything which will make tonight better for me.' She sobbed and lowered her head. 'I just want to go home and try to forget everything about this horrific night, and the people or things that have caused this.' She turned away as those words dug deep.

I stood up and went to go after her but felt the strong yet slender fingers of Tracey stopping me.

'Don't, Albert, now is not the right time,' the Bristolian said in the softest tones I had ever heard come from her mouth.

Jasper, who had a bleeding scalp, put his arm around my departing love. The look I received from him was one of sorrow, but he nodded, which just signalled 'I got this' as they walked up the stairs.

'Will she be okay?' I asked my friend.

Tracey hugged me. 'Yes, he's driving a Honda, and frankly it's a slow piece of shit,' she said with mirth dripping from her words. Our hearing then caught some grumbles coming from the departing doorman.

'WELL, DON'T WORRY ABOUT ME OR ANTHING!' boomed a voice with a very strong accent. We turned to see a very angry Russian baroness staring daggers at us.

I smiled. 'Oh hey, you missed all the fun.' I moved a bit too slowly to dodge the incoming fist.

Once we had managed to calm Sia down, we re-joined the butler and driver who were starting to complain about the damage to the property. Tracey blamed Jasper, who had become a bit of a wild man in typical Marine Corps fashion by using the expenditure of ammunition to get the job done.

Sia took us down to the vault and reclaimed her wealth while Tracey, two employees of the estate and I took a share of the rest. As we counted, I could hear my red-haired friend chanting, 'VEGAS! VEGAS! VEGAS!'

Once we were done we were driven back to my apartment in style, although we received dodgy looks from the doorman as we were still coated in dust, dirt and carrying big bags of loot.

We stumbled into the apartment and dropped the bags with exhaustion. The girls fell onto the sofas where I left them before heading to my room to think and hopefully sleep the day away.

I fell asleep alone and woke up with a pair of Vampiresses cuddled in next to me. As nice as it felt, there was only one person I wanted warming my cold body.

I was back to living alone as Tracey did what she always did: get some money, then go and have fun. I woke up to find a dirty pair of knickers on my pillow and a note saying 'Vegas baby!' with a lipstick imprint on it. God help Sin City.

The next day after a very nice night of dinner, dancing, drinking and other adult entertainment, Anastasia headed back to her motherland to look for the graves of her family and give them a long-awaited goodbye. Afterwards, she said there were several places she had visited as a child that she wanted to see again – oh, and some families of those who had betrayed her family. I noticed that some important Russian government officials went missing during her time on holiday.

I missed them both, Tracey and Anastasia, but I knew they would be back one day.

It was well over a week before I received a text from Rose asking me to meet her for a drink and chat. There was no banter or kisses on it, which didn't bode well.

I finally had a nice chat with Jasper on the way out of the building to see Rose and put some ideas to him about the future. Thankfully he was willing to help, especially as he knew the areas around here. I made it to the bar and there she was sat in our booth; it was a different barman again this time.

I bought our drinks, sat down and pushed the glass over to her. 'It's good to see you again, Rose. How are you?'

She took a sip of her dirty Martini. 'Apart from the fucking nightmares, Berty, I'm okay, thanks,' Rose said curtly, never once locking eyes with me.

'Well, I'm sure—' I started to respond, but I was stopped dead as she put her perfect hand over my mouth.

'Don't speak, this is hard enough for me to say as it is. I have never been so scared in all my life, and now I have to live my life knowing there are vampires out there – who, unlike you, will kill me without a thought,' Rose admitted, and I understood her reasoning. 'And like your friend Kelly, every time I look at you and into those eyes of yours, I will feel that monster's fangs against my flesh. He was so close.' Tears then flowed. 'You brought these monsters to my door; they threatened my whole family.' She wiped the tears from her cheeks. 'I saw you die. I know you didn't, but at the time it shattered my heart, and I can't go through that again, Berty.'

Darkness swirled in my mind and body again, but it wasn't the beast, this was due to the fact that once again I had lost someone I'd fallen for. I couldn't form the words I needed to beg her to change her mind.

'Thank you for not making this more difficult than it is,' Rose said, fighting emotions as she spoke. Then she picked up her glass and downed it. 'I really hope you find peace, Berty. Goodbye.' Without another word she stood up, walked past me and out into the night. I could hear her sobs until she got into a taxi; the slamming of the door had a certain finality to it.

Without a thought in my head, I ghosted through the city. Once again, I was alone and the emotions that ran through my body fed the beast. He was hungry and ready to play. So that's what we did. The criminal fraternity in New York and its boroughs fled for their lives that night. Thankfully, criminals are rarely reported missing, otherwise they would've broken the world record for missing people. That night sated the evil that slept inside me, for now.

During the next month I didn't see Rose, not once, and it left me adrift in life. Spring was coming, so the days were getting longer, but the things Rose said about a bar had me thinking about the future.

I carried out some research on the Internet and with Jasper's help we drove around the boroughs of New York. As it turned out, an owner of a dive bar had disappeared one night with several of its locals, and his long-abused wife just wanted rid of the place, so I bought it and moved out of my apartment to live in the spacious rooms above the bar.

Jasper joined me as bouncer and co-manager; I let him choose the chef. It was a themed bar which seemed to be quite popular again, so The Coven was born. It turned out the New York vampire scene was on the up, which made me laugh as all these pretend vamps were rubbing shoulders with the true creatures of the night. We sold good beer and fantastic food. I even kept the old waitress once I put her through rehab and gave her a pay rise.

It was when I told Anastasia about the bar and where it was that she laughed out loud, as it was the same bar she was attacked in, which I had already gathered. What I didn't know was that Anastasia had found the drivers' licences I had taken off the men who attacked us that night, so the girl had a night out to visit our friends for something to eat, and those men ended up as the main course.

One summer night I was walking through Manhattan when I heard my name called out – and there she was, Rose.

'Berty, how have you been?' she asked and strode towards me wearing a white cotton dress and sandals.

'Hey, I moved over to the Bronx – you know, a new start. You okay?' I asked, searching her face. I had missed her so much and was looking for any sign that she felt the same way.

She nodded. 'Yes, I'm fine. It took me a while, but I'm okay.' She looked at her feet. 'Are Sia and Tracey still with you?'

'Nah, we can't be around each other long term. Tracey is in Vegas doing quite well I hear, and Anastasia is touring around Russia. Somebody tried to kidnap her, which she enjoyed to a point, then she fought back, but she still writes,' I said and heard Rose laugh. How I had missed that laugh.

'You do know why I couldn't stay with you, Berty, don't you?' she asked.

'Yes, and I can't blame you, and I never will,' I replied with a sad sigh. 'But I do miss you, and that won't change.'

'I know. I miss you, too, but…I don't know, it's too hard to imagine how it would work between us,' she said, her eyes watering.

I gave her a weak smile. 'I understand, I really do.' I took out my wallet and found what I was looking for. 'I'm here for good now. That's my new address and number. Come for a coffee, or just to say hi, it's your choice.' I leaned in and kissed her soft and slightly wet cheek. 'Bye, Rose,' I said only just louder than the breath on her lips.

'Bye, Berty, take care.' We then parted, walking our separate ways. As I crossed the junction, I could hear the *slap, slap* of someone who either had flipper feet or was wearing sandals.

'Oi, Lord Lucan, what the hell is The Coven?'

I turned around and saw Rose standing on the other side of the road. 'It's my bar. Why?' I asked.

'You listened to me; you took my advice,' she said with a happy smile on her fragile face.

I laughed. 'Of course I did. I love you. Why wouldn't I?'
Then I heard the slapping of sandals and the beeping of horns and felt her body wrap around mine as swear words swarmed around us from disgruntled drivers.

Finally, I allowed a smile to grace my face again, and maybe it will stay this time…for now.

The End

Printed in Great Britain
by Amazon